CW01632603

[illegible] e air made [illegible] head and [illegible] ing a bright [illegible] ng the girl [illegible]

Casey remained crouched on the ground. Carl was holding the whip and raised his arm for another blow. The tongue sailed towards Laidlaw but landed on the girl, slicing deeply into her breast. Carl drew back his hand to strike again.

'Let the girl go, Laidlaw,' he shouted.

'Not while you're bloody lashing me. Have you gone mad?'

'I think you have.' Carl aimed again and scored another stripe across Laidlaw's cheek.

Laidlaw rolled across the ground and recovered his pistol. He pointed it at Carl. 'It's time I took what you owe me and got on my way.' Laidlaw walked over to the girl and kicked her in the crotch. 'Get up, wench.' Casey stopped at the fence and watched.

'I'll take this nigger with me.'

Also by Richard Tresillian in Sphere Books:

FLEUR
THE BONDMASTER
BLOOD OF THE BONDMASTER
THE BONDMASTER BREED

Bondmaster Fury

Being Book Four of the Bondmaster Saga

RICHARD TRESILLIAN

SPHERE BOOKS LIMITED
30–32 Gray's Inn Road, London WC1X 8JL

First published in Great Britain by
Arlington Books Ltd 1982
Copyright © Wordsman B.V. 1982
Published by Sphere Books Ltd 1983

TRADE
MARK

This book is sold subject to the condition that it shall not, by way of trade or otherwise, be lent, re-sold, hired out or otherwise circulated without the publisher's prior consent in any form of binding or cover other than that in which it is published and without a similar condition including this condition being imposed on the subsequent purchaser.

Printed and bound in Great Britain by
Cox & Wyman Ltd, Reading

For Eddy, Abe, Tony and Baba

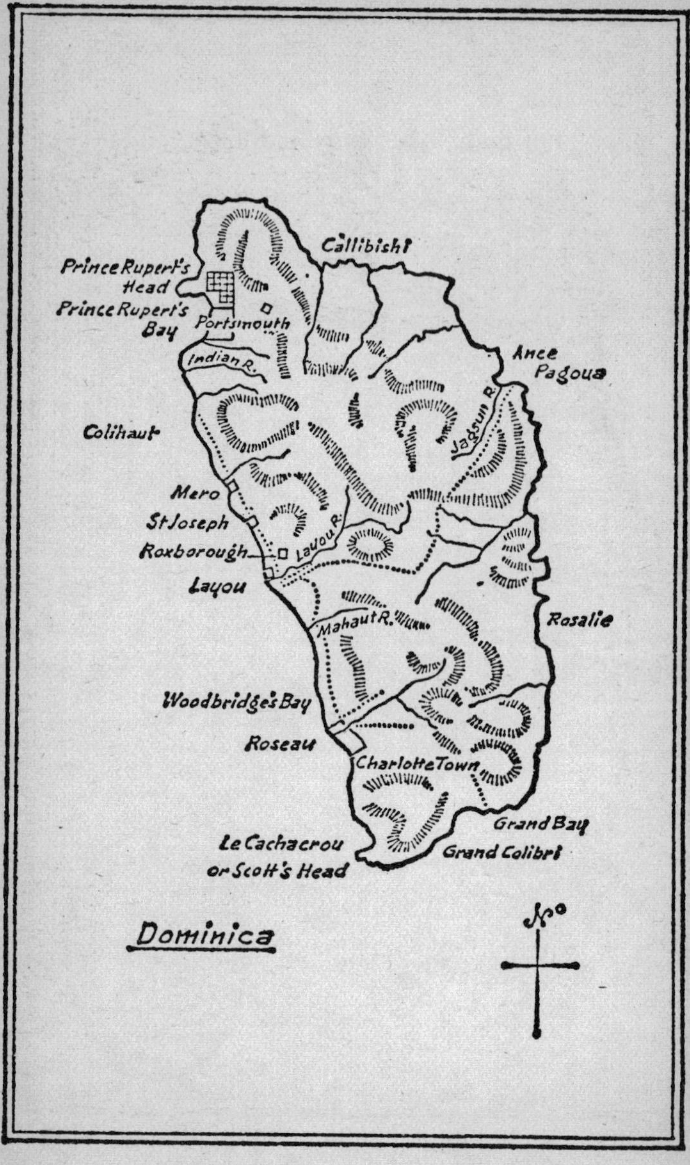
Callibishi
Prince Rupert's Head
Prince Rupert's Bay
Portsmouth
Indian R.
Ance Pagoua
Jagsun R.
Colihaut
Mero
St Joseph
Roxborough
Layou R.
Layou
Rosalie
Mahaut R.
Woodbridge's Bay
Roseau
Charlotte Town
Grand Bay
Grand Colibri
Le Cachacrou or Scott's Head
Dominica
No

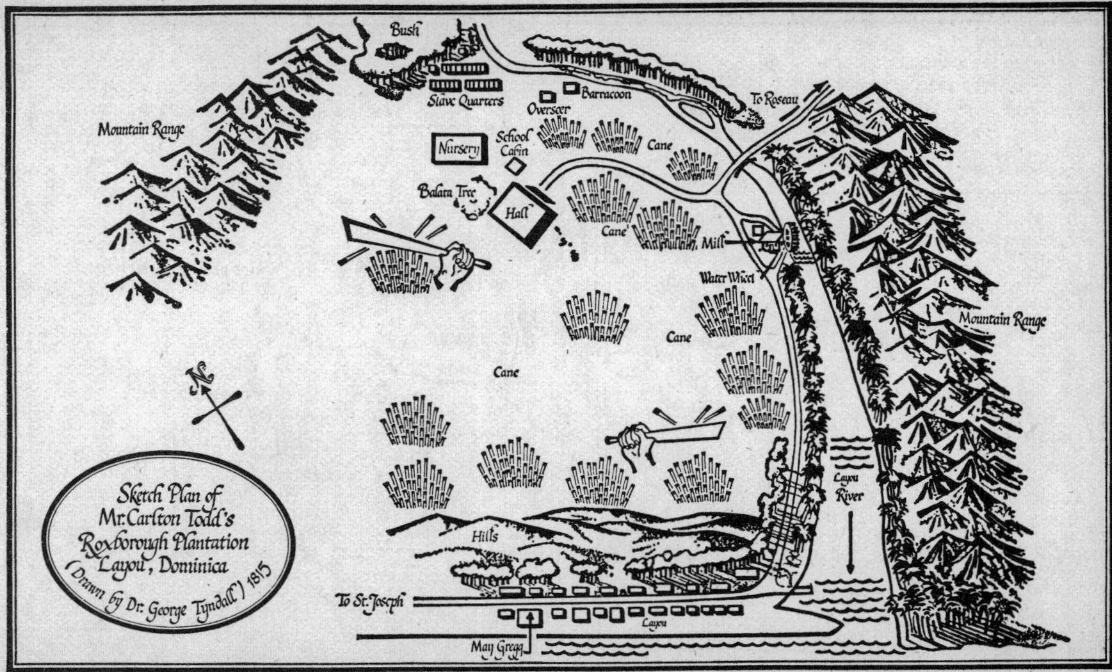
Sketch Plan of
Mr. Carlton Todd's
Roxborough Plantation
Layou, Dominica
(Drawn by Dr. George Tyndall) 1815
Mountain Range
Bush
Slave Quarters
Barracoon
Overseer
School Cabin
Nursery
Balata Tree
Hall
Cane
Cane
Cane
Cane
To Roseau
Mill
Water Wheel
Mountain Range
Layou River
Hills
To St. Joseph
Layou
May Gregg
N

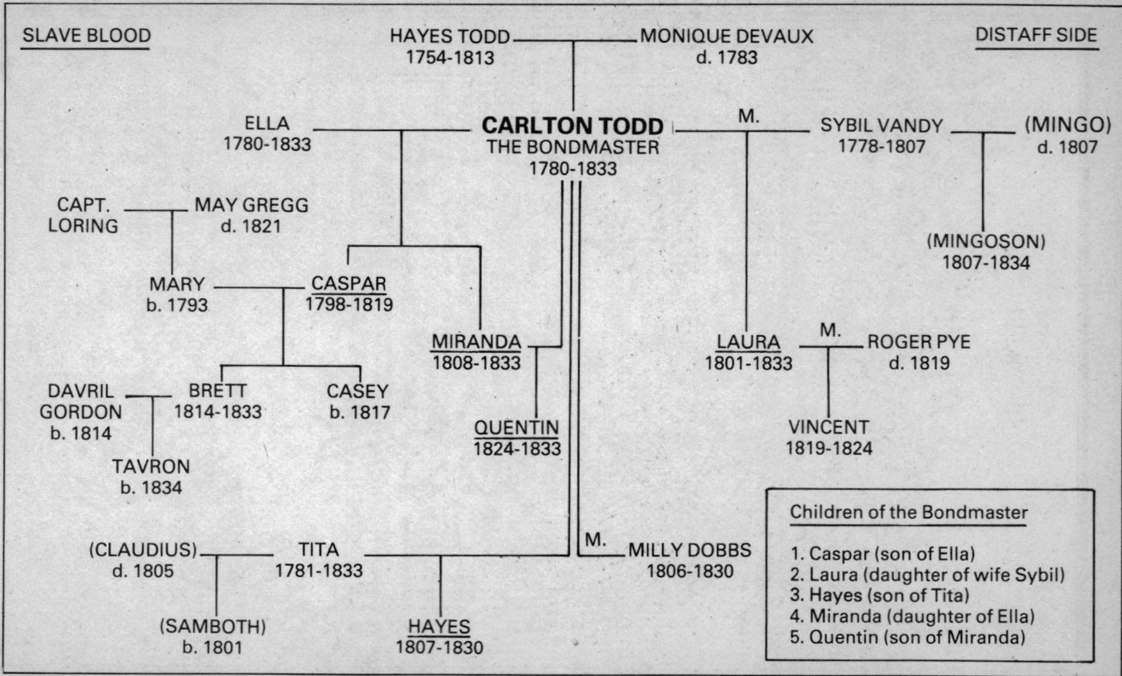

SLAVE BLOOD
DISTAFF SIDE
HAYES TODD
1754-1813
MONIQUE DEVAUX
d. 1783
ELLA
1780-1833
CARLTON TODD
THE BONDMASTER
1780-1833
M.
SYBIL VANDY
1778-1807
(MINGO)
d. 1807
(MINGOSON)
1807-1834
CAPT.
LORING
MAY GREGG
d. 1821
MARY
b. 1793
CASPAR
1798-1819
MIRANDA
1808-1833
LAURA
1801-1833
M.
ROGER PYE
d. 1819
DAVRIL
GORDON
b. 1814
BRETT
1814-1833
CASEY
b. 1817
QUENTIN
1824-1833
VINCENT
1819-1824
TAVRON
b. 1834
Children of the Bondmaster
1. Caspar (son of Ella)
2. Laura (daughter of wife Sybil)
3. Hayes (son of Tita)
4. Miranda (daughter of Ella)
5. Quentin (son of Miranda)
(CLAUDIUS)
d. 1805
TITA
1781-1833
M.
MILLY DOBBS
1806-1830
(SAMBOTH)
b. 1801
HAYES
1807-1830

CONTENTS

'Roxborough Estate in the Layou Valley was the most productive of Dominica's sugar plantations until it declined at the end of the eighteenth century when the Todd family started the first slave warren in the British West Indian Islands.

'The Bondmaster, Mr Carlton Todd, is reputed to have made a considerable fortune by his selective breeding of enslaved Africans for sale to the plantation owners of neighboring islands.

'A Roxborough slave became renowned throughout the West Indies as the elite of that subjugated race, and it is said that many of today's native citizens of prominence have descended from the line begun by the Bondmaster of Roxborough.'

From: *A History of the British West Indian Islands* by Sir Verne W. Bissett, Bart. Published by Shankland & Box, London & Cambridge, 1913.

Prologue

Dark Secrets, 1817

1

The bullock cart lurched along the track through the riverine village. A slave boy with only a dirty breech cloth wrapped around his waist and his black skin drenched and glistening with sweat, ran alongside the cart. He swiped at the bullocks with his larchwood switch and shouted at them to move faster. Two hogsheads of rum rolled against each other on the dray.

Caspar watched the wagon trundle past the step of the rum shop where he was sitting. "That's the order for Ma Gregg," he said.

"Her casino does good business, Caspar."

"Hah!" Caspar slapped his thigh and looked across at Samboth squatting on the trunk of a fallen palm tree. "Ma Gregg needs new whores if she wants my business!"

Samboth looked alarmed.

"Don't worry." Caspar chuckled at his friend's concern. "I'm not going to pay Ma Gregg for her white strumpets. I've got all the wenches I want at Roxborough."

Samboth's face ballooned into a grin. He slipped his hand between his legs and rubbed his crotch. "I wish you give one to me!"

"You!" Caspar shook his head. "If you broke the maid of the Bondmaster's virgins no buck could satisfy them again!" He held up his glass to the sun and peered at Samboth through the amber liquid. The boy hugged himself happily.

"Aye," Caspar said. "John-James doesn't water his rum like some." He gazed at the bullock cart where it had stopped outside Ma Gregg's casino. Two slaves were manhandling the hogsheads to the ground. They were strapping youths with the Roxborough brand, the letter "R", etched into their shoulders. Three white men outside the casino were watching the slaves.

"See those fools there," Caspar nodded his head in the direction of the men. "They're panting for a screw of that rum."

"It does be Roxbruh best."

"Not now Ma Gregg's got it. She adds half a cask of river water to make more profit."

"She does be old and mean, Caspar."

"Aye." He lapsed into silence. It was four years since Caspar had returned to Layou from England with the Bondmaster. He recalled how the Bondmaster made him strip off his new silk breeches in that casino so Ma Gregg could finger him. He was fifteen then.

He drained the contents of the glass and stood up from his seat on the step. He stretched his arms above his head and touched the roof beams of the shack with ease. He had grown a lot in those four years, in mind as well as body. He smiled to himself. If Ma Gregg were to strip him down now her fat face would swell and she'd break wind with greed.

He glanced at Samboth sitting on the trunk of the palm tree. He had befriended the boy the day he arrived back in the island. Samboth was a free negro, three years younger than him. He couldn't have chosen a better companion, unless it was a woman; a real woman, not a slave bed wench.

He sighed and Samboth looked puzzled. "Was thinking," he said, almost to himself.

Samboth jumped to his feet. "Where we going?"

Caspar shrugged.

"Sun setting soon," the boy said. "We done deliver all de rum."

Caspar nodded his head, aware of Samboth's attempt to humor him. He felt so strange these days yet he could fathom no reason for it. Roxborough Plantation was successful and his work as overseer was undemanding. His relationship with the Bondmaster had mellowed and Carlton Todd accepted him as his son even though his mother was a slave. And he had a son of his own, Brett, a bright-skinned child who lived in the pen with the slave whelps.

Yet he was troubled. He ran his hand through his mass of black curls and tried to shake off his mood.

"Caspar!"

Samboth's urgent whisper brought him back to the present. The boy was tugging at his sleeve with excitement and pointing down the track.

Layou was a prosperous village. The vast mouth of the river was a fine anchorage and there was usually a cluster of schooners moored behind the sand bar. They discharged cargo at night to escape the attention of the revenue men in the port of Roseau, twelve miles down the coast.

The village had grown with the informal trade until it was famed throughout the Caribbees for its casinos, its rum and its wenches. It was a lawless quarter bounded by the river to the south, by the sea to the west, and by the hills and canefields of Carlton Todd's Roxborough Plantation to the north and east.

Caspar gazed along the mud track between the wooden shacks and stone-wall taverns. Bare-backed negroes were sauntering up from the river bank while mulattoes slouched under the eaves of the bars and brothels. Tough white men bounded along the track in tight groups eager for gaming and wenches.

"What is it?" Caspar frowned, seeing nothing unusual.

"Look there! It does be Mistress Mary back from Trinidad."

Caspar suddenly felt hot. "I don't see her."

"Yes, you do! Look behind dat gang of matelots."

He saw her. She was surrounded by her cronies, a white girl from her whorehouse and two slaves dressed to look like ladies. She smiled encouragingly at the tars as she proceeded through the village. Caspar licked his lips nervously.

It was three years since he and Mary were sweethearts. It was madness, and they both had suffered for it. Brett had been born and became a Roxborough slave and Mary had not looked at Caspar since. It was as though the moments of passion they shared had never happened.

He scowled bitterly. She was white and a white man's

whore, and to be seen with him was bad for business. He hated Mary for she made him conscious of something he could never change: the color of his skin.

"She comin' here!" Samboth's shout of delight stirred him. He stepped back hurriedly into the rum shop.

"Ain't you gonna bid she howdye?"

He grimaced. Samboth meant well but he wasn't going to expose himself to public scorn. Let her go! He had done without her for three years.

"I declare!" He heard Mary's drawl, typical of the whites born in the Caribbean. A shiver touched his spine and he drew deeper into the gloom of the shop.

"Ain't yew Samboth?"

Samboth danced in the doorway of the shop, bobbed his head and grinned foolishly. "Yes, ma'am!"

Caspar glimpsed Mary's face and sighed. She was more beautiful than he remembered. Her lips were the juicy red color of sangaree. Her hair was silken and golden, falling in cascades around the cambric collar of her pink dress. Her face glowed and her eyes, a forlorn blue under her long dark lashes, sparkled with pleasure.

"How nice to see yew, Samboth. I was in Trinidad, yew know..." Her voice was husky and she seemed about to say something else but her companion was urging her to walk on.

"Fie on you for speaking to nigger riff-raff," Caspar heard the woman say. "What will the tars think!"

"What, indeed?" Mary's voice sounded sad. "If they knew..."

"Knew what?" The white woman's nose quivered at the scent of scandal.

"Nothing!" Mary's face hardened. "Come on," she snapped. "Can't dally here!"

Caspar bit his lip, fighting back the urge to call her name. He was breathless and weak, his legs scarcely capable of supporting him. He leaned against an up-turned rum cask and waited for the heat in his body and the hardness pulsing in his breeches to subside.

Mary Gregg looked around the reception room of her bordello and formed a moue of displeasure with her voluptuous lips. The room was heavy with shadows, the windows draped with brocade curtains and the single lantern burning low. The couches were occupied with clients and simpering whores.

From the bedrooms leading off the reception room came the squeals of her girls and the grunts of drunken men laboring for their money's worth. The wooden floor of the bordello, which was upstairs of her mother's casino, shook with the gyrations of her customers.

Mary turned and groped along the darkened passage to her chamber at the rear of the house. It would soon be dawn; she could sleep now. The dark hulk of a man loomed in front of her, blocking the door to her room.

"Miz Mary?"

"Yes, Apollo?" She sounded tired.

"Yo' a'right, Miz?"

"Of course. Let me in."

The huge slave opened the door and held it while Mary entered. He brought a burning taper and lit the candle for her. She sighed with relief. The room was small, prettily furnished with the *objets d'art* she had been given on her trips to other islands. Her bed was hung with deep red curtains, the sheets and pillow cases exquisitely embroidered. Five dolls, each with dresses far more modest than the one she wore, lay on the bed. Another doll, a black one dressed like a Regency dandy, lay with them.

The daintiness of her boudoir revealed a side of Mary's personality unknown to the bordello's clients. They saw her as a tough madam bullying her feisty whores, punching sailors when they were troublesome, and ruling her brothel with an attitude that allowed no nonsense. But Mary, behind the hard exterior which helped her survive in the rough world of her waterfront whorehouse, was a woman of tenderness.

She watched Apollo place the candle in its ormolu holder on the top of the escritoire. He was a magnificent black. The sight of him never failed to give her pleasure. His features were classical, his eyes dark and sultry, and he moved with a feline grace which befitted the discreet splendor of her chamber.

Yet tonight not even the presence of Apollo could still the sense of restlessness which bedevilled her. She dismissed him with a wave of her hand and he withdrew carefully, closing the door behind him.

Since she returned to the island, Mary had such a feeling of dissatisfaction. She undressed slowly while she considered the matter. Her heart was no longer in what she was doing. There was no fun any more in catering for the debauched whims of arrogant planters, merchants, sailors and sickly soldiers.

She picked up the dolls and placed them on the chair beside the bed. Playfully, she slapped the backside of the black one. "Yew naughty boy!" she said, trying to laugh. "Pestering my gals again." She climbed wearily into her bed and blew out the candle.

With her head on the pillows she reviewed her life. As the daughter of May Gregg and the old sea dog, Captain Loring, it was inevitable that she would enter her mother's trade. In time, May Gregg's casino would be hers. Anything would be better than having to lie with a different man every night.

A deep sigh wracked her body and she cupped her full breasts in her hands. It was too late now. Had she ever loved a man, she wondered, but she knew the answer even if she refused to accept it. There was one man, warm and loving, but young and naive...

She moaned with frustration and thrashed her body against the mattress. The door to the boudoir opened and closed quietly. Soft footfalls approached her bed and the mattress subsided with the weight of someone on it. She reached up and pulled the hard muscular body down beside her. It was Apollo and she clung to him, cradled in his strong arms, and rested her head against the softness of his hairless cheek. Tears streamed down her face.

"Hush, hush," Apollo said. He stroked her hair and hummed a lullabye.

"Hold me, Apollo," Mary choked in her sobs. "I feel. . . "

"Dere, dere. Hush nuh!" Apollo patted her shoulder as she pressed her naked body close to his own. She wrapped her legs around his sturdy thighs and squeezed him in despair. He cradled her and she wept.

He could do nothing else; he had been gelded by the Bondmaster when he was ten. Clasped in his arms, Mary fell into a troubled sleep as the first cock crowed and dawn began to drift into Layou.

2

The rain fell ceaselessly, pelting the cobbles and splashing back again in dull sprays. It was typical London weather and the boy watching from the basement window of the terrace house with his eyes at pavement level, stared listlessly at each splash.

The rain gathered strength and joined up puddles into a rivulet which coursed along the paving stones. It found the steps leading from the pavement and surged down them, creating a pool in front of the basement door. The boy grimaced as the pool grew in size.

The boy wanted to play. He didn't like being confined to the basement. His mother said he was lucky to live in a grand house but if he wasn't allowed upstairs and had to keep as quiet as a mouse, it wasn't much luck at all.

He knew that his mother's employer, James Stephens, was a great man but his greatness was very inconvenient. He couldn't play in the nursery upstairs because his mother was a servant to the great man.

"Upstairs" assumed a major importance to the seven year old boy because "upstairs" and the people who lived there kept him downstairs. Other people rode around London in their carriages but the boy was trapped like a prisoner in the basement. London was a city of riches and opportunity, but not for him.

The pool of water began to seep under the basement door. The boy got down from the chair on which he had been standing with his nose pressed against the window, and walked out into the passage way. The mat which lay against the door was soaked and water swirled around it. The boy shrugged, jammed his hands into his pockets and idly kicked the door.

"Carl! What are you doing?" The boy looked up sulkily as his mother hurried down the stairs. "Why didn't you tell me the rain's coming in!"

Carl pulled his hands out of his pockets ready to protect himself if his mother belabored him with the broom. She always carried that broom in her hands when she went upstairs. But she didn't use it on him this morning. Instead she pushed him out of the way and began to clear up.

He watched her curiously. When she got down on her knees she was no longer taller than he was. She turned on him suddenly.

"Fetch a pail!"

Carl didn't answer. He sauntered into the scullery, pulled a bucket out from under the sink and dragged it, clanging on the flagstones, to his mother.

"For gawd's sake, stop that row, Carl!" His mother sounded distraught. It was a danger sign. He handed her the bucket and smiled.

"You finished upstairs?"

"Yes, thank gawd."

"Mum! I don't know what to do."

"Play with something."

"How can I when I'm by myself?"

His mother stood up, clutching her back. She glared at him. "Poor little bastard," she said half to herself. "Come on, I'll make you some hot milk."

He settled down on the old couch, a worn one which had come from upstairs, and sipped his milk. His mother sat at the other end, her shoes kicked off and her feet stretched out in front of her.

"I've got one hour," she said, "then I've got to go upstairs again." She closed her eyes.

He looked from his mother's face to the window. It was still raining. He looked at his mother again. Her head was lolling forward. Her hair was gray, strands dangling down untidily under her cap. Her pinny was untied and she seemed exhausted. He finished his milk, got up from the couch and carried his cup into the scullery.

"If I had a dad," he thought suddenly, "he would tell them my mum isn't going upstairs again. Ever." He ran back to the old lady on the couch and sat next to her, wrapping his arms around her frail body. He hugged her.

"You little bugger!" she said angrily. "You woke me up."

"Don't go upstairs, mum. Stay here with me."

Mrs Brady relaxed and he snuggled up to her quickly. "If I had a dad, he wouldn't let you."

"Crikey!" Mrs Brady was scornful. "You can forget about your dad!"

"That's what the under footman said. He said I had a silly name."

"Did you tell him your full name?"

Carl noticed his mother's eyes spark. He sensed he was on dangerous ground, but he didn't know why. "Yes." He was cautious. "I told him my full name's Carlington."

"What did he say?"

"He said it sounded like a place, not a name."

Mrs Brady muttered under her breath.

"Mum, why's my name Carlington?"

"Oh gawd! Won't you let your old mum rest?"

"Tell me!" He sensed there was some mystery here. The rain outside and "upstairs" were forgotten. "Is it a good name? It's not like Malcolm or Peter, is it?"

"No it ain't." Mrs Brady tucked her legs under the couch and pulled him close to her. "It's a very special name that I chose myself."

There was silence, apart from the drumming of the rain, the clatter of carriages on the cobbles, and the noise of the kitchen servants preparing luncheon. Mrs Brady began to speak as though she was telling a story.

"One day, just before you were born, a gentleman came to call on Mr Stephens. He came from far away. His skin was tanned by the sun and his hair was fair like a field of wheat. He was dressed simple, but it was easy to see he was a man of consequence. He was a bluff fellow and spoke to us servants like we was his own.

"He had a way about him. We were charmed. It's not often we see a gentleman so considerate. He complimented Cook and, would you believe it, he gave my bottom a pinch."

Carl's eyes widened and he looked at his mother in amazement.

"He tickled my fancy, son, you can be sure of that."

He held his breath, willing his mother to continue.

"This gent came several times to see Mr Stephens. They had dreadful arguments in the drawing room. I couldn't understand head nor tail of it, and sometimes the gent would leave in a temper. He looked so handsome when he was angry. But he always had a sweet word for me. If he didn't chuck me under my chin, he'd squeeze my elbow."

Mrs Brady paused again and her harsh features softened when she gazed into the past. Carl decided that he liked this man who was so kind to his mother.

"I remember the last time he came here," she continued after a few sniffles. "Mr Stephens said he was coming and I was in the hall when the butler opened the door. I was shocked when I saw the gentleman had someone with him."

"Who, mum?"

"You'll never guess."

Carl thought. "His wife?"

"No. His wife was dead. He had his son with him, that's who. But his son was half a negro!"

Carl was speechless.

"Well, Mr Stephens was taken aback. I don't know what was said in the drawing room although I dusted the hall until it shone while I tried to listen. After some time, the son came out. He looked ever so proud, but he was black, wasn't he, so I paid no attention to him."

"I've never seen someone black, mum."

"No more had I, not close up. Cook and I questioned him. He told us his father owned the greatest plantation in the Caribbean. He said his father was so rich, he had treasure buried under his house. His father had a farm of slaves and bred them to sell to other planters."

Carl shivered.

"The half-negro said his father was the Bondmaster because he owned so many bondsmen. Mr Stephens is an Abolitionist, so I believed what the boy said was true. The Bondmaster had been visiting Mr Stephens to acquaint him with life on the plantations.

"The boy was called Caspar. He was a cocky little fellow, no more than twelve. He sat here on this very couch where you are now." Mrs Brady laughed suddenly.

"We had a skivvy with us then. I forget her name but she was a rude girl. She wanted to know if Caspar was black all over. He said yes and opened his britches to show us. He had the biggest prick I've ever seen!"

"Oh mum!"

"It's true. Well, Mr Stephens had an awful row with the Bondmaster. It didn't matter how rich the gent was, Mr Stephens told him to leave the house for ever. It was a big scandal in the Crescent."

Carl could scarcely contain himself. "What was the Bondmaster's name, mum?"

Mrs Brady paused, then said slowly, "Carlton Todd."

"But that's like my name!"

"Yes, son."

He looked at his mother's face, lined with years of worry and hard work. It was difficult to imagine that she was ever young, and once had her fancy tickled by a wealthy stranger from the Caribbean.

"Is he my father, mum?" he asked in a whisper.

"That's my secret," she replied and pushed him away.

3

Carlton Todd sat on the gallery which girt Roxborough Hall like a corset preventing the sagging wooden walls from bulging. His chair was tilted back, his legs extended so that his heels were hooked on top of the gallery rail. He sipped reflectively at a sour rum punch. The end of the year was nigh and he could look back contentedly on his affairs.

His slaves flourished; they were well fed, muscular, fit and healthy. A Bondmaster negro was a pleasure to the eye, a superb specimen of lusty nigrescence. Prices were high because planters needed new slaves now none reached the islands from Africa. His breed were creolized and trained, and in demand throughout the Caribbean.

He savored his rum punch and beamed with self-satisfaction. He loved his blacks. They were the finest crop a man could have. His herd brought him a fortune while the other planters, relying on sugar and coffee, sank deeper into debt each year.

He withdrew his feet from the balcony rail and sat up. To his right, the sun was positioned for the dive into the sea that heralded nightfall. He caught a glimpse of Caspar swaggering along the path to the sugar mill. Carlton was proud of the boy. Although he was only half white, it was Carlton's blood in his veins and that was stronger than the black blood of his mother.

He scowled as a thought occurred to him. It was all right for a white man to drain himself into a black wench but not for a negro to poke his pecker into a white conny. No, sir! The very idea made his cheeks color with anger.

He stood up and gripped the railing, his knuckles white

against his tanned skin. He had seen so much at Roxborough and things had happened which ought never to have happened. A black man was an animal to be admired like a pedigree race horse. White women and soft-hearted Abolitionists didn't understand that.

His thoughts were interrupted by a giggle. He heard a whispered warning and the giggle was stifled. He looked down. Three girls were emerging from the kitchen under the house. They hurried across the courtyard with their eyes on the flagstones.

The sight pleased him. Slaves had to be terrified to make them do whatever their master wants. He squeezed his crotch happily. "You, there!" His voice snapped out into the sultry afternoon and the girls stopped.

"Turn around and raise your heads so I can see you." The girls' fingers fumbled for each other and they moved closer together before shyly gazing up at him.

"Where are you going?" He surveyed them with interest. "Speak up!"

"De pen, massa." It was the tallest girl who spoke. She was ebony black with a crown of frizzy hair and the outline of young breasts prominent under her osnaburg shift.

"De pen, massa," chorused the other two. He dismissed them from his mind.

"What's your age?"

The girl faltered. She was in the center and looked at her companions. There was some whispering. Carlton drummed his fingers on the top of the balcony rail. The girls could have gone another way to the pen if they hadn't wanted him to see them.

"Twelve, sah."

The girl sounded bolder now. One of her companions giggled. Carlton's throat tightened.

"Those chits can go on their way. You, come here!"

The girls parted, the younger ones linking hands and running off into the bush. The ebony one approached the house, her youthful hips swinging.

"Back step," said Carlton, clucking with annoyance. "Slaves use the back step."

The girl raised her face. Her tiny pink tongue flashed against her lips. She ran off around the house. Carlton grinned to himself and sank back into his chair. He fondled his crotch.

"I's here, sah."

The girl was standing in front of him. She had a full body, well proportioned and gleaming. Her shift barely covered her thighs. He blinked. "Hmm!" was all he could manage to say.

"Yassah?"

He swallowed. "Name?"

"Uraline, sah."

He frowned, trying to place her. "Know your mam, do you?"

"No, sah."

"Sire?"

"No, sah."

That didn't surprise him. Whelps were taken from their dams even before they were weaned. The mothers went back to the fields and the suckers were raised in the Pen by wet nurses. That way they had a chance of survival and the dam could be mounted again.

Carlton sniffed. "I could check the stock book," he said. "But you look pleasing enough. Coromantee, I expect." He was proud of being able to tell a slave's blood line by its features. Some tribes made better slaves than others. He sniffed again.

"You bathe today, gal?"

"Oh yas, sah!" There was a glint of amusement in the girl's eyes. Carlton was puzzled.

"Someone tell you to bathe?"

"Miz Ella, sah."

Ah, so that was it. Ella never let him down. "What else did she tell you?"

"To be respec'ful, sah." The girl gained confidence. "An' to do what yo' does tell me."

"What would you like to do, Uraline?" Carlton uncrossed his legs and covered his swollen crotch with his hand.

"Anyt'ing, sah."

"Hmm." The sun was poised to sink into the sea. There were no clouds on the horizon. "You see there," he said, pointing. "Watch the sun."

He glanced at her to see if she understood. The sun was a deep gold and lit up her face. Her complexion was smooth, the rich color of a pure African, like midnight velvet. He turned away and gazed at the sun. It plunged gracefully out of sight into the ocean as he held his breath and fingered himself absent-mindedly. The green flash was so quick, he almost missed it. His eyes were full of stars.

"Did you see it?" he asked eagerly. "The green light?"

"Yassah."

The girl's answer lacked conviction. He sighed. It was always the same. There were only two things slaves were good for: breeding and toil. And they needed constant lashing to make them do the latter.

"Are you a virgin?"

"I does not know, sah."

Carlton raised his eyebrow. "Anyone mounted you yet? Caspar? Any of the bucks from the barracoon?"

The girl seemed to be considering what answer Carlton wanted. "No, sah," she said hopefully.

"One way to find out," he said. "Shuck off your shift!" Not for the first time, Carlton wished he had a white companion at Roxborough. His enjoyment of his slaves, like that of any collector of beautiful objects, was heightened when he could show them off to someone.

The child stepped out of her shift. She was used to being naked and seemed to know that her body was forming in the special way that made bucks want to touch and enter it. He beckoned her.

"Stand here." He indicated the space immediately in front of his chair. His legs were opened wide and he leaned forward. His left hand held her buttocks firmly as his right hand began to trace a pattern over her naked body.

He passed his hand over her shoulders, across her chest and held her young breasts in his fingers, squeezing them. He stroked her flat stomach and then gripped her crotch. Tears came to her eyes and he grinned. He shoved his fist between

drifted down and rested on her hair.

"You're a quick wench," he murmured. "Get me a fancy and I'll give you a bolt of cloth."

"Fancy?" She uttered the word without comprehending it.

"Aye," he spoke softly, almost tenderly. "Bright-skinned whelp. He'll sell for more money."

"Money?" The girl thought about that. "Ah, yes," she said with a sigh.

There was something in her tone which alerted Carlton. He boasted of his sixth sense where slaves were concerned. He claimed to know what they were thinking before they knew it themselves.

"What's in your mind?" he asked sharply, opening his eyes. He gripped the girl's slender neck in his fingers, leaving no room for doubt that he would snap off her head like a flower if he felt so inclined.

"Sah?" Terror entered the girl's voice.

"What do you know about money?"

"Nothing, sah!" The child's bleat did not satisfy him.

"Who told you about money?"

"De slaves, sah."

He waited for her to continue.

"Dey does say yo' does hab muh money dan anyone. Yo' is de Bondmassa, sah!"

Carlton was almost satisfied. He released the girl and picked up the glass of punch. He sipped thoughtfully. The child edged across the floor dragging her shift with her. "Stay!" he shouted.

There was something wrong. Why should his slaves discuss his fortune among themselves? Did they have more intelligence than he credited them with? An insurrection could start at anytime. There were escaped slaves, maroons, in the mountains. He had to be alert.

"Uraline!" His soft voice startled the girl. Oh yes, how slaves hate to have their names known in case there is punishment in the offing.

"Yes, massa?" she said unhappily.

"Tell me about this money."

"What, sah?" Even in the dark, without seeing her eyes, he could smell her fear.

Rippon rolled his tired eyes. "He does be lyin' in de still room, missus, clutchin' his belly and cryin'."

"Tell the monkey I'll give 'im something to cry at!"

"Perhaps he dyin', missus."

"I'll stuff 'is carcass and use 'im as a door stop if 'e does!" She dismissed Rippon and looked around her, gauging the mood of her patrons.

Seamen, merchants, overseers and all the riff-raff of the island flocked to her casino for the rum and wenches she and her daughter supplied. She wheezed with delight. She was too fat to circulate but she liked to see her customers enjoying themselves. A fiddler played on the tiny stage across the room and some of the men were dancing with each other. She didn't allow women in her casino. They were to be had upstairs, for a price.

May had earned a reputation for being fearless. Men drank, gambled, danced, fought and even died while she remained unflinching in her chair. Actually, she needed three slaves to prize her from the chair so she remained immobile in times of commotion because of expediency rather than courage. But men regarded her as a rock and even the bravest came to her for comfort. Her huge bosom harbored countless secrets.

There was a disturbance in the crowd. It rippled through the groups of drinkers as a man pushed his way in her direction. Her tiny eyes narrowed with consternation. "Law, lummee!" she said in astonishment when she saw who it was. She blinked.

"Carlton Todd!" she wheezed deeply. "Oo'd 'ave thought you'd ever come 'ere?"

Carlton shrugged and took the chair a slave handed to him. He sat down at May's table, flicking his fingers under the slave's nose. "Grogg," he said crustily. "None of your piss. I want the best screw in the house."

May waited while Carlton poured rum out of the jug which the slave brought him on a pewter tray. She watched him throw the liquid down his throat. He pursed his lips, savoring the taste.

"It'll do," he said grudgingly.

She was gratified to see his eyes moistening. "We put red peppers in the best rum. That's for real men!"

"Aye." Carlton took the jug from the tray and placed it on the table between them. He waved the slave away.

The years had been kind to him, May thought. His face was gaunt and tanned, his once blond hair showed signs of silver which lent dignity to his hard appearance. She let a sigh escape her lips. It wafted the odor of rum and rotting teeth over Carlton.

"It grieved me that we 'ad words, Carlton."

"No doubt."

"Mary would 'ave been ruined if people knew she was carrying a 'alf-breed's child."

Carlton leaned closer, his eyes holding her own. "Caspar's my son, May. Your purse is as fat as your arse so you had no reason to squeeze me by blackmail like you tried."

May panted with delight, her fat tongue hanging out at the side of her mouth. "I'm so 'appy to see you, Carlton," she said when she caught her breath and her jowls stopped shaking like a blancmange. She remembered how he threatened to close down the casino if she insisted that he hang Caspar for raping Mary.

She raised her hands in the air in a gesture of forgiveness. "I ain't got no 'ard feelings!"

"You ain't got no feelings at all," said Carlton, sipping his rum with respect. His glance wandered around the casino.

"What's wrong?" May was surprised to notice that her question startled him. He put his goblet on the table and looked at her.

"You don't grow no smaller, May."

"You didn't come 'ere to pay me compliments!"

"I'll pay you something better than that."

May's massive thighs churned under the table. She was shrewder than Carlton but she couldn't guess what had brought him to her. He was proud and wilful. It must be a matter of importance or profit.

He could have read her mind. "Got tired of me own company, May."

"You ain't come for an 'ore!" May's chins wobbled with amazement.

"Ain't a white strumpet that can match a hot niggerling." He sipped his rum. "Ain't that I'm talking about."

She was intrigued. "You planning something lustful?"

"No, May." He managed to smile. "Get your filthy mind off fornication."

"It's my business."

"Aye, and mine's niggers. We're a pair."

"Whooh! I never dreamed the day would come when the 'igh and mighty Bondmaster would couple 'imself to a fat old 'ore!"

"You ain't making it very easy for me." Carlton poured more rum from the jug, spilling some on the table. She tapped her glass.

"What about me?"

Carlton looked as though he were seeing her for the first time. He sniffed, and poured some rum into her goblet. That glance told her what she wanted to know.

"You're a cool bugger, Carlton Todd! You've come 'ere to get something out of me."

He seemed relieved. "It's true! And I'll pay."

"What am I selling?"

"Hah! I knew you'd not let me down. If recompense is involved, you'll do anything, won't you?"

"There ain't nothing I never done in me time."

Carlton smiled at that, gesturing at the hubbub of the people packed into the casino. "Your business is good, May. You could use an extra couple of slaves."

"So that's it! You've got some useless niggers you want to get rid of!" Her eyes gleamed. "I ain't taking none of your rejects."

"Not rejects. That wouldn't be good propaganda for the Bondmaster breed." He sounded offended.

"I know slaves like I know men, Carlton. You've got some devil's scheme in your 'ead!"

Carlton sat up, his back straight. "Glad you know slaves, May. I've got a pair for you to inspect."

"I'm not buying."

"I'm not selling." He snapped his fingers and the skull-like face of Rippon emerged at his side. Carlton spoke to him and the slave looked at May. She nodded her consent, curious at what trick Carlton was planning. She wondered if this was his way of getting revenge after three years of emnity between them. Rippon disappeared to the back of the bar.

She sipped her rum without speaking. Carlton, too, was lost in thought. She eyed him curiously. There was an insatiable rage burning in the man, and a searing loneliness.

"Please, missus."

May turned to see Rippon pushing forward two slaves. The male was the color of copper, naked except for a strip of breech cloth around his loins. His body was sleek and gleaming; his face, young and eager, had a pleasing smile and fine features.

His companion was a female whose shift showed off her slender, ripe body and proud breasts. Her hips were wide with thighs made for passion. She was dark and comely. May gasped, unable to speak.

"A pair." Carlton's cold voice interrupted her astonishment. "The buck is sixteen, bursting with sap. Got Fulani blood in him. The filly's twelve, in heat already. Cross them and you'd get a litter of bright-skinned whelps you could sell for a small fortune."

May couldn't take her eyes off them.

"Finger them if you like. Not a flaw to be found. Wench ain't a virgin, of course. Broke her maid myself."

May found her voice. "I ain't buying," she said weakly.

"I know that. Never known you to part with currency if you can get it for free."

"Are these free?"

"They're yours if you want them. Uraline," he spoke to the girl. "Drop your shift for Ma Gregg."

"No!" May lifted her hands. "You'll start a bloody riot."

"You're an evil old bitch, May, but you have your price. This pair is double your price but they're yours. If you do something for me." He took some documents from his pocket. Two were festooned with red ribbon and his seal, and the third was a piece of vellum folded in quarters.

"What's that?" she asked sharply.

"These are the title deeds to the slaves. Take them." He pushed two documents into her hand. "The slaves are yours."

"What do I do?" She was overwhelmed and suspicious that Carlton had out-maneuvered her.

"Take this." He passed the third document to her. "It's sealed. You just agree never to open it."

She took the paper and inspected it dubiously.

"May, if anything happens to me, I want you to give that document to my heir."

"That's all?" She tucked the vellum in her bodice where it was swallowed up by her ample breasts. "Are you sure that's all?"

"Yes, May. Do you swear you'll keep it secret?"

"Lumme, Carlton," she said, tapping her chest and glancing at the two young slaves. "I'll swear anything you want for a piece of that buck. See 'ow 'e's 'ung!" She sighed with disbelief. "I'd do anything too!"

The casino was empty of standing customers and the slaves picked their way over the ones lying drunk on the floor. May Gregg shook and a huge sigh of relief wobbled through her. She had dozed for the last two hours, trapped in her chair by her ponderous weight and her duty. She believed her presence in her casino until the last customer had staggered out was necessary. It helped to make her a legend, and preserved some sort of order.

She beckoned the slaves around her and watched owlishly while they counted the takings and showed her the credit book and the stock registers. Only when she was satisfied that there were enough receipts to cover the drinks consumed, did she relax.

Her body was in a turmoil. Ever since Carlton had left earlier in the evening, she had been longing to inspect the two slaves he'd given her. Now that the casino was closed, she could study them at her leisure. She would worry later about the real reason for Carlton's extraordinary gift.

She flapped her hands impatiently while a slave cleared the coins into a coffer and another stood behind her to hold her chair. Rippon and a boy grasped her arms and pulled. She came out of the chair with a whoosh. The momentum was sufficient to propel her off the dais in the direction of her chamber and because of her excitement, she waddled as fast as she could after the slave bearing the takings. Rippon and the boy gripped her arm to steady her in case she keeled over.

Once in the chamber, there was the ritual of positioning her on her commode. This accomplished, she farted with contentment while she watched the money being secured in its hiding place in the wall. She gave Rippon the two slave deeds to put in as well. She was too tired to dig in her bodice for the other document.

When the keys to the safe had been handed to her, she shook herself dry and allowed Rippon and his helper to haul her off the close-stool and deposit her on the bed. That was the time for the slaves to withdraw so she could sleep.

"Send in the chit and the new buck," she told Rippon. The old slave shuffled out and May ignored the censure she fancied she saw in his eyes. She squeezed her thighs together and quivered with anticipation.

The buck came in first. He stayed in the center of the room where the light from the lantern highlighted his features. He was naked to his breech cloth and his young muscles seemed to be sculpted from polished gold. His arms were folded across his chest and he stood with his legs apart. His smile was mischievous and knowing. May gloated.

The girl pushed herself forward. "Mah name does be Uraline, miz," she said. "Dis buck does be Tony."

May's eyes darted from one to the other. They were both perfect. The girl's smile was pleasant and, if she was a little bold in speaking without being asked, it suited May Gregg. She didn't like dullards around her. The girl seemed to be a veritable black sprite, probably a tigress when she was under the covers.

Someone coughed by the door.

"What the 'ell is it, Rippon?"

"Beg pard'n, missus. Bambute done die."

"Shove 'im through the window into the sea!"

"Yo' ain' gonna stuff him, missus?"

"I'll stuff you, Rippon, if you don't get out and shut that door!"

"De slaves..."

"They're sleepin' 'ere with me, Rippon. Put 'im out, boy!" She was astonished when Tony spun around on his toes, put his arms around Rippon, picked him up and threw him out of the room.

"Whooh!" she said, hugging herself with delight. "Now close the door."

He did so immediately, returning to stand, like a prize fighter, under the lantern, alert and waiting for her next command.

May's mind was racing. She had never owned a slave who would do everything without a sour expression or ill-concealed reluctance. It was a heady feeling.

"Now you!" She looked at Uraline. "You've got a tongue in your 'ead, I know. Let's see if you do as you're told."

"Oh yes, miz."

"Right! Step out of that shift."

Uraline's eyes lit up. Quickly, she loosened the shift and wriggled her shoulders so it fell to the floor. She glanced at May expectantly.

"Come here." May began to pant. "On to the bed."

Uraline sat on the bed facing May. She looked at her to see if she was doing the right thing.

"Yes, yes," said May, her bosom heaving. "But move closer, I can't reach."

She clapped her heavy hand on Uraline's shoulder. Her fingers probed lower and pummelled the girl's breasts. She was enraptured by the girl's apparent pleasure at being fondled. She dropped her hand between her legs and squeezed. The girl sighed with ecstasy and wrapped her slender arms around May's neck.

"Whooh!" said May, shaking. She opened her eyes and looked at the boy still standing in the center of the room. He was jumping from one foot to the other, his breech cloth sticking out in front of him.

She released Uraline and pushed her off the bed. "That brute needs you, gal. Take off 'is diaper."

She watched, almost choking as a feeling of desire stormed through her.

Uraline approached Tony slowly, like a cat stalking its prey. She put out her hands to touch him and jumped away playfully when he snarled at her. May clapped her hands and wheezed happily.

"'is pants, gal!"

Uraline tugged at the cord holding Tony's breechcloth and it fell loose. She teased him with her fingers as she pulled it away from his thighs.

May gawked. Blacks had a reputation for being well hung but Tony outdid every rumor. He was colossal and yet not so monstrous as to be repulsive. It was solid beauty, a rod of burnished copper which pulsed gently in the glow from the lantern near his head.

Tony and Uraline, standing naked side by side, were watching her. She pulled her frock up to her waist and opened her thighs.

"Come," she said hungrily. "Both of you, come!"

5

The trail from Roxborough Hall to the Layou River was a broad avenue. On either side were royal palm trees growing tall and straight with their gray trunks smooth and patterned as though carved in alabaster. Bougainvillaea and hibiscus bushes filled the spaces between the palms and the borders of the road were lush with spongy grass imported from Bermuda.

Caspar sauntered along the trail lost in thought. The Bondmaster had ordered him to go to Layou and see May Gregg. He couldn't understand the object of what he was to ask her but he dared not question Carlton's orders.

He took the right fork on the trail, walking alongside the river, passing the cane mill with its lumbering water wheel. The mill was concealed from the track by the thick clumps of sugar cane growing around it. On his right, the cane pieces stretched right up the hillside.

He didn't notice the scenery as he walked, nor hear the birds singing in the mild morning. He was troubled by Carlton's instructions and didn't want to enter May Gregg's tavern. The cantankerous old bitch would probably throw him out. Was that his father's intention – to remind him of his inferiority?

He sucked his lip. The only bright side was that he might see Mary. He wondered what she'd say. It was the message that he was to deliver to her mother that perturbed him. It didn't make sense yet he knew that Carlton always had a reason for his actions. He was supposed to ask May Gregg if she had stored the letter carefully. He wondered what letter? He couldn't help feeling that it was some silly jape which would end in him being humiliated.

He flung the stick he was carrying into the trees and listened with satisfaction as it crashed through the leaves and fell into the river. He was approaching Layou.

It was mid-morning. He walked slowly past the jetty where blacks, both free and slave, were unloading lighters. The sugar warehouse, where he used to make love to Mary, was opposite. The sight of it made him think of her again. At that hour, she would still be in bed. With a white client!

"Caspar!" The rough shout startled him.

"Samboth, I didn't see you!"

"Dat because you have more sense in your pants dan in your head." His friend studied him. "You does look troubled, Caspar."

He nodded his head at the warehouse. "I was thinking of the time you used to bring Mary to meet me in there."

"I will again if you want."

He stared at Samboth. "What do you mean?" Samboth smirked and danced away.

"Come here, Sam! Don't joke with me." He lunged forward and caught the boy by the scruff of his neck. He lifted him from the ground until he squealed with pain.

"Put me down, Caspar. I'll tell you!"

"Go on." Caspar walked to the shade of a huge mango tree and waited out the moments while Samboth straightened his torn shirt with deliberate slowness.

"Something I hear." Samboth grinned, cocking his head on one side. "Maybe it ain't true."

"What, what?"

"You sure burstin' your britches for dat wench!"

He gripped Samboth's arm tightly. "Tell me!"

Samboth chuckled. "Last night I does be screwin' a maid from de bordello." He held up his hand when Caspar began to protest. "I free to poke my piece where I want, Caspar. You know dat!"

"Go on!"

"De maid say Mary Gregg ain't lay wid no man since she come from Trinidad. She say she see her write you a letter."

Caspar's heart leaped. "That's a lie!"

"No, it ain't." Samboth shrugged his shoulders. "Maybe she didn't feel to send it. Tell me why you in de village at dis hour?"

"Mas Carlton sent me to see Ma Gregg."

"Now dat strange . . ."

Caspar was aware of Samboth watching him quizzically. "A letter, you say?" He shook his head. Mas Carlton had mentioned a letter. It seemed there was some scheme afoot and he was worried.

"Damn it, Samboth!" he said angrily. "It ain't for me to reason things. I'm just a stupid half-breed!"

May Gregg tried to ignore the knocking on her door. She rolled on to her side and nearly capsized the bed. She brushed a mosquito off her backside and tugged her dress down so that it covered her thighs. She was hot and sticky and the stench in the room made her wrinkle her nose with disgust.

The knocking on the door continued. She half-opened her eyes.

The shutters were fastened over the window. Daylight filtered into the room through cracks in the woodwork and gaps in the tiles of the high-gabled roof. She was alone in the chamber and wanted to piss. Her head hammered in time to the blows on the door.

"Shut up!" she shouted but it came out as a hoarse whisper. The knocking continued. She rolled to the edge of the bed and groped on the floor for something to throw at the door. Why didn't the fool come in!

There was a thud as the bed skated on to its side and May tumbled out. She clutched at the commode to break her fall and the box slid over, tipping its contents on to her face. The door burst open and Rippon hurried in.

May was apoplectic. She lay gasping in a stew of excreta, her limbs flaying under the bed sheets and the mattress lying on top of her. Slaves rushed into the room to stare at her.

"'Elp me, you bozal bastards!" she screamed.

It took them time, but the slaves managed to haul her out of the room and into the casino. It was empty except for a youth standing by the door. May took no notice while the slaves dabbed and dried her and poured coffee liberally laced with rum, down her throat.

When the coffee had stabilized her and her body had stopped quaking with indignation, she glanced around the casino. There was a raft of dazzling light floating in from the open door but the windows were still shuttered. She blinked at the slaves hovering around her.

"Mas Caspar does be here, ma."

May blinked again. The sight of Uraline's bright face and Tony standing eagerly at her side, mollified her. She grinned at the memory of the night before, then frowned. "'Oo the 'ell's Caspar?"

"At your service, Ma Gregg!" The youth who had been standing by the door strode across the floor. "I apologize for the rude awakening." He bent low with a bow which had an air of mockery about it.

"Ballocks!" May stared at him unhappily and flapped her

arms at the slaves. They withdrew leaving her alone on the dais. She had a premonition that this visit meant trouble. She knew she shouldn't have accepted the slaves. She shuddered.

"Mas Carlton asked me to come."

She studied Caspar. He had grown quite handsome. His nose was straight and his eyes were the piercing yellow of his father. He was watching her closely, damn him.

"Shut that door!" she said to Rippon. "Too much light in 'ere."

"You don't want people to see me, I suppose. Bad for business?" Caspar shifted uncomfortably.

She stared at him and wondered what he was talking about.

"That's what you told Mas Carlton when I was loving your daughter."

She sighed. So that was it! Carlton had trapped her by giving her those slaves so that Caspar could renew his liaison with Mary. She patted the sweat off her face with a stained handkerchief.

"Times change, Caspar," was all she could think of saying.

"Mas Carlton asks if you have the letter in a secure place. His exact words."

"Letter? Does he want it?" May's chest churned and a numbness spread up her left side like a bullet had struck her heart. She dared not breathe. She gripped the arms of her chair and stared at Caspar, as immovable as a mountain.

"I'm sorry to give you such trouble." Caspar looked embarrassed. "That's all Mas Carlton told me. He said you'll know what he means."

Oh yes, she knew. Carlton said his letter was for his heir. Good lawd! Caspar was his heir. She gulped.

"He wants to know if the letter is safe."

"Oh yes," she lied. "Quite safe. You can tell Carlton it's quite safe."

Caspar turned to go. He really was a splendid looking youngster. May wondered what to do to show she understood Carlton's unspoken request. The letter was obviously only a pretense and the fact that she'd lost it didn't matter.

"Caspar!"

"Yes?" He raised his eyebrow.

"Why don't you call on us more often?" She paused, her eyes on the pair of slaves she'd been bribed with. "Mary would be pleased to see you. Any time."

Mary had been told by her maid who had been told by Samboth that Caspar was in the casino. She sat on the balcony wearing a bonnet to keep the sun from scorching her pale complexion. She held a sampler and stitched clumsily, her eyes on the street below instead of on the embroidery.

"Damn!" she said when the needle pricked her finger. She scowled at Apollo who leaned over the railing at the other end of the balcony watching the casino door. "I don't think I'll ever get the hang of these ladylike pastimes."

"He does be comin'."

Apollo's loud whisper threw her into a panic. The sampler fell off her knees onto the floor. She bent to retrieve it and knocked her bonnet askew. "Damn, damn, damn!" she muttered under her breath, sitting up and trying to straighten it. Her heart was thumping so loudly, she was certain Caspar would hear it.

Then she saw him and her nervousness died. The years of doubt, when she hated him but still wanted him, vanished. He was her Caspar! Her intention of being cool and ladylike was forgotten. She leaped out of her chair and gripped the balcony rail.

"Caspar!" Her shout could be heard from one end of the village to the other, but she didn't care.

When he lifted his head in astonishment and stared at her, she knew she was in love with him. That cute nose, those eyes steeped in sadness, that brow, his black locks and that russet glow. And under the rough elegance of his plantation-tailored breeches and coat, was a body she had lived without for too long.

"Caspar!" This time it was a whisper only he could hear.

He gazed up and down the street as though considering flight. She wanted to tell him not to go, but that would have to be his choice. She opened her mouth to engage him in amusing conversation but she couldn't think of anything to say. She just stood there staring down at him, willing him to be hers.

"Mary?"

"Yes, yes!" She had forgotten the pride in his voice, the manliness.

"Are we to give a tableau for the village?"

"No, I mean . . . oh, I'm so flustered."

"Ask Mas Caspar fuh sang'ree, miz."

"Thank yew, Apollo," Mary said with relief. "Go down and show him up at once." She began an elaborate mime to show Caspar that Apollo was coming for him. He slapped his thigh and shook his head at her silliness.

Then suddenly he was sitting in the drawing room on one side of a low table and she was on the other. Mary prayed that her whores would stay in bed.

"You were in such good voice when I was in the street, now you say nothing?" Caspar was amused. Her heart melted. He was so close, if she extended her foot under the table she could touch his.

Apollo strode in with a tray and a decanter of sangaree. He placed it down on the table with two of her best silver goblets.

"I'll pour," she said hastily. "Yew can go now."

"Yas, miz." Apollo rolled his eyes at Caspar and grinned broadly.

"He's the only kind of buck to have with all the women here," said Caspar while Mary poured the drinks.

"He is a comfort."

"You get no problem with him? With your clients, I mean."

Mary's throat dried. "No," she managed to say. She sipped at the sangaree and felt bolder. "I don't actually have clients myself, Caspar."

"Oh?"

"No, Cas." She tried the term of endearment she used to use when they were together. He hardly noticed. "I don't really like that life. It's because of Ma."

"I see." He hadn't touched his drink.

"Now we are successful, I just keep the books." It sounded

stupid but she wanted him to know how she had changed. "Cas..."

"Yes?"

"Do yew still --"

"Do I what? Still mount the Bondmaster's virgins to get him bright-skinned whelps to sell in Trinidad?" He sounded bitter. "No, Mary." He shook his head sadly and reached for his glass. She felt his foot on hers and wondered if he knew it was there.

"I never was any good as a breeding stud."

"I wasn't any good as a whore."

Caspar and Mary, walking arm in arm down the mud street in the late afternoon, became a regular sight in Layou. The whites were scandalized but Carlton Todd said nothing. He avoided his white neighbors and perhaps never heard the gossip about Caspar and Mary.

"What about Captain Loring?" Caspar asked Mary one evening when they lay side by side on his bed in the overseer's cottage on the plantation.

"Dad?" Mary turned in surprise to look at Caspar.

"Doesn't he say anything? He must know about you and I. Even if Ma Gregg doesn't object, he might."

Mary laughed. "What a strange notion. I haven't seen Captain Loring since I was eight and he dangled me on his knee and stuck his finger in my conny. He's scared of Ma. Besides, he's got a mistress in every port from here to Havana. He couldn't care less about me."

Caspar loved the way Mary laughed. It was a raucous sound, full of animal joy. She was no beauty and her demeanor was hardly ladylike. He adored her toughness, her zest and her vast appetite for him. He found nothing false in her attitude, none of the hypocrisy of the white women he had met when he was in England with the Bondmaster.

"Yew are so thoughtful tonight." Mary tapped him on his nose. "Why do yew worry what people think of us? We should live our life, not theirs."

He put his arm around her shoulder and she nestled closer to him. She smelt like sour limes, that tang which characterized white flesh in the tropics. He loved that odor and it never failed to arouse him.

"I'm only thinking of you. I'm a plantation slave. I'm the lowest form of animal life, apart from a bozal. You're a free white lady. People can hurt you."

She laughed again, running her hands over his bare chest. He squirmed at her touch and pulled her closer. It worried him. "I don't want anything to happen to you, Mary, because of me."

Her fingers strayed across the rippling muscles of his stomach and tugged at the waist band of his breeches. He moved away.

"Cas, what's wrong?"

He didn't know. Was it wrong for him to be so happy? Was it wrong for him to love a white woman?

"Oh, Mary!" he sighed, rolling back and clasping her in his arms. "What are we going to do?"

"I know," she said, her eyes glinting.

He smiled, relishing the warm moistness of her kisses on his cheek. Her tongue toyed with his nostrils then darted between his lips. He opened his mouth to speak but she blocked his words with her own mouth.

He was troubled by the problems of their relationship. He yearned to escape, to carry Mary with him to a paradise where they could feast on each other for ever.

While his thoughts wandered, his fingers were feeling their way under the crushed tulle of Mary's skirt. He stroked the inside of her thighs until she was writhing against him. He probed her tenderly and she bit the tiny lobe of his ear and shuddered.

"Cas, Cas!" she cried, seeking release.

He covered her lips with his mouth and penetrated her slowly. Blood spurted on his back where her finger nails raked his flesh. His own hands branded her body with the fury of his passion.

"When our child is born," said Mary, sitting on the side of the bed and combing her hair, "what shall we do?"

"You won't have a child." Caspar turned over lazily. His

breeches were at his ankles. He didn't bother to pull them up. He raised his hand to stroke Mary's neck.

"Don't do that, Cas! I must get ready to go." She shivered under his touch. She ached for him. "Will you walk with me to the village?"

"Why don't you stay here?"

"Don't change the subject." She placed the comb in her reticule and turned to face him. "Oh, Cas!" she laughed. "Do get dressed."

"You don't usually complain."

"I want to be serious."

He shrugged in the foolish way she adored. She had difficulty keeping her hands off him as he pulled up his breeches and swung his legs over to sit on the edge of the bed beside her.

"Cas . . ." She faltered, hating to spoil their happiness. "I'm pregnant."

He said nothing but she noticed the sudden pulsing of a vein in his neck. She loved him all the more. If he had protested, she would have killed herself, and the child.

"We're going to have a baby, Cas. Our baby. What shall we do?"

He touched her stomach tenderly. "What do you want to do?"

She was surprised. "Are you pleased?"

"Of course I am. It's what I want. Our child."

"Ours?"

"Yes, ours. Not the Bondmaster's whelp this time, but our baby. I don't want the Bondmaster to have him!"

"Oh, he won't, Cas, he won't!" She lay her head on his shoulder and began to weep with happiness.

"He'll be our secret. We can hide him in Layou. He'll be free, Cas. He'll be *our* child, the child of our love!"

Caspar patted her shoulder and stared over her head into space. She wiped her tears and chattered gaily about their future together.

But within months he was dead.*

* See *Blood of the Bondmaster*

Book One

Heir Apparent, 1833 – 1834

6

Carl carried the silver tray into the drawing room and set it down on the table between Mr and Mrs Stephens. A fire blazed in the hearth and its warmth added to the air of tranquility in the room. Through the long windows overlooking the Crescent, London was gray with the damp chill of autumn. Mr Stephens turned the pages of *The Times* unaware of Carl's presence. His wife glanced at the contents of the tea tray and nodded.

"Will that be all, madam?" Carl spoke with the deference expected of him.

"You may draw the curtains."

"Yes, madam." Carl's dull blue eyes were expressionless. He glided across the carpet to the windows and in seconds his presence in the room was forgotten. He gazed at the darkening street where people hurried to shelter from the cold and carriages trundled along with lanterns blazing in the twilight. He drew the heavy velvet curtain across the scene and moved silently to the next window.

"I say!" Mr Stephens was speaking to his wife. Carl glanced at him. He was holding out *The Times* to her. "There's been another dreadful massacre by those poor slaves in the Caribbean."

"Really?" Mrs Stephens raised her eyes politely.

"Listen!" Mr Stephens adjusted his pince-nez. "It happened in Dominica. A man known as the Bondmaster. You remember him, don't you?"

"Do I dear?" Mrs Stephens poured the tea.

Carl went rigid and his hand froze on the curtain. He held his breath. For sixteen years since the day his mother told him of the glamorous stranger he was named after, he had dreamed of his hero in the Caribbean.

"Carlton Todd," said Mr Stephens. "He came here to tell me about his slaves. Proud of them. Even had a son by one of them."

Mrs Stephens handed a cup of tea to her husband. "You meet the strangest people, James."

Mr Stephens placed the cup on the table and turned back to *The Times*. Carl remained motionless by the window as he read aloud.

"The body of Mr Todd was found on the balcony of his home. It is believed that he was poisoned. The bodies of his housekeeper and butler lay close by."

"Well, I never!" Mrs Stephens sipped her tea.

"There's more." Mr Stephens stabbed the paper with his finger. 'The bodies of his daughter and grandson were found lying in the courtyard. They had been horribly mutilated.' "

"Horribly mutilated!" Mrs Stephens gasped and the cup clattered in her hand.

" 'The murders were discovered by the residents of the nearby village of Layou'," Mr Stephens read, unaware of Carl drawing closer to listen. " 'It is reported that the plantation was raided at night by a gang of runaway slaves known as maroons who live in the mountains. A search is being made by soldiers of the Seventh Regiment for the killers.' "

Mr Stephens paused and Carl stared at the back of his head, willing him to continue.

"That's quite extraordinary! It says here that the maroons tried to get the slaves to run away with them but they refused. No one knows what will happen to the plantation as the Bondmaster's family was killed too. There's no heir."

"Oh." Mrs Stephens fanned herself. "I thought slavery had been abolished. Didn't you draft a law about it?"

"Yes, dear," Mr Stephens leaned over and took his tea. "Perhaps the news hasn't reached the slaves yet. The law doesn't come into force until August next year. There will be a period of apprenticeship for them to adjust so the slaves won't be completely free until 1840."

"You're so clever, dear."

Mr Stephens smiled. "I wonder what will happen to the Bondmaster's fortune?"

Carl drew the last curtain and slipped quietly out of the room. He leaned against the dresser in the hall, stunned by the excitement rising in his breast. Carlton Todd had died, leaving a fortune! Carlton Todd had no heir!

"Are you all right, Mr Carl?"

"Yes, yes!" He opened his eyes and saw the chambermaid watching him.

"I hope you aren't sickening, Mr Carl. There's a lot of sickness at this time of the year . . ." The chambermaid followed him as he walked to the servants stairs. He didn't hear a word she said.

Carl was twenty-three and had been in the Stephens' service since his mother died when he was ten. He had been put to work in the kitchen then and rose rapidly to become the family's butler.

He was a sobersides, not given to excesses. He and Cook ran the Stephens' establishment with firmness and efficiency. He suspected that he was not liked by either the Stephens or their servants. He didn't care. What no one knew was that he was really Carlington Todd, son of the Bondmaster. He had no papers to prove it, but it was true. Hadn't his mother named him Carlington after Carlton Todd?

His secret had sustained him through his years of drudgery. Now, by the grace of God, his waiting had come to an end. It was a sign.

In a daze, Carl opened the door to his small bedroom. He had often dreamed about the day he would arrive in Dominica. Carlton Todd would be waiting for him. "Son," he would say, taking him in his arms, "all this is yours."

The door burst open and a hefty woman stood with her arms akimbo glaring at him. Two maids twittered behind her.

"Mr Carl," said Cook loudly. "Betsy says you're sick. We have eight people for dinner so you can't be sick!"

Carl held his head. "Terrible headache," he said. "It will pass. Must rest. Half an hour. Be all right."

"Hmm!" Cook snorted with suspicion. "You haven't had a headache before."

"Please leave me alone. Hurts."

"Very well! Half an hour, no more. Betsy will collect the tea tray." She ushered the maids out of the room and threw a glance of scorn at Carl before she closed the door.

He reached for the valise under the bed and opened it. He had a sorry collection of clothes, nothing fit for a gentleman. His savings from his meager wages over the years amounted to a few pounds, barely enough for the coach to Bristol and a few nights at an inn while he looked for a ship.

Looked for a ship? The thought stunned him. Yes, he decided, this was the chance he had dreamed of. By fair means or foul, he would reach Dominica and claim the Bondmaster's fortune!

The atmosphere on the plantation was solemn in the bright sunlight. It was three days from Christmas but there was no sense of happiness in the air. A few slaves at work in the fields moved lethargically, and the drivers' whips were silent. It added to Warren Gordon's despondency as he rode up the avenue of royal palms to Roxborough Hall.

The house was shuttered as it had been since the Bondmaster's brutal murder seven weeks before. The sight of it caused Warren to grit his teeth with anger. Today was to have been the wedding day of his daughter, Davril, to Brett, Carlton Todd's mulatto grandson. The boy had died with his head cleaved in two, butchered by the maroon Mingoson. It was a tragic waste of life. Brett had been a talented youth whom Warren was training to be a leader of his people.

"Morning, Mr Gordon." The voice which broke into his thoughts was sour and obsequious. He glanced down and was surprised to find he had reached the overgrown courtyard of the house, right where Brett had been slain.

"Fine day," the voice said. "Slaves are well occupied."

Warren raised his eyes off the ground to stare at the man who had spoken. The man wore the practical outfit of the professional planter: strong boots, breeches, linen shirt, fawn jacket and a wide brimmed hat to keep the sun off his face. In his belt were two pistols, evidence of the precautions necessary after that night of terror.* Warren heaved a sigh before he spoke.

"Laidlaw," he said to acknowledge the man. "Everything all right?"

"Yes, Mr Gordon." Laidlaw snapped his fingers at a slave standing behind him. The old negro came forward and held the bridle of the horse while Warren dismounted.

"Ah, thank you, boy. What's your name?"

"Caliste, sah."

"Caliste." Warren repeated the name and tried to remember it. He had done the same thing on every visit to Roxborough during the last seven weeks. There was so much to remember.

The slave led the horse away and he walked slowly up the wide steps to the balcony of the house. He half expected Carlton to be sitting in his usual chair ready to greet him with a coarse joke.

"Sit here, Mr Gordon." Laidlaw ushered Warren to a chair by the table set up in the shade. "I've nearly finished the inventory." He waved at the ledgers on the table.

"Good." Warren knew he had to complete this distasteful task. He had been Carlton Todd's friend and as a planter himself, he was aware of the importance of re-establishing white authority over the slaves.

"Do the slaves show any signs of restlessness?"

"No, Mr Gordon. They're as docile as zombies. They miss their Bondmaster!"

Warren frowned. "How odd."

Laidlaw sniffed and sat on a corner of the table. He stared across the plantation with hard, steel gray eyes. Not a slave could move without him knowing. "Carlton Todd raised them," he said. "The slaves are lost without him."

Warren snorted. "Freedom is coming to the slaves, Laidlaw. Don't they want that?"

"They didn't take it when Mingoson and his maroons slaughtered the Bondmaster."

*See *The Bondmaster Breed*

"Mingoson escaped, Laidlaw. Doesn't that worry you? You could be next, or me. My plantation's only four miles away. I've seen the smoke from the maroon fires in the mountains." He shook his head. He had worked toward ameliorating the conditions of the island's blacks and yet, with freedom in sight, they committed such savagery.

Laidlaw scanned the sugar cane rolling down to the coast. A ship, its sails down, drifted slowly past the sand bar into the deep anchorage of the river. "Mingoson won't come back," he said. "His attack on Roxborough was personal. That's why the slaves didn't support him."

Warren huffed and opened the ledger in front of him. "Maybe," he said, turning the pages idly.

"That's the equipment book, sir. Everything is itemized."

"Good. I hope to get the Letters of Administration in the New Year. Carlton left no heir so the plantation will be mine. And all the slaves." His voice dropped to a whisper.

"What will you do with them, Mr Gordon?"

"What?"

"With the slaves? With emancipation coming, they'll be a liability."

"You're right. I'm taking the plantation for my daughter. She's in bloom, Laidlaw."

"I don't listen to scandal, Mr Gordon. My job is to keep this plantation shipshape and the slaves busy."

"Brett left her with child, Laidlaw." He sighed. "The Bondmaster's blood will live on in her baby. With the slaves freed, I want to get this plantation back to its best days for the heir he never saw."

"You'll need a fortune to pay the slaves' wages."

"A fortune? The Bondmaster had that."

Laidlaw's eyes showed emotion for the first time that morning. "I haven't seen it!"

Warren frowned at the overseer. "There's a fortune in gold buried here somewhere. I want you, Laidlaw, to stay when Roxborough is mine. You've done well. You deserve a chance to find that gold."

Laidlaw stroked his chin thoughtfully. "I'd appreciate that," he said, a far-off look in his eyes.

7

A boy lolled against the stone wall of the bake house and watched through half-closed eyes as Warren Gordon entered the village. He recognized the white man by his straight back and the pious way he rode his horse. He was picking his way with care through the negroes, dogs, chickens and carts cluttering the mud street.

The boy smiled to himself when Warren Gordon stopped his horse outside the casino. However respectable a white man pretended to be, sooner or later he found his way to his mother's house.

Casey raised his eyes to the sky. It was that breathless blue which heralded hours of heat, with the sun high over the sea. He shifted comfortably; the leafy shadow of the mango tree shielded him while the delicious smell of newly baked bread wafted from the bake house.

Warren Gordon disappeared into the casino without a backward glance. Casey was intrigued because most of the white men looked furtively about before trying to slip in unnoticed. Not Gordon. He tied his horse to the post outside thereby announcing to the village that he did not care who knew his business. Casey grinned again. He liked that strength in a man.

Casey prized himself from his perch and jammed his hands in the pockets of his pantaloons and sauntered around to the front of the bake house. Large-bosomed black women gossiped and jostled at the entrance while naked children clutching straw baskets and bitts in their hands, struggled to find a way between their legs.

Casey caught a tow-haired kid whose black body was gray

with salt dried on his skin after bathing in the sea. "Give me your basket," he said.

The boy yielded the basket and proffered the bitt he was holding. Casey shook his head and winked.

"Keep the money," he said, and eased himself in to the press of clamoring women.

A bulky matron with a red bandanna knotted on her head stuck out a huge arm. "Where yo' does be goin'?" she demanded hotly.

He didn't answer but faced the woman and smiled.

"You!" The woman's vexation dissolved into a rude grin and she pulled Casey in front of her. His shoulders rubbed against her enormous breasts and she chortled with delight.

In the bake house, another gigantic female, her shift sticking to her statuesque body and her black flesh shiny with exertion, raked hot bread from the floor of the oven. The small loaves were crisp, golden brown on top but dark with ash underneath. They fell from the oven into a pannier and a girl dusted the ash off them. The huddle of people at the doorway waited impatiently for the girl to complete her task and start selling.

Casey crouched beside the girl at the pannier and picked out some loaves he liked. He did so with mock concentration and a grin for the girl who was eyeing him adoringly. He filled his basket and stood up. His pantaloons were rucked around his thighs and his crotch level with the eyes of the squatting girl. Her lips parted.

He nodded his thanks and ambled out of the bake house; the women in the crowd eased to let him pass and he laughed at their lewd remarks. The small boy was waiting for him.

"Take some to my mam," Casey said, handing over the basket. The child ran off.

Casey looked along the street again. Warren Gordon's horse was still tied outside the casino. He strolled toward it. An ox cart, its bell jangling and its driver riding with the load, swayed down the street. Casey patted the animal as it lurched past him and winked at the driver.

"Oy! Oy!"

Casey reached at the sound. Two men were jogging

toward him, one behind the other. They carried a pole slung between them from which hung a heavy bundle of shingles. The men greeted him cheerily as they staggered past with their burden. A fish seller followed them, his basket of wet fish balanced on his head. He stopped in front of Casey and asked him to help ease the basket to the ground.

Casey reached up and carried the basket to the shade under the casino gallery. He picked up the man's conch shell and blew it lustily. Its flat, mournful sound echoed through the village saying that fish was for sale.

"Casey!" His mother's strident voice drowned the conch shell lament. He pretended not to hear.

"Yuh mam does be callin' yo', Casey!"

"I know." He grinned at the fish vendor. "But you haven't given me fish for my breakfast."

"Aw, Casey! No need to ax." The fish seller thrust two of his biggest fish into Casey's hands.

"Casey!"

He grinned ruefully as his mother called again. Nodding his thanks, he ran around to the kitchen at the back of the casino. "Here, Uraline," he said to the negress fanning the wood fire in the open grate of the ajoupa. "Fry these fish for my mam."

The cook beamed. "Does be a pleasure, Casey."

He felt her eyes on him while he dashed water on his hands and dried them on his pants. He smirked impishly and was amused when Uraline turned away with a heavy sigh that sounded something like, "Ah declah!"

He ran up the back steps two at a time to his mother's quarters above the casino. He pushed open the rear door and drank in the smell. He loved the stale odor of powder and face paint, lingering verbena, dried sweat and the mustiness of exhausted females. The smell of the whorehouse meant home to him.

He strolled along the passage to the balcony. His mother had the largest chamber at the rear of the house. Her guard, an old gelded negro called Apollo, slept on a mat outside her door. In the room next to hers was an English girl called Diana and two French whores who pretended to be twins.

Opposite was the chamber of the lady he knew as Aunt Sarah, a dried up creole who was not his aunt but the bordello's cashier. Two other rooms housed a selection of mulatto girls.

He himself slept in the casino downstairs. Until he was four he had lived in his mother's chamber but when his grandmother, old May Gregg, had died, he moved down to her room. It suited him, although he preferred the warm security of the whorehouse to the rough lifestyle of the casino.

Casey glanced at the balcony. His mother was silhouetted against the glaring brightness of the morning. Mango trees and the hills rich with Roxborough sugar cane lay behind her. Warren Gordon sat opposite her, his back straight and his hat balanced on his knees.

Casey was suddenly apprehensive that Mr Gordon's visit was a threat to him. Since the death of the Bondmaster, many strangers came to Layou. The militia had been billeted in the village for three weeks while they searched the hills for Mingoson and his gang of maroons. The soldiers, from the Seventh Regiment, were pathetic, sweltering men led by a braying officer who downed rum like it was a purgative.

Officious men had interviewed the white inhabitants, sneering behind their hands at private jokes among themselves. Casey had been offended by their attitude but his mother soothed him saying that was the way of the English. Warren Gordon, he knew, was English too. He owned Batalie Plantation, had lived on the island for twenty years, and had a reputation among the negro folk for being soft hearted. He had a newspaper in his hand and was showing it to his mother.

Casey watched Mary's face to see if she was distressed. If she was, he would ask Gordon to leave. He was not afraid of any white man, least of all an English busybody.

A bedroom door opened and Diana peered out into the corridor. "Oh, it's you," she said sleepily. "How nice."

He grinned. Diana was not at her most fetching in the morning.

"Gawd, I feel awful!"

"I'll massage your back if you like."

"No, dearie. I think that's what caused it." Diana's nightgown fell open. "Coming in?"

He shook his head. "My mam wants me."

"Ooer!" Diana stepped back when she saw Warren Gordon through the open balcony door. "A screwhead so early!"

"I doubt it." He kissed her and his nose tingled at the whiff of dried semen on her cheek. He pinched her bottom affectionately and walked to the balcony door. His mother looked up with pleasure when he strode on to the balcony but Warren Gordon drew back stiffly.

"This is my son, Casey," she said.

For a moment, Mr Gordon stared as though he had seen a ghost. Casey saved him embarrassment by not offering him his hand to be shaken. Although by law mulattoes in Dominica were supposed to be equal to whites, Warren Gordon's face showed his dismay at being introduced to him.

"Mr Gordon is paying us a courtesy call, Casey," his mother said archly. "Sit down."

"That's all right, mam." Casey was uneasy in Gordon's presence and sitting down would make him worse. He shuffled under the white man's glance. He sensed that Gordon was trying to evaluate how freely he could speak in front of him. At night, in the dim lanterns of the casino, the seamen, soldiers and merchants assumed he was white like them. But in the glare of the morning sun there was no mistaking the yellow hue of his skin, and the wiryness of his hair which betrayed his mixed blood.

"You must forgive my rudeness, young man." Mr Gordon put out his hand and Casey shook it shyly. "I was taken aback . . . the likeness to Brett . . . but, of course, from your mother . . ." Mr Gordon stammered into silence.

Casey was amazed. He had not expected that Warren Gordon would be nervous. He tried to put him at ease. "Gentlemen callers are no strangers in this house, Mr Gordon."

"Ah . . . er . . . no." Mr Gordon blushed, putting his finger under his collar and tugging it.

His mother frowned when Casey winked at her. They

enjoyed jokes at the expense of those embarrassed by her profession. "Mr Gordon has been telling me about the Roxborough affair," she said.

To Casey, his mother looked stunning this morning. She wore a new white dress of imported jaconet with four rows of embroidery on the skirt. Her corsage was high and finished with a tucker of fine lace and with sleeves gathered at the wrist. At her waist was a blue sash and she had blue ribbons tied in her hair. Her elaborate appearance made Casey remember that she had anticipated Warren Gordon's visit. She had been told by Laidlaw, always indiscreet when he was drinking, that Gordon was visiting Layou today.

"I know that the late Carlton Todd would have liked me to call on your mother." Mr Gordon looked solemn. "To acquaint her --"

"Hah!" Casey snorted with derision. "The Bondmaster can rot in his grave for all we care!"

"Hush, Casey! Don't be so disrespectful in front of company."

"Sorry, mam, Mr Gordon." He kept a straight face but he knew what his mother was thinking.

"May I talk in front of the boy?"

"Lor', Warren, of course! Casey knows all my business."

Mr Gordon looked more uncomfortable. He blushed and took a deep breath. "You were Brett's mother so it's courtesy that I should inform you that I have applied for Letters of Administration to Carlton's estate. It's here in the announcement from the Marshall's office in the *Dominica Colonist.*" He waved the newspaper in front of him.

"May I see it, please." Casey's request seemed to surprise Mr Gordon.

"Can you read, young man?" He handed over the paper reluctantly. "It's on page one, top left hand corner."

"I see." Casey read quickly. He had learned from the Methodists and his brain was alert in spite of the impression he gave of insolent laziness.

"What does this have to do with me, Warren?" Mary's drawl was pronounced as she considered what Gordon had said.

"Since Brett compromised my daughter --"

"That's nothing to do with my mam!"

"Casey!"

"I understand that, young man. I'm aware of the circumstances. I know that your mother er . . . sold Brett to the Bondma--"

"She didn't sell anyone!" Casey clenched his fists in anger.

"It's all right, Casey." Mary laid her hand on Mr Gordon's arm and the white man flinched. "I was obliged to relinquish Brett to the Bondmaster's control, Warren. That's how Carlton explained it."

Mr Gordon stood up hastily. "I merely wanted you to know that as my daughter's position is somewhat invidious, I have taken certain steps. She was to marry Brett but now she is an unmarried widow and her child will be fatherless."

"Now ain't that a shame!" Casey put his hands on his hips and sneered. His mother rose from her seat and slapped him a stinging blow across his cheek.

He lowered his head, flushing deeply. "Sorry, mam," he whispered, bridling with shame at being humiliated in front of the pompous white man. He stole a glance at Gordon and was relieved to see the man seemed as distressed as he did.

"I'm sorry, Miss . . . er I mean . . . Mrs . . . Miss Gregg."

"Lor', call me Mary like everyone else! Now, go on."

Mr Gordon remained standing. "I'm arranging to administer Carlton's estate for his descendants. I'm sure that's what he would have wanted."

Casey pricked up his ears when he heard his mother cluck her tongue and say sharply, "His descendants?"

"Yes, there's one direct heir only, the child my daughter Davril will be having. There's no question that Brett was the father and he was Carlton's only heir."

"Only heir?" Casey stepped forward and handed the newspaper back to Mr Gordon.

"Yes, that's right. I'll manage the estate until the child is twenty-one and the income will help alleviate the disgrace of --"

Mary stood up and held out her hand. "Thank you,

Warren, for your visit," she said grimly. "Forgive my son for his rudeness. He takes after his grandfather."

"Ah . . . er . . . yes." Mr Gordon looked baffled.

"My grandfather is Captain Loring," Casey said with a smile.

Mr Gordon edged toward the gallery steps. "Really? Er . . . I believe I knew him. Please," he said as Casey moved toward him, "don't bother. My horse is below. Long ride, must be going."

Casey and Mary watched Mr Gordon, his back now bowed in confusion, stumble down the steps.

"Poor dear," said Mary. "He should have asked me who your father was."

Casey snorted with laughter and wrapped his arms around his mother's waist. "He's too eager to get his hands on the Bondmaster's gold."

"But if Caspar's children are the real heirs . . ." She stared at him in amazement and then began to laugh.

"Casey! I love yew!" She reached out for him and kissed him firmly on his lips.

"Mam," he said, pulling away and giggling. "I love you, too!"

8

Casey and Mary Gregg made a striking couple as they walked arm in arm along the High Street. Apollo, grandly dressed in a client's cast-off clothes, strolled behind holding a parasol. The thoroughfare was the capital's main road but it was no more than a cart track with grass growing between the ruts. On either side, the wooden shacks of recent settlers leaned against the stone buildings of merchants and gentry.

From windows and galleries, people stared at the couple.

"They think you're a queen," said Casey, patting his mother's hand.

Mary smiled without speaking, her head held high, the plume on her bonnet bouncing proudly as she walked. She had dressed deliberately for the impact she would have on Roseau's citizens. The bonnet was of rich silk with a deep edge of black lace adding luster to her fair hair which billowed beneath it. Her dress was made of green brocade with a full skirt. It was unsuitable for the capital's heat but it was the latest fashion and one that the English ladies of the town could ill afford.

She carried herself gracefully. The extra ounces of middle age that, in other women would have been fat, gave her a mature beauty. Casey noticed how every man they met turned his head to watch them pass.

"If they think I'm a queen, they must take yew for a prince," Mary whispered.

Casey was no less striking than his mother. He was taller than her with a sleek and muscular body. His handsome face glowed with vitality and his alert eyes were a pale bronze, startling in his olive features. His clothes had been tailored especially for the occasion. He wore them with arrogance in spite of the discomfort his full-skirted coat and leather boots were giving him. His trousers were fawn, his stock a peacock blue, and he looked like a dandy.

"Unless they think yew are my lover!" Mary cackled with laughter.

The idea appealed to Casey. He shared his mother's contempt for the hypocrisies of the island's gentry. He had been raised by whores who had slept with everyone, so he knew by sight all the island's important personages. If they were shocked by the parading around Roseau of Mary Gregg and a youthful mulatto lover, let them be!

"We mustn't disappoint them," he said, patting her hand again.

"Especially now yew are going to be rich." Mary squeezed his arm. "As the Bondmaster."

She didn't see the flicker of concern that crossed his eyes

and he blinked it away quickly. He had no real desire to change his life and the possibility of becoming the Bondmaster was disturbing. He had only come to Roseau for Mary's sake.

They had arrived in the capital that morning by canoe, a four hour pull southward down the Leeward coast. He knew that the people gawping at them were wondering about their destination. The house of Governor Schomberg was at the end of the High Street. The Governor was new to the island, a Royal Naval officer, and it would have scandalized the populace if he and Mary went to Government House.

"I see the idea pleases yew," said Mary. "We'll show these buggers who's who when the Bondmaster's title is yours."

"Yes, mam." He kept his misgivings to himself.

The Marshall's office was next to Government House. Casey led his mother to the doorway, gratified by the stir they had caused. Children were frolicking around them with awe, and even the bullocks pulling carts showed them respect by giving them room. He told Apollo to wait on the step and bowed Mary through the door.

They found themselves in a dreary office no bigger than a slave hut. Mary looked about her disdainfully. Her dress filled the floor, and the people who sat waiting on a bench huddled into a corner to get out of her way. The room was hot and smelled of damp. Casey perched at the top of the step and peered past Mary. There was no official in sight.

"I declare!" said Mary at the top of her voice. "Christmas gone ten days and no one at work here. Is this the way Governor Schomberg governs us?"

The people in the corner elbowed each other. A large white lady who had seen better days, sniffed and said, "We've been here since last week. You'll need an appointment."

"Appointment!" said Mary in a voice the whole street could hear. "I'm the one who gives appointments to those who think they can afford me." She rapped on the counter. "Come now, yew within. Get without!"

A door was flung open and an official in clerical gray sporting a watch chain across his stout stomach as a badge of office, hurried into the room.

"What's all this noise," he said. "Can't you read the notice? Silence!"

"Silence indeed!" Mary stared haughtily. "I'll give yew silence between your legs. Yew the Marshall?"

"No, I'm not the Marshall. If you want to see him you must come back in two weeks."

"Why, is he fornicating?" Casey turned away and the clerk looked shocked.

"He's busy. Please leave the office. You're creating a disturbance."

"I'll create a disturbance, all right." Mary leaned over the counter and grabbed the clerk by the lapels of his coat. "Aren't yew the pansy who couldn't get it up when yew came to see one of my gals?" She pushed him aside and opened the door to the inner office. Casey followed.

A slim man sitting behind a desk looked up in alarm.

"Yew the Marshall?" Mary demanded.

"Yes, yes."

"Want to see yew!"

"I'm rather busy. My clerk will give you an appointment."

"Won't take that long." Mary sat opposite and glared at him across his desk.

The Marshall sighed. Casey closed the door shutting out the clerk, and stood behind Mary. The Marshall eyed him anxiously. "What's this about?"

"About my son's inheritance." Mary opened her reticule and brought out a folded newspaper. She pointed to an advertisement. "Are yew Nisbet?"

"Yes, yes."

"Marshall in ordinary? Whatever that means."

"Yes, yes."

"Did you sign this notice in the newspaper?"

"Let me see." He held out his hand and withdrew it quickly when Mary gave him the newspaper. "Yes, yes," he said, his confidence returning to him. "This is the application of Mr Warren Gordon for Letters of Administration. No heirs alive. No problem at all."

"Yes, yes!" Mary's mocking tone was also threatening.

"Why, what's the matter?" Nisbet cowered nervously in his chair.

"My son here," said Mary triumphantly, "is the grandson of Mr Carlton Todd!"

"I don't understand." The Marshall paled.

Casey took the newspaper. "It says here that Warren Gordon is applying for Letters of Administration for my grandfather's plantation, goods and chattels, rights and credits. He wants what's mine!"

"He ain't going to get it, Nisbet!"

"Yes, yes. Keep calm, madam." The Marshall drummed his fingers anxiously on the desk top. "I'm sure it's perfectly simple. A mistake --"

"Bloody well is a mistake!"

"Yes, yes. Please . . . Er, can you, er, prove that this ah . . . " Nisbet peered up at Casey and shifted uneasily. "This . . . ah . . . young man, is the late Mr Todd's grandson?"

"Prove he ain't!"

"In law, madam --"

"To hell with the law. Casey here is my son by the Bondmaster's own son, Caspar. I raised him in secret but he's the grandson all right."

"What do you suggest we do?" Casey tried to be polite to calm the Marshall's growing distress. He laid his hand on his mother's shoulder. "Mr Gordon didn't know about me when he put in his application."

"This petition has to be heard in court," the Marshall said, shuffling the papers on his desk. "The next of kin and all others having, or pretending to have, any rights can appear then and show why the petition shouldn't be granted."

"Who decides that? Not yew!"

"His Excellency Sir Charles Marsh Schomberg, the Lieutenant Governor, will consider the petition."

"Then our business with yew is done, Nisbet!" Mary stood up and the Marshall leaped to his feet as though he expected a blow.

"Thank you, sir," said Casey, opening the door and escorting his mother out.

"Why are yew so polite, Casey? Don't yew see it's a plot to deprive yew of your --" Mary was cut off by a hurrah from the people in the street when she appeared on the step. Apollo looked worried.

"Crikey!" she said as the poor whites and mulattoes crowded around to congratulate her.

"You showed them, ma'am," an unshaven man with rotten teeth crowed cheerfully into her face. She blenched and clung to Casey as Apollo cleared a way through the crowd. Mary waved rudely at the gentry staring down at the commotion from the safety of their galleries above the street.

Casey was surprised by the attention they attracted until he saw how neglected Roseau was. In its heyday, the town had been a freeport, founded on the slave trade and commerce. Now it showed the damage from hurricanes and the loss of prosperity caused by wars and changes in colonial policy. New arrivals such as he and Mary were a welcome distraction for the poor whites who remained after the wealthy ones had left.

He was relieved to reach the hotel and hurried up the steps while his mother gave a final wave to the crowd who had followed them. A portly white man stood with his arms folded across his chest, blocking the entrance.

"Where do yer think yer going, boy?"

Casey grinned cheekily at the man's pomposity. "We want two rooms and quarters for our slave."

"No rooms here for yeller bastards."

"How now, Henry Gold! Is that the way the high and mighty of Roseau repay hospitality?" Mary said loudly.

Henry Gold stared at her. "What hospitality?"

"You remember," said Casey unabashed. "The night you spent at my mother's whorehouse."

"Good Lord!"

"Quite a night, wasn't it, Henry? I've still got the toothmarks." Mary snickered.

"What the devil do you want?"

"I told you," said Casey. "Two rooms and quarters for the slave."

"It's payment in advance."

"Of course." Casey stepped forward and Mr Gold let him through reluctantly. "We'll be staying one night. My mother would like the best room and I'll have one next to her." He spilled some coins into Mr Gold's outstretched palm.

Mary pulled the proprietor by his sleeve. "Let's have a screw, shall we, for old time's sake?" She led him across the room to the saloon. Two merchants sitting in the settles in the corner stopped talking and watched dourly as Mary arranged herself at a table. The three officers in the scarlet uniform of the Seventh Regiment standing disconsolately by the window, cheered up when they saw her.

Mr Gold sat down and Casey edged into the settle beside him. He enjoyed the man's discomfort and boldly ordered rums for them all. He let his mother talk while he glanced around the saloon. It was as large as the casino in Layou but furnished with tables, chairs and settles. Thick curtains covered the glass windows and kept out the sun's glare. The floor was polished boards and the slaves attending them glided silently over it with their drinks.

"A nice place, Henry."

"Yes." Mr Gold didn't sound very happy.

"Yew've done well for yourself. A lot of class."

Mr Gold's narrow eyes watched Mary suspiciously and his fat fingers grasped and unclasped his glass. He looked from Mary to Casey and back again. Casey grinned.

"My mother don't mean anything unwarranted, Mr Gold."

"We're celebrating today, Henry." Mary beamed but her smile had a hint of menace.

"Oh yes?"

"My son, Casey here, is going to inherit Carlton Todd's fortune."

"What!" Mr Gold's glass slipped from his fingers and fell to the floor with a crash. The soldiers tensed and the merchants looked anxious.

Mary raised her eyebrows. "Oh, dear, have I surprised yew?"

The proprietor's face turned red as he opened his mouth to gulp for breath.

"Mam, you mustn't say that. It ain't certain."

"Of course, it's certain. Governor Schomberg only has to

issue the Letters of Administration and yew're the Bondmaster."

Casey was worried. "No, mam . . . "

Mr Gold was spluttering. "I don't believe it! Gordon said he'd got that tied up."

"Did he?" Mary chuckled. "He didn't know about Casey although anyone can see he's Carlton's grandson."

"Huh!" Mr Gold thumped the table. "Warren Gordon's got his comeuppance now!"

"What do you mean?"

"What do I mean, boy? Well, yer a half-breed, aren't yer?"

"Yes . . . " Casey tensed.

"It was Warren Gordon who persuaded the Assembly to allow mulattoes, half-breeds like yer, equal rights to whites. He said whites created yeller bastards, so whites got to look after them!" Gold laughed dryly. "If he hadn't got that law passed then yer'd have no chance of inheriting the Bondmaster's fortune. Poor Carlton, he must be turning in his grave."

The door of the hotel creaked open and a man peered in. He was dishevelled and he blinked as he tried to see in the dim light of the interior.

"I say," he said to no one in particular. "Is this the hotel?"

"It is," said Gold, pushing past Casey and hurrying to block the entrance.

The stranger sighed with relief. "I've just arrived. The voyage . . . "

He sank into a chair and Casey studied him. He had dark, straight hair, a weak face and a slight build. He appeared to be in his twenties, pale and sickly, fresh from England. Another ne'er-do-well packed off to the colonies to get out of trouble, he thought.

"I need a room," gasped the stranger. "To rest. What a relief . . . glad to get off that ship . . . "

Mr Gold scowled. "Payment in advance!"

"Oh dear," the man hesitated. "I've just arrived. I have people to see...perhaps tomorrow?"

Mr Gold drew himself up to his full height, a smile curling across his fat face. "Our policy is payment in advance!" He sniffed. "Unless yer have someone to vouch for yer."

"No one."

"Then I can't help yer, Mr . . ."

"Carlington Br--." The man paused and seemed to recover his strength. He rose to his feet and glared at Mr Gold as though he had suddenly realized he was being insulted.

"I'm Carlington Todd. Son of the Bondmaster of Roxborough!"

9

Carl liked the sound of his new name: Carlington Todd. But he didn't anticipate the reaction of the pompous innkeeper. The man's face drained of color, his cheeks sagged and he flopped into a chair.

"Sir, are you all right?" Carl bent forward solicitously before he remembered he was no longer in service. He drew back and curled his lips in the manner he thought the Bondmaster himself would have used.

"Come, come, my good fellow! I see you know my status. A bed, if you please."

The innkeeper's eyes swivelled to the saloon. Carl saw a youth rise from a table and hurry over. The innkeeper's expression changed when he saw him. "Hah!" he gasped. "Now you've got your comeuppance too." He seemed to gloat.

"Yes," the youth said with a grin. "We were speaking in jest, Mr Gold, nothing more. Here!" He pulled some coins from his pocket. "My mam will pay for Mr Todd's lodging."

The sight of gold galvanised the innkeeper into action. He scrambled from the chair, proffered the register, Carl signed it and accepted the key he was handed. The innkeeper shook his head, mumbling under his breath.

"Strange fellow," said Carl as he followed the youth across the hall to the saloon. "Thanks awfully, you really shouldn't . . ."

"It's our pleasure," the youth said, beaming. His friendliness comforted Carl. If everyone is so easy to impress, he thought, life in Dominica would be even better than he imagined.

The youth led him to a table where a formidable woman glowered at him. "This is my mam, Mary Gregg. I'm Casey." He indicated the settle for Carl to sit down.

Carl bowed. "I'm honored to meet you, madam," he said. "I'm Carlington Todd." Again, he experienced the thrill of using his new name but his pleasure vanished when he saw the hatred in Mary Gregg's eyes. He sat down hastily.

"Carlton Todd was your father?" Mary Gregg's voice was sharp with disbelief.

"Yes, I --"

"No one knew he had a son!"

"A white son," added Casey, seemingly delighted with the news, in contrast to his mother.

Carl shifted uneasily. He was tired but his instinct warned him to tread carefully with this fiercesome woman. "You knew my . . . my father?"

Mary Gregg snorted. "You don't look like him!"

"I . . . I take after my mother."

"Huh!" Mary Gregg sneered. "If Carlton had a son, why didn't he tell us, eh? Why weren't you at Roxborough with him all these years? Why, eh?"

"Give him a chance to explain, mam."

Carl swallowed nervously, grateful for Casey's intervention. "My . . . my father didn't know he had a son. He left England before I was born. My mother --" Carl hesitated.

Mary Gregg's face hardened. "Bah!" she said. "My son here, well Carlton Todd was his --" She shrieked suddenly and glared at Casey. "Yew little bugger!"

"Sorry, mam. My foot slipped. Did I hurt your ankle?" Casey looked contrite. "My mother was saying that Mr Todd was our neighbor. We live by the boundary of Roxborough Estate."

Carl should have given the matter closer attention but he was tired. The voyage from England had been long and unpleasant. "Forgive me," he said, standing up. "I'm quite fatigued."

Mary Gregg scowled at him without speaking. Casey stood up. "I'll show you to your room, Mr Carlington."

"Thank you." Carl liked Casey. He would make a good houseboy. "Why don't you call me Mr Carl. It's not such a mouthful and I'm sure we're going to be friends."

"Pleased to, Mr Carl. This way."

"Yew bugger!" Mary glared at him when Casey returned to her table. "Why did yew kick me like that?"

"I didn't want you to tell the white man about me."

"Why not?"

Casey was exasperated. "Oh mam, don't you see? All my life you've kept my father's name a secret. Now the Bondmaster's son is here, it doesn't have to change."

"Casey, yew're foolish. Yew must have what's yours."

"Roxborough ain't mine, mam. It belongs to the white man, Mr Carl."

Mary sniffed. "Like the Marshall said, he's got to prove it."

"Please, mam. Let's forget it."

"Hah!" Mary lapsed into thought. "All right," she said after a while. "If that's what you want, I'll say nothing now. We'll bide our time."

Casey sighed with relief. He didn't want to be the Bondmaster. He was happy at home in Layou with the whores and his village friends.

"Let's go upstairs."

Casey escorted Mary across the saloon. Mr Gold scratched his head when they reached him.

"Don't play no japes like that on me again, yer yeller bastard," he said. "Yer and yer mother!" He growled at them like an angry bear.

"We nearly fooled you, didn't we?" Casey winked.

"It's Warren Gordon who's going to be fooled!" Mr Gold rubbed his hands together. "Set such a store on getting

Roxborough. But this new one ain't like the Bondmaster. He would have had a black wench up the back passage and in his bed by now. Thought I didn't know!"

Casey drew his mother away. He sensed her disappointment. Perhaps he wasn't like the Bondmaster either. He kept quiet while he walked up the grand staircase at her side and they were both deep in thought when they entered the room where Mary was to sleep.

"Was my father like the Bondmaster?" he asked suddenly.

"What?" Mary looked at him in surprise.

"Was my father --"

"Your father was a very special person, Casey. I can't describe him." She unlaced her bonnet, glanced at herself in the mirror, and sighed.

"Caspar was a prince. Really!" She sat on the bed and held out her hands. Casey took them and kissed her fingers. He sat beside her. He wanted to make her feel good.

"Caspar's mother was a Royal Batutsi. She was descended from one of the kings of Africa."

He put his arm around her shoulder and she snuggled closer to him.

"Your father was proud, like his mother, but he was headstrong like the Bondmaster." She rested her head on his chest. "He was handsome and strong. Perhaps he was weak too, but his body was . . ."

Casey stroked his mother's hair, his fingers caressing the back of her neck. She looked up at him.

"He used to do that." She twisted out of his arms and glanced around the chamber. "Takes me back years. We never made love in a room so fine as this."

Casey frowned, unable to fathom the affection he felt for his mother at that moment. Her strength had vanished; she seemed vulnerable and in need. The lace curtain at the window fluttered in the breeze and the gasp of cool air was refreshing.

"Am I like him?" he asked.

Mary considered the question while he waited anxiously. He couldn't see what images flashed through his mother's mind, but eventually she shook her head and sighed. She lay back on the pillows. "Come," she said.

Casey understood her need. First the disappointment about him not inheriting Roxborough, after such excitement, and now his questions about Caspar. She was always touchy when he asked about his father. He wondered if he would ever be the man Caspar was.

"Some times yew remind me of him," she said, touching his chest. "Take off that coat. Yew look like a remittance man!"

They both laughed. He drew the coat off and tossed it on a chair. He leaned against the pillow and Mary unfastened the buttons on his shirt. With her face so close to his, he could kiss her.

"Yew have his body, Cas," she murmured, opening his shirt so his chest was exposed. "Yew're fairer than he was, but yew have his shape." She ran her finger down his throat and traced circles over his chest.

He giggled. Her fingers tweaked his nipples and she rubbed them slowly until they hardened and protruded darkly against the honey glow of his skin. An awareness of a deep yearning swelled through him and he stirred lazily.

Mary's hair fluttered around his shoulders when she bent her head to his chest. He felt the sharp bite of her teeth on his flesh and he winced. A warm moistness lapped him where her tongue caressed his chest. A strange sensation swam through his body. He quivered and grasped her shoulder to stop himself floundering.

"Mam--"

She pulled up her head but the feeling stayed, soaring through him. He lay back and closed his eyes.

"Caspar wouldn't cry, Casey. He'd hold me in his arms and smother me with kisses."

His hands lay heavily on his mother's shoulders. He wanted to please her. He had lain with wenches since he was six. The whores in the casino had shown him how, treating him as their toy, playing with him until he was hard. With the village girls in the cane fields, he had experimented with what the whores had taught him. But he had never known this overwhelming euphoria, a desire to yield himself completely.

Mary's hands crept lower, rubbing his flesh so that he trembled. He rolled his head from side to side, squirming under her mouth. Her tongue tasted the sweat caught in the hair under his arms, then traced a line across the hard muscles of his stomach to probe his navel. Every touch triggered off explosions of a new sensation within him. He cried out and suddenly Mary was on him, pushing her tongue between his teeth and demanding him.

He embraced her and was amazed when his hands touched her naked shoulders. Somehow she had shed her clothes. He groaned.

"Cas," she whispered. "You're sweeter than he ever was."

He shuddered. Another sensation erupted deep in his loins. He opened his eyes. His mother removed her lips from him and raised her head.

"Caspar!" She smiled.

"No!"

He twisted out of her grasp and leaped off the bed. His trousers were bunched around his ankles and he fell with a jolt to the floor. He lay startled, gasping with shock. Mary followed him, entwining her hand around his neck, the other reaching between his legs.

"Caspar!" she breathed.

"No!" he shouted and dragged himself to his feet. He pulled up his trousers and tucked himself in with difficulty. "No," he said, controlling the rage surging through him. "I'm not Caspar!"

Mary crawled across the floor and reached up for him.

"No, mam! Caspar is dead. He's been dead for years. You can't bring him back through me!" He wanted to cry.

"I know who you are, Casey."

"Then why . . .?"

"To help yew."

He was puzzled. "I thought I was comforting you by letting you do that."

His mother stood up and laughed coarsely. "I raised yew, boy. I've drained hundreds of men. Yew think what yew've got between your legs could comfort me?"

"You were depressed! Because I don't want the Bondmaster's fortune!"

"Hah!" Mary pulled on her dress. "Yew have high ideas about yourself, Casey. I don't care a damn what yew do."

"But I love you, mam." He was baffled.

"Yew love only yourself! I've sheltered yew from the day yew were born. Caspar wanted it that way. Yew ain't never gone short of anything yew wanted. Yew're just a spoiled, selfish brat!"

"I'm not, mam, I'm not!" Casey put up his hand to fend off the blow he expected.

"Get out!" Mary advanced on him, rage and frustration blazing in her eyes.

He opened the door and paused, his eyes pleading. "Mam, I do love you."

"Go to hell!"

10

Carl was pleased when he woke late the next morning and stepped out of the hotel for a walk, to find Casey waiting for him. "Where's your mother?" he asked, glancing around with apprehension for the redoubtable Mary Gregg.

Casey shrugged his shoulders. "She's gone back to Layou."

"Aren't you going with her?"

Casey idly scuffed his boots in the mud of the street. "I'll go later. Thought you might need some help. Being as you're new here."

He clapped Casey on his shoulder. "Dashed kind of you! Let's take a turn around the town."

Carl's excitement at having reached Dominica after a great deal of scheming and swindling, soon evaporated in the heat of the town. He realized Roseau was a desolate place. Its fine houses were closed and grass grew lushly in the heavily rutted streets.

There was a river at the north of the town and the streets, although ill kempt and deserted, were long and spacious, intersecting each other at right angles. There was one square with a well in it which was never used.

"The maroons were butchered here," Casey explained as Carl stared at it. "Twenty years ago. Their blood ran over the stones into the well. It's defiled."

"Maroons?" He was puzzled. "What are they?"

"Negres marrons, we say in patois. Escaped slaves, run-aways. There are a few of them left. They live in the mountains. Mingoson is one."

There was a note of awe in Casey's voice that intrigued Carl. "Who is this Mingoson?" he asked.

Casey's eyes widened with amazement. "Don't you know? He's their leader. It's Mingoson you have to fear. He killed your father!"

Carl shuddered involuntarily. His clothes were clinging damply to him and his body was prickly with cold sweat. "I thought he'd been caught," he said nervously.

"Oh, no!" Casey seemed amused. "The militia don't even try. Scared of the bush."

Carl became thoughtful as he peered at the well no one used. It had never occurred to him that the man who killed Carlton Todd was still at large. Would he look for him too?

"They say Mingoson returns to Roxborough at night," Casey said in a hushed voice. "To stir up the slaves."

Carl raised his eyes anxiously. Two blacks trundled a wheelbarrow across the square, and a merchant and his clerk sauntered by, nodding their heads in greeting. He drew strength from the normality of the scene. "I won't let a wild man from the bush upset me, Casey," he said, patting his recently-acquired pistols that were slung under his coat.

"He'll be dead as soon as he sets foot in Roxborough once I'm there."

Casey smiled sympathetically. "I hope so, Mr Carl," he said, leading the way out of the square to the water front. "I hope so!"

The trading establishments in Roseau varied in character from the dingy shops of the side streets to the great merchant houses lining the bay front. The tiny shops, six feet square where a customer was unable to stand erect, were operated by free black or mulatto women. They retailed provisions, candles and cottons to the slaves.

Carl was eager to inspect them but he deferred to Casey's insistence that gentlemen did not patronize such shops. He allowed Casey to lead him to the bay front. Roseau had no careenage and ship passengers were subjected to a thorough drenching when they landed on the beach in open boats. Merchandise suffered the same fate before it was stored in the warehouses that supplied the plantations.

Carl followed Casey into the warehouse of a broad shouldered Scotsman called Shillingford.

"I've heard about ye from Henry Gold," Shillingford said, almost crushing Carl's fingers with his firm handshake. "Ye'll no' be wantin' credit."

"Well, actually . . ."

"Och, an' ye the Bondmaster!" Shillingford turned away abruptly. He waved at the goods piled up behind him. "I've got salt fish, grain, rice, tobacco, wine, pitch, tools, lumber, everything a planter needs." He sniffed loudly. "Ye da' knew what he was about."

"I'm willing to learn, Mr Shillingford." Carl gulped. "It's a noble tradition --"

Shillingford spat at his feet. "There are so many rogues in this country who never pay their debts! The Bondmaster did. I have to make the honest men pay double, or I couldn't live."

"We could find another merchant."

"Aye, ye could." Shillingford scowled at him contemptuously. "Ye da' would'a loaned me a slave wench for an hour. Many's the doxie I've rogered on the rice bags while Mrs Shillingford was at kirk. Grand one for kirk, Mrs Shillingford."

Carl glanced at Casey for help but the boy just grinned inanely. "Well, I'll see what --"

"Guid. It'll be fine doin' business with ye." The merchant turned on his heel and disappeared into the depths of the store.

Carl sniffed. "The whites here don't seem to be from the top drawer," he said sadly. "Was the Bondmaster like them too?" He picked his way daintily through the sand and mud of the street, keeping in the shade of the stone warehouse.

"You'll learn to be hard, Mr Carl. If you want to survive."

"Oh dear," Carl muttered, dismayed that his island paradise was turning out to be rather unpleasant.

"Here's the slave factor." Casey stopped before a rotting wooden fence. A gate hung open onto a dusty square of dried mud. The dead heat of afternoon hung heavily over the compound.

Carl grimaced. "What's that smell?"

"Nigger shit."

He leaned weakly against the fence. It sagged under his weight and Casey pulled him off. "I don't think I feel well," he said.

"You'll get accustomed." Casey urged him inside the gate toward a wooden hut. There was a platform in front of it. "That's where the auctions take place."

Carl stared around the square, uncomprehending.

"The slaves strip down and stand on that platform while the planters bid for them."

"Not any more, they don't." A small sad-eyed man limped out of the hut. Carl was struck by the man's air of failed duplicity, as though he no longer cared if he lied or not. Tufts of gray hair stuck out from the sides of his shrunken head, and he wore a bedraggled sweat-stained suit of brown linen. He hobbled over to Carl and peered at him briefly, then appraised Casey. Saliva bubbled at the corners of his mouth.

"Fine buck!" he said with a gurgle of regret. "Time was I could get a thousand for a lively colt like that. He yours?"

"I'm no one's." Casey spoke softly. "I was born free."

"Ah, me! That's how it is now. Everyone is free. In the old days, every negro was a slave."

"Slavery's finished now, Mr Henderson." Casey turned to Carl. "This old bag of wind and bones is Jonas Henderson. He's the auctioneer."

"Nothing to offer you today, young sir." Henderson peered at Carl again. "Nobody wants to buy slaves now. Can't even give one away. Come August, planters have to apprentice their slaves. Pay them with currency instead of the lash. Did you ever hear the like!"

"I'm the new Bondmaster of Roxborough," Carl said, appalled by the old man's whining.

"Bondmaster!" The auctioneer brightened. "Carlton Todd was lucky. He died before slaves were freed. Would have killed him to do it! Business ruined. Future gone."

"What do you mean?"

"Obvious, young sir. Can't sell a slave, and that's the only crop Roxborough has. Slaves! Got to feed and mollycoddle them now. The expense!"

"There'll be compensation, won't there?"

"Pshaw! It will be less than the commission I'd get if I sold them at their real value." He wiped the saliva from his mouth. "The Bondmaster knew his slaves. Finest flesh I ever handled." He drooled. "Sold the Bondmaster his own daughter once. He broke the chit's maidenhead that same afternoon."

"Roxborough has at least a hundred slaves," Carl said. "What am I going to do?"

"Ah! If you were the Bondmaster, you wouldn't ask that question, sir. Oh no!"

Carl blushed. "What do you mean?"

"The Bondmaster found ways to turn everything to his profit. He was a creole, you see, born here, not an Englishman like you, still wet behind his ears."

Carl felt himself reddening, but didn't know what to say.

The auctioneer moved toward Casey. "I'd like to finger this colt for old time's sake."

"Get your filthy hands off him!" Carl brushed Henderson's grasping fingers from Casey's crotch and pulled him away.

"He didn't mean any harm." Casey was amused. "It was a compliment really."

"That's disgusting!" Carl hurried out of the compound. He was sweating and felt miserable. He wondered if he would ever get accustomed to the heat, the stench, the flies and the coarse behaviour of the white people. He began to wish he'd never come to Dominica.

Casey said nothing, which suited Carl very well because he could feel himself getting irritable. It seldom happened in the past, unless Cook was being particularly truculent or Mr Stephens was working late and kept him out of bed. He had learned to curb the early frustrations he knew as a child by sublimenting his passion into dreams of the future. Strong emotion was unsuitable for a gentleman's gentleman.

But now he was a gentleman himself! In the airless heat of the town, in his unsuitable clothes and subjected to the disparaging remarks of the uncouth whites he encountered, he allowed his fury to grow. Even the grinning face of Casey got on his nerves. The boy laughed like a nervous negro at the slightest thing. He didn't realize that he, Carl, was just as fearless a man as the Bondmaster. He was the Bondmaster!

These thoughts stiffened his resolve. He was grateful to be able to relax at last in a cool, dark corner of the saloon of the hotel. Mr Gold glowered at him from another table where he was in conversation with some army officers who, to Carl's mind, were a disgrace to their uniform with their sloppy appearance and disgusting manners. He felt sure they were talking about him.

"Mr Carl."

"What's that?" Carl sipped his lime juice to hide his confusion. He had been unaware that Casey was speaking to him. The boy's face looked serious for a change.

"I hope you'll forgive me for asking."

"Asking what?" He suspected more criticism.

"Are you a Willyforce man?"

"What the devil!"

"I don't mean to be disrespectful."

Carl believed the concern in Casey's face. He gulped the juice and brought his temper under control. He knew he must have a rest; it was the heat and the despondent air of the town and its people that annoyed him. And perhaps the realization slowly dawning on him that he may have made a mistake in forsaking the orderly life of a butler for this doubtful existence in a disease ridden, bankrupt, godless Caribbean island.

"What do you mean, Casey?" he said wearily.

"Are you an Abolitionist, Mr Carl? You don't seem to have the guts of the Bondmaster's son."

Carl pushed against the back of the settle, his palms on the edge of the table. His eyes blazed and his mouth curled into a sneer. "Boy! I'm going to show this island such things as they've never seen. I'm going to rule Roxborough with terror. Maybe slavery is ending, boy, but I'm not a Willy-force man and I'm going to get a fortune out of those slaves before it does.

"People are going to respect me, Casey! From pompous innkeepers to the Governor himself. Ain't no one going to doubt that I'm the Bondmaster!"

Casey grinned.

The hearing of the petition for the letters of administration to the estate of Carlton Todd was a brief one. Warren Gordon formally withdrew his application, then the Governor questioned Carl.

His training as a servant had accustomed Carl to dealing with people in authority and he was at ease with the Governor. He recounted how his mother, a lady of quality, had met Carlton Todd at Almack's Assembly Rooms in Piccadilly.

"She was an innocent young girl, your Excellency, when this flamboyant planter, a romantic figure from an exotic island, swept her off her feet."

"Quite so, quite so," the Governor clucked. It was obvious he held a poor opinion of creole slave breeders.

"I don't know what lies this man told when he forced himself on my mother and destroyed her innocence. What chance did she have? She slipped from virtue and paid dearly for it. She died minutes after I was born." He dabbed his eyes with a scented handkerchief and was delighted to see the Governor's sympathetic expression. The court was hushed.

"Her parents were old and would have nothing to do with me. My father, Carlton Todd, returned here to his plantation. He was never informed of my existence. A friend of my mother's cared for me, paid for my education and helped me to get established in society."

He thought it was going very well. He had deliberately embellished the story because there was nothing to be gained from everyone knowing his mother was a chambermaid.

"It is only recently that I discovered the name of my father," he continued. "I was preparing to come here to meet him when I learned of his horrible death."

The Governor asked a few questions which Carl answered easily and with respect. The legal matters were considered and Carl produced an affidavit. The Governor read it, studied the signature closely and then scrutinized Carl in astonishment.

"Mr Carlington Todd," the Governor intoned. "This affidavit is signed by James Stephens." There was a pause. Carl held his breath anxiously.

"It vouches for everything you have told the court. Mr Stephens is well known to this court as Legal Adviser to His Majesty's Colonial Office. An affidavit signed by Mr Stephens is irrefutable.

"Petition granted!"

11

Carl sat in the dug-out canoe and gazed in awe at the rugged coast as the small craft neared the Layou River. He ignored the spray showered over him by the Wagenie oarsman. The slaves laughed at him and he smiled back; he was so happy.

Casey sat facing him gloomily.

"Come now, boy," he chided him. "Aren't you pleased to be going home?"

"I've enjoyed keeping you company, Mr Carl." Something seemed to be wrong with Casey and Carl tried to read his mind.

"I suppose you're sad because we'll part now I'm the Bondmaster and going to live at Roxborough."

Casey shook his head. "It's the slaves, Mr Carl." He inclined his head to the Wagenies. "You mustn't let them get the better of you. Negroes are cunning."

"No fear of that!" He was brimming over with confidence. "I can handle servants."

Casey grimaced and Carl turned away from him and studied the coast line. The canoe was approaching a promontory protruding into the sea. He followed it with his eye back into the interior of the island. It was an awesome range of mountains with a waterfall scouring its side. It was covered with tall trees; the foliage of one merging with another to present a panoply of dense, impenetrable jungle. Smoke rose lazily from a solitary fire high up in the hills.

"That's Mingoson's camp."

Casey's remark quelled his excitement. He watched anxiously as the canoe rounded the headland into a vast river that flowed from the forest into the sea.

"Your house is on the hill, Mr Carl."

Carl stared in horror. A tumbledown shack with a roof of shingles nestled on a shelf of flatland at the crown of a hill. It was almost swallowed up by the tall grass and towering coconut trees surrounding it.

Below, to his left, there was a cluster of cabins and shacks and, on the right, the mountain range.

"That's Layou!" Casey pointed at the shacks. "That's the Roxborough boundary." He indicated the mountains. "All that cane behind the village, it's yours, Mr Carl."

Now he was there, Carl was disappointed. The plantation was not what he had imagined and the house appeared to be a native shack quite unsuitable for a gentleman. He was dismayed that his dream seemed worthless.

"Who are all those people?" he demanded sulkily.

Casey laughed. "They're your neighbours, the villagers."

Carl was aghast. The tiny jetty was packed with negroes. They were shouting and caterwauling and screaming and jumping with arms raised, pushing and shoving for a better view. What a foul mass of stinking black savages!

"My neighbors?" He shrank back into the canoe. Neighbors were civilized people but these were animals. He shouted at Casey above the din. "What do they want?"

"They've come to see the Bondmaster."

"Tell them to go away!"

Casey chuckled. "You tell them, Mr Carl."

The canoe scraped against the wooden supports of the jetty. Black hands reached down to grab him. The combined heat, smell and clamor overwhelmed him. He turned helplessly for Casey. The boy had gone.

He was pulled from the canoe and stood on his feet on the makeshift jetty. He was mauled by dozens of hands as he stared wildly about him. Black faces with shining teeth bared in fierce grins stared back at him. He clutched at someone in panic but his fingers slipped off the man's sweaty body. He was lost and frightened as he was tossed like a bag of flour from one black bogeyman to another.

He screamed but the sound was drowned by the noise of the crowd. Too late, he remembered his pistols. He reached for them but they had gone. The crowd surging around him became a blur of black faces, mocking eyes and snarling teeth. It was inhuman. He screamed again.

Suddenly there was silence. He was stunned. He was standing on the outside of the crowd, in the center of the track, by a flat cart. A hand, brown and sinewy but belonging to a white man, was extended to him. He grabbed it and scrambled up into the cart, spluttering his gratitude.

The man gave a practised flick of his wrist and his whip lashed out over the heads of the blacks. They fell back at the sound, their eyes blank. A negro jumped on to the tail of the wagon with Carl's box. The man cracked his whip again and the two horses moved forward through the gap which opened in the crowd.

"Laidlaw," said the man, lashing the horses again.

Carl clung to the edge of the seat to stop himself falling. The trail was rough and the wagon jerked from side to side. "Yes," he managed to gasp. "You laid down the law."

The man's face was heavily tanned. He pushed back his hat with his free hand and revealed a half moon of white where his brow had been protected from the sun. His face was dour as he glanced at Carl.

"Laidlaw," he said flatly, "is my name."

"Oh! How do you do!" Carl had to cling to the wagon with both hands so he couldn't shake Laidlaw's hand. He was being bounced so much his teeth banged together. "Th . . . thank you," he shouted.

Laidlaw growled at him which made Carl feel he had made an unfavorable first impression. He turned to look behind. A negro was sitting on his box watching him darkly. He smiled at him.

"Hel . . . hello!" he managed to say.

"Yassah, massa sah!" The negro bobbed his head repeatedly.

Laidlaw cleared his throat and spat into the wind. Spittle showered on to Carl. "Nigger's a slave," he said curtly. "One of yours."

"Oh!" The sarcasm in Laidlaw's voice added to Carl's confusion. He was bruised, angry and humiliated. He dared not say that he'd lost his pistols. He clenched his teeth and prayed he would soon stop being hurtled from side to side by the jolting wagon.

There were so many trees overhanging the trail that the sun was blocked out by the leaves. It was eerie on the path and damp. Over the screech of the wheels and the cacophony of the forest hemming them in, he heard the sound of water. He peered through the trees but glimpsed only reeds waving and shimmering in the breeze.

"Mill's over there," Laidlaw waved his whip in the direction of the sound.

"What's that?" Carl asked, to show his interest.

Laidlaw frowned and looked where Carl's finger was pointing. He pushed his hat further back on his head and scratched his scalp. "What's what?" he asked and sucked his teeth noisily.

"Those tall reeds. Some sort of plant?" Carl desperately wanted to win the approval of the odious man.

Laidlaw gaped and his eyes narrowed with suspicion. "That's sugar cane," he said gruffly. "You didn't know?"

"Oh yes, yes, of course, how silly of me." Carl's shirt pricked him and his stock seemed too tight. He loosened it to cover his shame.

"I mean, is all this mine?"

"S'pose so."

"Those negroes at the jetty - are they mine too?"

Laidlaw shook his head. "Free niggers. Roxborough slaves aren't that fresh. Not yet, anyway." He glanced with contempt at Carl.

"What's your job here, Laidlaw?" The wagon turned left at a fork in the trail and was forced to slow down by a steep incline.

"Overseer."

Carl swallowed, dismayed at the man's insolence. "Who engaged you?"

"Warren Gordon."

Well, I'll sack you the first opportunity I get, thought Carl.

"Mr Gordon said you'll pay me for the past six months so I reckon I'll stay here until you do." Laidlaw slashed at the backs of the horses, and the cart jerked over a ridge.

Carl gazed up the avenue of palm trees. "Is that ruin your house?" he asked, afraid to hear the answer.

"Yours. Roxborough Hall."

"Looks like a chicken coop."

"Suited the Bondmaster for forty years."

Carl fell silent. The air was oppressive. Although the sun was shining and the sky, where he glimpsed it between the overhanging boughs of the trees, was a glorious blue, clouds hung over the hills which hemmed in the plantation. There was a feeling of despair, emphasised by the gloomy faces of the slaves who stood silently in the undergrowth watching his progress up the hill. A wisp of smoke hung over the trees deep in the interior.

"You've got no money, have you?"

"I beg your pardon?"

"I'll have to stay until you get some." Laidlaw urged the horses over the final slope and brought them to a halt at the edge of an overgrown courtyard.

Carl took a deep breath. "It would give me pleasure to dismiss you now, Laidlaw," he said. He jumped down from the wagon into the weeds. "You haven't done much work here, have you?"

Laidlaw spat at his feet. An old negro hobbled over and took the horses' bridles. Laidlaw climbed down and waited while the slave led the horses away. He stared at Carl across the space between them where the wagon had been.

The two men were equal in height. Laidlaw tore off his coat and flung it over his shoulder, pushing back his hat. He wore a wide belt, breeches begrimed with dirt, and scuffed leather boots. He waited, his sleeves rolled up and a scowl on his face.

Carl swallowed nervously. His most formidable opponent in the past had been Cook when she tried to challenge his authority in the kitchens of the Stephens' house. She and Laidlaw shared the same unpleasant countenance. The similarity gave him confidence.

"Come, come, Laidlaw," he said, clapping his hands as though shooing Cook to her stove. "This won't do at all. Your idle days have finished. Show me around!"

Laidlaw glowered but he spun on his heels and walked toward the steps. Carl followed, raising his eyes with trepidation at the gray stone walls and the weathered boards of the ramshackle house which was now his home.

If Carl knew anything at all, and Laidlaw clearly doubted it, he knew about house management after his years of service for the Stephens. He knew what needed to be done, and he told Laidlaw what to do. The surly overseer was taken aback but rounded up some slaves. Under Carl's direction, they swarmed through the old house opening up doors and windows, dusting, polishing and arranging furniture.

"The place isn't as bad as it seems," he mused aloud during

a pause in his inspection of the premises. He was weary but in his element. Laidlaw's arrogant swagger had been replaced by perspiration and anger.

"There are some interesting pieces of furniture and the house has a certain charm." He stood on the gallery with its view over the sugar cane to the river mouth.

"Trifle damp after being closed for so long." He turned to Laidlaw. "In a few days I shall have it presentable. No shortage of staff, what?"

Laidlaw mopped his brow with the edge of his bandanna. His hair stuck to his scalp, patches of skin showing through where he scratched frequently. "Staff?" His voice was tense.

"Servants."

Laidlaw scratched and looked bemused.

"Sorry, I forgot. I'm supposed to call them slaves because they're not free yet. Ha! Ha!" He sighed when Laidlaw ignored his attempt to lighten the animosity between them. He resorted instead to his chivvying-the-chambermaids voice.

"Go and organize something to eat, Laidlaw, there's a good chap. I'll take my supper here on the gallery." He turned to look at the view then swung around suddenly. "By myself, of course." He dismissed Laidlaw with a wave of his hand.

His weariness prevented Carl from identifying by name the slaves who shuffled warily through the house. There was a collective edginess in the air. He knew the feeling. At the Stephens' house, the servants were sometimes unsettled until the mood of Mr Stephens and his wife had been established.

He sat in a low armchair with a wicker seat and a deep pitch that laid his head so far back he was obliged to raise his feet and hook them over the gallery rail. It was the perfect way to relax. The heat had died and a breeze wafted gently down from the mountains. Far out at sea the sun was slipping away. He closed his eyes.

There was a soft cough at his elbow. He blinked. A black face peered down. He was alone on the gallery with a slave standing beside him balancing a small tray in the palm of his huge hand.

"What do you want?" Anger at being disturbed, as though the slave had eavesdropped on his thoughts, gave his voice a sharp edge.

The slave faltered. "Ple . . . please, sah!"

"Speak up!" Carl was firm, using the tone the giggling scullery girls understood.

"I done mek some sang'ree fuh yo', sah."

He pulled himself upright and looked at the glass on the tray. It contained a scarlet liquid. He studied the slave's face. It was a deep blue-black, with eyes a brown so dark, it was impossible to read their expression. Yet the slave seemed friendly, his voice kind.

"What's sang'ree?" he asked, taking the glass.

"Red wine, sah. An' lime an' water an' sweetening."

He sipped. "How very refreshing. A little more water next time, I think."

"Yes, sah." The boy beamed.

"What's your name?" He had seen the boy busy in the house earlier in the afternoon. He seemed eager to please.

"Dale, sah."

He noted the slave's torn shirt and patched breeches. There was a lot to do before he could live like a lord, and be served like one. "Do you want to be my butler, Dale?"

"I don' know, sah."

He sipped his sangaree again. "You know, my house boy."

Dale's face lit up with an enormous smile framing his dazzling white teeth. "I gonna serve yo' good, massa!"

Carl replaced his feet on the gallery railing and sipped his drink. Dale ushered in two slaves with a table, then he served dinner. It was a stew whose ingredients Carl couldn't identify but he washed it down with more sangaree. He didn't see Laidlaw again and soon sought his bed.

"Dis way, sah." Dale guided him through the drawing room by the light of a candle. "We ain't got no lanterns yet, sah. Dere does be plenty t'ings we does need for dis house, sah."

The slave stopped in front of a door. "Dis does be de Bon'massa's bedroom, sah," he said reverently.

The back of Carl's neck began to tingle. He turned around but in the dark beyond the light of Dale's candle he could see nothing. He experienced a sensation of eyes watching him from the shadows. He thought again of the smoke rising from Mingoson's camp in the hills.

He pushed open the door and strode into the room. A candle flickered beside the bed. He stared. Behind him the door closed without a sound.

Lying on the bed, uncovered and naked, was a girl the color of gold. She was smiling, her black hair lustrous and sparkling in the candle light. Her breasts rose and fell gently. Her nipples, deep russet, drew Carl's eyes like magnets. Tiny curls of dark brown crowned her lower abdomen, a private spot he had never seen before, on any woman.

He blushed and lowered his eyes. He was rooted to the floor.

"Come, Master Carl," the girl said softly.

"Who . . . who are you?" he asked, his voice squeaking like a schoolboy's

"I'm yours." The girl rose from the bed, tiptoed across the floor and took his hand.

"I'm the Bondmaster's."

12

Carl followed the naked girl across the polished boards of the chamber, his boots echoing loudly in the forced silence. He sat, as directed, on the bed. The girl laid her finger across his mouth, sealing his lips. He had no strength, nor will, to protest.

He watched her sink to her knees and felt her fingers plying the soft leather of his boots. He leaned back on the bed and the girl eased off his boots, then his stockings. Her hands massaged his feet, creeping up his leg to his calf. He sat up, bunching himself forward with his elbows on his knees. He was dismayed by the pressure mounting within his breeches, threatening to burst out. He tried to hide it.

The girl raised her head and her eyes glimmered. "My name is Sabina." She paused. "Master."

The huskiness in her voice and the depth of meaning she gave the word 'master' made Carl soar. He hunched forward, blushing with shame at his reaction.

Sabina seemed not to notice. She smiled and stood up. Carl found to his amazement that his eyes were level with her abdomen. He glimpsed a hint of her female pride and raised his head quickly. Sabina's hands were caressing his shoulders, easing off his coat. He lifted his arms when she touched them, and she drew the coat over them leaving Carl feeling naked in his shirt and breeches.

"Why . . ." His voice was a strangled whisper. He tried again. "Why are you here?"

Sabina climbed on to the bed and pushed his head down on the pillows. She loosened his stock and then Carl realized she intended to strip off all his clothes.

"No," he said weakly but the stock was already drawn from his throat and her fingers were tugging his shirt. "No . . ." He frowned. ". . . Please!"

Sabina's beautiful mouth puckered with disappointment. She massaged his chest gently which made him aware of the throbbing of his body and his inability to control it. He tried to roll over but Sabina rolled with him bringing her lips close to his.

Never in his loneliest moments of fantasy had Carl dreamed that his body was capable of receiving so much pleasure. His dignity and morals were shattered under the skill of the black girl's embraces. He succumbed, slowly at first, and then with eager response. Soon, to his shame, he was demanding her as lustfully as any animal.

When he woke, hours later, a firefly illuminated the room with its soft green glow. The candle had burned out. Sabina lay in his arms, her delicious body with her lithe brown limbs and savage energy, pressed to his. He was deeply shocked by what he had done. What had happened to his propriety, his modesty, his soul? He shuddered.

Sabina's hand slipped between his legs and he groaned with pleasure.

In the morning, she was gone when he woke, and he was embarrassed to realize he was naked. He reached for the coverlet and pulled it over him. His clothes were folded neatly on a chair and a dish of coffee steamed on the table beside him. He hesitated to think of the night before. He reached for the coffee and sipped it cautiously.

Was this love, he wondered. He could feel the girl on his thighs. His penis pulsed as though it was still within her. His shame dissolved and was replaced with a feeling of mastery surging through him.

He jumped out of bed and flung open the shutters. The sun pushed in with a brilliance which made him blink. The window opened on to the balcony and beyond it were the rolling acres of Laidlaw's sugar cane. Not Laidlaw's; his.

He heard the overseer shouting orders with a flourish of curses. He backed away from the window, found his shirt and pulled it on. The door gently swung open.

"Mornin', massa." Dale bobbed his head and grinned.

Carl clutched his breeches in front of him. "I'm not dressed!"

Dale ignored him and strolled over to the coffee dish. "Mas Laidlaw does be waitin' fuh yo', sah."

He turned his back on the slave and started to put on his breeches. "I'll have to teach you some manners, Dale," he said over his shoulder. "How to speak, and how to serve a gentleman."

"I does 'preciate dat, sah."

He wondered if the boy was being sarcastic but when he turned he saw the slave watching him keenly. He fastened the buckle of his belt and sat in the chair, reaching for his boots. Dale put down the coffee dish to help him.

"That's all right, I'll do it myself."

"Yes, sah." He stood back, waiting.

"Dale, last night . . ."

"Sah?"

"A girl, here." He blushed.

"Sabina, sah?"

"You know!"

"Was she pleasin', sah?"

He concentrated on his boots so the slave would not see his embarrassment. "Well, yes . . ." he said. "Pleasing." He longed to see her again. She was his; he loved her. He stood up and stared out of the window.

"What, er, does she do?"

"Field slave."

"Ah." He strolled thoughtfully into the drawing room, his mind on Sabina. A field slave! Had he lost his heart to a field slave?

"You rise late!" The harsh voice startled him. Laidlaw was standing at the doorway, leering.

"Good morning, Laidlaw." How he loathed the man!

"Enjoy the wench, did you?"

"What?" He gripped the back of a chair, his stomach churning.

"The bed wench. Hot little chit, isn't she?" Laidlaw sneered. "Thought she'd drain you properly." He turned and sauntered on to the balcony.

Carl hurried after him. "You sent her?"

"That's the custom here. You're a visitor. Always give a wench to a visitor. Might get a light-skinned whelp."

"I am not a visitor!" Carl said, his heart racing. "This is my plantation!"

"Maybe it is, but you won't stay." Laidlaw threw himself into a chair and gazed up at him. "I know your sort. A few weeks poking the niggers then you'll be off to England."

"Get up!"

"Huh?" Laidlaw cocked his head in surprise.

"I didn't give you permission to be seated." He was sterner than he'd ever been with Cook. But this man was repulsive!

Laidlaw leaped out of the chair and bowed mockingly. "So sorry, sir. Forgot my manners. Forgot you're an English gentleman."

"Forget it again at your peril, Laidlaw." Carl gazed out

over the cane. "Where do the field slaves work?"

"In the fields."

"That girl. Last night. Where does she work?"

"Hah! Tasty wench, ain't she? Rode her last week myself. You can have another tonight and I'll have her again."

The bile rose in Carl's throat. He gripped the balcony rail to control his rage. "I'll choose the girls I want." He felt sick at the thought of the overseer making love to Sabina.

"Girls!" Laidlaw's snort of scorn echoed into the house. "You've got a lot to learn, friend. Sabina's a wench, a slave, a nigger. She works in the cane with her frock tied around her waist and her titties hanging out. She'll rut with any buck and be back holing cane in five minutes. She's an animal, friend, not a girl." Laidlaw aimed a stream of spittle over the balcony rail.

Carl moved to his seat. "It will take me time to become accustomed to your own animal ways," he said. "I want to know everything about this plantation and I want to know it today. The quicker I can dispense with your services, the better."

"Oh yes, you sound very fine, friend. But you need me. You can't control niggers. I can. No one knows cane better than me. You're going to need sugar to pay your debts."

"That's as maybe." He waved his hand. "I'll start with the house. I want kitchen staff, chambermaids, footmen."

"House slaves!" Laidlaw sneered. "Planters here make do with a boy and a cook."

"When I want your advice, Laidlaw, I'll ask for it. That young lady, Sabina, she'll work in the house."

"I know what work she'll be doing! Best to keep her in the field gang and send for her when you fancy a piece of black pussy."

Carl swallowed his anger. "The young man here in the house, Dale. What do you know about him?"

"The black one? Troublesome bugger! Needs thrashing."

"Indeed?" Carl clapped his hands sharply and called: "Dale, come here please."

"Just shout 'boy' when you want a nigger," Laidlaw said. "They don't understand politeness."

"I wonder if you do, Laidlaw?"

Dale stood hesitantly in the door way. "Yes, massa Carl?"

"Come here, Dale, if you please. Don't be shy of the overseer." He felt kindly toward the slave who had shown him far more respect and understanding since he arrived than Laidlaw had.

"How old are you?" he asked.

"I does not know, sah." Dale bit his lip. "It does be in de stock book, sah."

"He's about twenty." Laidlaw fingered his whip.

"What's a stock book?"

The overseer ignored the question but Dale leaned forward eagerly. "It does be de ledger wid de slaves in it, sah."

"Why haven't I seen that?"

"I was going to show you," Laidlaw said sulkily. "There are ledgers for the distillery, stores, clothes --"

Carl held up his hand. "Get them! Get them all!"

"I ain't had breakfast."

"Then you'll have to do without." Carl drummed his fingers on the arm of his chair. "I'm making Dale here my major domo. He'll be in charge of the servants and will take any slave he wants from the plantation to serve me in the house."

"That's my job!" Laidlaw gaped at Carl. "You can't give a nigger that responsibility. He'll be the master and you the slave."

Carl waved his hand to shut him up. "The ledgers, Laidlaw, if you please!"

Carl's session with Laidlaw trying to read some sense into the ledgers, was a stormy one. He disagreed with every notion Laidlaw had, and the overseer ridiculed every idea he advanced. According to Laidlaw, the plantation was on the verge of bankruptcy. Slaves had to be emancipated in seven months. From August, they could no longer be coerced into work by judicious use of the whip. They would be protected and must be paid.

"Todd's only crop was slaves," Laidlaw said. "They ain't worth a whore's fart now."

The overseer's solution was to work the slaves to their limit in the remaining seven months in the hope of expanding the sugar crop.

"If they're going to be freed, they won't want to work, will they?" Carl was shaken. The heat was too much for him and he was sitting in the shade with a lime squash in his hand. "How the slaves even move in this heat is beyond me."

Laidlaw gloated. "Niggers got thick skins. Tougher than you. They got to be made to work however hot it is so you get the money to pay for their feed."

Carl was puzzled. "I thought Carlton was supposed to have been a rich man?"

"Maybe he was." Laidlaw thumped a ledger. "Don't understand figures much. There's credit with Colquhorns, the London agents, but no currency here." He scratched his head. "Credit ain't paying me."

Carl said nothing. He remembered his mother's tale about treasure buried beneath the foundations of the house.

"I need every slave there is to get that sugar crop in. I'm taking them out of the Pen too."

"Heavens! What's that?"

"Breeding pen. Where the whelps are kept."

"No!" Carl had no reason to refuse Laidlaw other than his determination that the overseer was not going to bully him. He wasn't even sure what a whelp was. "You'll do nothing on this plantation without obtaining my consent first."

Laidlaw let a loud raspberry rip from his lips.

Carl blenched. "I've heard the sugar trade is not that profitable. I need to consider all aspects before I give you my instructions."

Carl's original plan was to find the Bondmaster's fortune and return to England to enjoy it. But Laidlaw's contempt rankled him. He decided to show the overseer that he was quite capable of handling slaves and revitalizing Roxborough.

"I believe I understand these black chappies," he said. "Lashing and cursing them isn't the answer. It wouldn't work with servants in England."

Laidlaw jammed his hat on his head and stalked off the

balcony without a word. Carl was relieved to see him go. He picked up the stock register and idly turned the pages to calm his nerves.

Listed in the book were the names of every slave on the plantation. There were breeding charts that showed the slave's name, his tribe, and who he was crossed with, and the female's tribe. It was a history of the Bondmaster's attempts to reproduce strong, healthy slaves who were tractable and willing workers.

Notes, which must have been written by Carlton himself, detailed the characteristics of different tribes. "Coromantees -- strong, bellicose, virile. Beware fierceness; escapers." From Whiddah came "Papaws -- industrious, agriculturists; dread pain." A note said that a crossing of a Coromantee and a Papaw was likely to produce a good field slave. House slaves could be bred from Yoruba – "best in physique and intelligence" – and Fulani – "slender built, reddish skin."

His glass was empty. He got up from the table and strode to the end of the balcony. There was a slight breeze at the corner and he let it ruffle his neatly combed hair. He wore his coat despite the heat. It was important, he believed, for a master to maintain a good appearance in front of his servants. Servants? No, they were slaves. They were bred to be slaves.

He paced the balcony dismayed at the neglect around him. No attempt had been made to clean the grass and weeds that overgrew the courtyard. The plantation, he realized, as he gazed out from the gallery, was in a dilapidated state because Laidlaw wanted to concentrate on growing sugar cane.

Bah! He wouldn't allow it! Roxborough was not an ordinary plantation. The cream of slaves was raised here, that was Carlton's legacy -- and it was his!

He gasped with excitement as an idea hit him. He sat down, got up, took a turn along the balcony, and sat down again. Yes, it would work. He was about to develop the idea in his mind when a voice broke into his thoughts.

"Yo' sen' fuh me, massa?"

He raised his head irritably but his scowl faded to a shy smile and he shifted uncomfortably in his chair. "Hello," was all he could say.

"Yes, master?" Sabina looked more beautiful than he remembered. She wore a loose shift of nondescript slave material. But her face was alive, her hair glowed in the sun, and her body seemed to quiver with anticipation. He put his hand out to touch her, but she recoiled.

"What's wrong?"

"Are you going to beat me?"

"Good heavens! Why should I want to do that?"

"Maybe I don't please you?"

"Come here!" Carl jumped from his seat. Sabina shrank against the wall. "Don't be frightened. Of course you please me. Oh hell!" He was lost for words.

"I'll wait in your chamber."

"Stay!" He lowered his voice. "I like you, Sabina. I mean more than . . . you know . . ."

She nodded. "Yes, sir."

"I want you to work in the house."

"Yes, sir."

"You don't sound pleased."

"What ever you say, sir. It's you."

"Damn it all, I'm taking you out of the canefields. Out of that hot sun."

"Yes, sir."

He hit his brow in exasperation. He expected Sabina to be delighted. "I'll give you new clothes! You can prettify yourself. Be quite the young lady."

"Yes, sir. I'll wait in your chamber," she said, gliding off the balcony before he could stop her.

He realized then that he didn't understand slaves at all.

13

"I don't understand yew, Casey!" Mary threw her hands up in the air in despair. "Haven't yew got any ambition?"

"Aw, mam," Casey shook his head, showering water around him. He had just emerged from the sea and he stood in front of his mother on the sea wall behind the casino. In the bright morning sun, drops of water glistened like diamonds on his lightly bronzed skin. His wet breechcloth clung to him, revealing the outline of his proud physique.

"Lazing and fooling around all day, Casey! Yew aren't doing a thing to help yourself."

"Mam!" Casey wiped himself dry with his hands. The sun warmed him and he was content. "I don't want to go to Roxborough today."

"I think yew should."

He caught the note of disappointment in his mother's voice and looked at her closely. She was wearing her walking dress, a light cloak and a matching bonnet. Her face was rouged and powered but perspiration was already seeping through. She twitched her skirt with annoyance.

"I'll come, mam. For you."

"Run and change!"

He glanced down at himself and laughed. "Can't I come like this?"

"Yew ain't one of his slaves. Those breeding wenches will rip the drawers off yew," Mary clasped her parasol and stepped carefully off the wall. "The carriage is coming."

He ran to the back of the casino and rolled the wet breechcloth over his thighs and down his legs. He stood naked in the doorway and relished the sun on his body.

"Uraline," he shouted. "Bring mah breeches an' a clean shirt fuh me, nuh!"

The cook's grumbling stopped when she rounded the corner of the house and saw him naked. "My gawd! Casey, yo' does be ou' yuh mind. Dere does be ladies here!"

"Whores ain't ladies, Uraline." He pulled his clothes from the cook's hands. "Only you." He stepped into his breeches and tucked himself in.

"Yo' wan' me help yo', Casey?"

"Uraline, it ain't fuh yo'." He dragged his shirt over his head, chuckling to himself.

"Ah does be a fine wench fuh pleasurin'." Uraline eyed him coyly. "Ah done serve de best! De Bon'massa himself!"

"You told me already." He put his arms around Uraline's ample waist, and kissed her cheek. "Take that for now."

"Come back later, boy. Ah make one nice calaloo."

"Maybe!" He laughed and ran off to find the carriage. Mary was sitting inside. She stared at him in horror.

"Yew ain't coming like that!"

"Why not?"

"Yew ain't dressed. Where are your shoes?"

"Mam, let me be. Mas Carl won't mind."

"Well, sit on the coach box." She sank into the seat of the carriage and sighed loudly.

Casey climbed up and winked at the coachman. The negro whipped the horses into motion. Mary Gregg had hired the village conveyance especially for the visit to Roxborough. She wanted to pay her respects in style. To Casey, it was a waste of time and money.

It was a month since he came from Roseau with Carl. He had befriended him in the capital because his mother made him angry. Now he had a suspicion that it had been his mother's intention all the time to bring him and Carl together. She was still determined to see him get something from the Bondmaster's legacy. This neighborly courtesy call was another ploy.

The trail along the riverside through the plantation was being tended by a gang of slaves. They waved at the carriage and Casey was surprised to see them leaning on their hoes and smiling. Drains had been cleaned, pot holes filled, and the trail cutlassed.

"Road is better," he said to the coachman. "Laidlaw's taken the slaves out of the cane. Odd."

"Ver' odd." The coachman rolled his eyes. "De new massa, he does hab new 'proach. 'T'ain' right! Slaves is slaves."

The coach turned into the grass boulevard leading up the hill to the house. A gang of children, all naked and shrieking with laughter, ran to meet it. Some of them leaped at the coach, and a bold one landed on the coach box beside Casey. He grabbed him so the boy wouldn't fall off. The other children ran gaily beside the coach.

"Hello," said Casey holding on to his captive. "Where did you come from?"

"De pen!" The boy bounced delightedly. "Ah ain' neber ride a cart like dis." He was black and sturdy, ten years old and cocky.

"You'd better get down, young feller. The Bondmaster will beat you."

"Not he! Mas Carl does tickle mah balls. He don't beat no one."

"Ain' right," said the coachman gloomily.

"Go on, get down!" Casey held the boy under his arms and dropped him to the ground as the coach slowed. They were coming into the courtyard. It had been freshly swept, the cobbles and flagstones gleamed in the sun. Flowers were growing in wooden tubs by the newly painted grand steps.

A youth ran forward as the coach halted. He grasped the bridles and chattered to the horses to calm them. An older man followed him and opened the door of the carriage.

"Welcome to Roxbruh, Mistis!" the old slave said, unfolding the steps. "Ah does be Caliste."

Casey watched with astonishment while Caliste helped his mother alight. He hardly recognized the slave in his livery with his hair combed and his face shining. Another slave descended the grand steps. He bowed low, stood up and straightened his coat.

"Welcome to Roxborough, ma'am." The slave enunciated

every word with care. "Please come wid me."

Casey and the coachman exchanged glances. "'T'ain' right," the man said.

Casey wasn't sure what to do. His mother cast a scathing glance at him as she swept up the steps. She reached the balcony and twirled her parasol with delight as Carl greeted her and bent to kiss her hand. He said something and Mary waved in the direction of the coach. Casey heard his name being called.

"Casey! Why don't you come up?"

He jumped down from the box and grinned. "My mam doesn't think I'm properly dressed!"

"My dear boy!" Carl turned to a liveried slave standing beside him. "Show Mrs Gregg to a seat, Dale. I'm sure she'd like some refreshment." He nodded to Mary before bounding down the steps and seizing Casey by his hand.

"Come up! There's nothing wrong with your outfit."

Casey shrugged and followed Carl. "The slaves --."

"My servants, Casey. In uniform. What you and I wear is our affair." Carl himself was coolly elegant in buff trousers and a cotton shirt. "See, I've no formal wear. Your mother must accept us as we are."

Casey was overwhelmed by the attention. A slave held his chair for him. Dale, whom he knew, looked so pompous in an outfit of gold and scarlet. He was directing the flow of slaves bringing sangaree and lime juice and sweetmeats. Mary watched open-mouthed.

"I declare yew have house-trained every black in sight."

"Thank you." Carl crossed his legs and settled back confidently. "I'm trying to."

"Whatever for?"

"For domestic service."

Casey mouthed the words silently to himself. "What's that?" he asked.

Carl waited until Mary and Casey had been served and the slaves had taken up their positions again. There was an air of preparedness in the house which Casey found alien to the normal lethargy of plantation life.

"I realized," Carl said, leaning forward and tapping him on

his knee, "that Roxborough has the greatest resource of any plantation in the Caribbean."

"Sugar or coffee is all you have," said Mary coldly.

"No. Roxborough has something better; slaves - the human resource."

"Carlton would never have called slaves human."

"Maybe not, Mary. But he believed in them. He raised these slaves himself, and trained them too."

"Trained them for field work." Mary sipped her sangaree and gazed askance at the young blacks in their English style finery.

Carl spread his hands. "When slavery finishes, can you imagine any negro working in the cane fields of his own free will?"

"It's all they know."

"They have the intelligence to learn more! I've inspected all the slaves on this plantation. I've chosen, tested and evaluated them all. I'm going to train them to be house servants, domestic staff."

"Well, I never! I could use a couple for the casino."

"You shall have your choice, Mary. At a price, of course." Carl was serious.

Casey hadn't touched his drink. "Slavery finishes end July!" he said loudly. "You can't have slaves then."

"Yew keep out of this. I'll buy niggers if they're house broke."

Carl turned to Casey. "Don't forget there is going to be a period of apprenticeship, six years, for every slave to serve when slavery officially ends. So your mother will get six years of service, at least, out of every one of my domestic slaves she buys."

Casey felt a chill of apprehension spreading through him. "You make abolition seem like a trick," he said. "You can't sell slaves now!"

Carl shrugged. "I can."

"Then if I were a slave, I'd start an insurrection."

"Casey!"

"I understand the boy, Mary," Carl said calmly. "Because he's free, he thinks a different way. But I don't believe slaves really want to be 'free'. Do they want to fend for themselves, live off wages and have no one to care for them?"

"I don't understand."

"Don't look so glum, Casey," Carl said indulgently. "My slaves have been reared since birth for ownership. They are rooted by custom to slavery. They need owners! I'm going to give them the opportunity to acquire owners even when slavery is abolished."

Casey bit his lip and said nothing. A fury was rising within him.

"There's something else." Carl had a twinkle in his eye. "I'm going to breed."

"Crikey!" Mary spluttered into her drink.

"If I can get more whelps out of these slaves before I sell them, I'll train the suckers from birth. By the time they are six, they'll sell for more than the finest field buck."

"But they'll be free. You can't sell a free man."

"I can." Carl spoke slowly, his face hard. "I can't sell slaves stripped down on the auction block but I can place my trained servants with people who are prepared to pay me a consideration to get them. By private treaty."

"Good lawd!" Mary sat back. "You sound like the Bondmaster himself!"

"It ain't right," said Casey bitterly, unconsciously echoing the sentiments of the coachman.

"Of course it's right." Carl sounded offended. "I'm giving the slaves a chance to better themselves."

"And yourself a chance to make a fortune."

"I hope so, Mary. I'm up to my eyes in debt. The clothes, the supplies, the provisions . . ."

Mary snorted. "Yew must be the richest man in Dominica."

"That's not true." Carl's cheek twitched. "There is some credit with Colquhorn's in London but no currency here."

"Perhaps Mingoson stole it." Casey hoped he had.

Mary's eyes narrowed. "There were coffers of gold here! Caspar told me. If Mingoson had that gold, all the blacks in Layou would know. So would I!"

"Did Caspar say where the coffers were hidden?"

Mary sniffed. Casey thought she was crying. "No," she said firmly. "He didn't."

The conversation died. Casey's mind was in a turmoil about Carl's plans. He was relieved when his mother stood up and gathered her cloak around her. She advanced across the balcony while the slaves bowed and curtsied. Two slaves danced down the steps in front of her as she descended to the carriage.

Carl walked beside Casey and tried to put his arm on his shoulder. Casey moved away. "I hope you'll come again."

"I won't."

"Suit yourself."

Casey paused at the foot of the steps. He looked at Carl and saw how the young Englishman had changed. There was a manic glint in his eye. The softness of his features had been burnt out by the sun. He seemed to be a man who had discovered himself but what he'd found wasn't pleasant.

"If Roxborough was mine," Casey said, "I'd free the slaves now. I'd give them the gold, the plantation, and their liberty. It's their flesh and blood that gave the Bondmaster his fortune. It's theirs, not yours."

Carl laughed sarcastically. "Noble sentiments! But there's no fortune."

Casey's skin tingled and he wanted to strike Carl. He mounted the coachbox quickly.

"Let me give you a filly, Casey. You look like you could use a wench!"

"Drive!" Casey scowled and nudged the coachman in his ribs. The carriage leaped forward as the whip struck the horses' backs.

He glanced with pity at the children laughing and gambolling beside the trail. He was consumed with hatred for Carl and his evil plans when he considered how the slaves were being duped. How could they let their freedom be stolen from them for a promise of silk breeches and pretty pinafores?

He cursed bitterly the twist of fate that had nearly put Roxborough in his hands and then taken it from him. The Bondmaster still ruled the plantation, even from the grave.

14

For days after his visit to Roxborough, Casey was troubled by what he heard there. It disturbed him that Carl had found some immunity from the laws that governed the other plantations.

The island was agog with the preparations for emancipation. In Dominica where the power of the whites had been eroded by miscegenation, the idea of apprenticeship was scorned by the slaves. If a female slave was three degrees removed from black, her child by a white man became free. The island was unique in having the Brown Privilege Act which conferred status equal with whites on mulatto offspring.

Now there were new laws and visiting English officials explained them enthusiastically. Casey listened, and spent hours in the shade of a mango tree by the river mulling over what he'd heard. This was his favorite spot, a place where he could sit without being disturbed and plan what he could do for the Roxborough slaves.

One afternoon, three weeks after his visit to Roxborough, he was lying on his stomach, his chin supported on his hands, gazing at the river. The fast flowing water had a hypnotic effect. It calmed his mind and the tranquility of the glade soothed him. He was absorbed when a girl's voice shattered his thoughts.

"What a lazy bones!"

His heart sank. "Go away!" he said in despair without turning to see who had spoken. He was vexed that one of the casino whores had discovered his hiding place. Now he would have to find another, further up the river, on Roxborough land.

"All right."

There was silence. He concentrated on the river again, watching coconuts bobbing past and the eddies around the boulders at the water's edge.

"It's a lovely river, isn't it? Nicer than the Thames."

The interruption shocked him. He rolled on his side. "I told you to go --" He gaped in amazement. "I'm sorry, I didn't know . . ." He sat up quickly and drew his knees to his chest to conceal his hardness where he had been pressing his body into the earth.

The girl blushed. "I didn't mean to make you angry."

"I'm not."

He wondered who she was. She sat on the trunk of a fallen palm tree, her skirt carefully arranged but showing a trace of ankle under its voluminous folds. Her dress was white with red ribbons, and her sensible bonnet was loose. Her hair hung down like silken gold, framing a face of the most delicate beauty he had ever seen. She smiled hesitantly.

"Are you sure?"

"Yes."

Neither spoke. He watched the girl's eyes, an English blue like sapphires in the fair setting of her gentle face. He felt those eyes on his own and he smiled. When her gaze dropped, he shifted uncomfortably, suddenly ashamed of his wet breechcloth and his bare body. He probably looked like a maroon to her.

"I'm sorry," he said, sitting up on his haunches. "I'll go."

"Don't do that!" The girl put her hand to her mouth. "You really are angry with me."

"No. I was going anyway. I came here to think." He gestured at the river. "You can watch --" His voice died under the pressure of the girl's blue eyes. They were pleading.

"Don't go . . . " she said. "Is it very bad?"

He knew what she meant. "You are alone?"

"Yes. I saw you from my window so I told mother I was going for a walk in the village."

"You followed me?" He was intrigued.

"It's the only way I could speak to you."

"You must be very wicked."

Her frown vanished and she laughed. It was like a bird's song, joyful and carefree. "Yes, I am. That's what mother says. She doesn't want me to speak to a --"

"A black boy?"

"Yes."

"I'm black," he said, wondering if the girl assumed his light skin was because he was a creole white. "And my mother's a whore."

"I know. I really must be wicked." The girl laughed again then hid her smile quickly behind her hand. "Oh dear, I hope you don't think I'm laughing at you."

"Are you?" He was acutely aware of his dishevelled appearance. "I've been bathing, I've --"

"Don't! You shouldn't apologize. I'm the one who's intruding on you."

"I'm used to it."

"A braggart as well as handsome, I see."

"I mean, the whores, where I live . . ."

"Oh." The girl blushed.

There was silence. The girl seemed to be struggling to get her thoughts under control. Her glance darted nervously from him to the river, to the mango tree and back to him. Then she smiled.

"Why did you want to speak to me?"

The girl eyed him carefully. "Because you are so, well . . ." She shrugged her shoulders. "You interested me."

He pursed his lips. The girl was his age. She had an air of sophistication but he sensed her nervousness. He liked her.

"You haven't told me what you think about," she said suddenly.

"You almost caught me out," he said, embarrassed. "Do you go to school?" He asked the question more to divert her attention than to pry.

"Do you feel if I go to school then I'm not old enough to hear what you think about?"

"Of course not. I've never seen you before, that's all."

"I've seen you every day."

"Every day?"

"Yes. I watch you when you walk down the street. When you go to the bakery, when you see your friends. I know so much about you."

He wasn't pleased.

"Now I've upset you! I'm not spying on you, please don't think that. I sit at my window and dream that one day we could be together on the river bank like this."

"Why?" He picked up a stone and threw it at the water. It skimmed over the surface like a bird.

"Just because."

"I've never seen you. How long since you came?"

"Three weeks. My father's the stipendary magistrate."

"One of those English men who explain about emancipation?" He was excited.

"I suppose so. Is that what you think about?"

He didn't answer.

"My father is very understanding, Casey . . ." She said his name slowly as if she had been practising it. "Why don't you visit and talk to him about slavery? He doesn't know many ordinary people."

"Ordinary people? Is that what I am?" He threw another stone.

"People who aren't planters and slave holders. He needs to know all sides. He'll be here for two years at least."

"Shall I walk you back?"

"Yes," she said, surprising him.

"What about your mother?"

"She'll find out what a wicked girl I am." She laughed. "Besides, you're coming to see Daddy."

"I am?"

"Yes. You've got something on your mind."

"How do you know that?" He turned away and picked up another stone.

"You told me. Come on!" She tapped him lightly on his shoulder.

Her touch startled him and he let the stone slip from his fingers and swung around to face her. His throat dried when he saw the rise and fall of her bosom under the high neck of her corsage. The fragrance of her perfume roused him and he stepped back in confusion. A yearning gripped his guts and his heart pounded. He couldn't speak and stood as though trapped.

"You feel it too! I know you do!" The girl's fingers slipped into his hand. "Oh, Casey!"

"Go home," he said thickly. "I'll come to your father's tonight." A ray of sunlight shone through the leaves of the mango tree and caught in her golden hair.

She turned and ran out of the glade. He watched her until he could no longer see the flashes of the white and red ribbons on her skirt through the trees. He stood motionless for a long time savoring the scent of her perfume lingering in the soft stillness of the afternoon. He felt the gentle pressure of her hand still tingling his fingers.

He walked slowly to the river and dived in, swimming with strong, powerful strokes to the center. He rolled on to his back, letting the sun caress his chest and thighs as he floated in the swirl of the river to the sea.

"On August first," the magistrate said, "slavery will be at an end. From that date, all freedmen above the age of six will be classified as either agricultural or domestic servants." The magistrate held up his hand to forestall any interruption.

"The classification will be decided on the basis of the type of labor that the slaves performed twelve months before the passage of the Abolition Act last year."

Casey's head spun. He was sitting on the balcony of the house which the magistrate rented in Layou. Lanterns blazed at both ends of the balcony and Casey was aware that both he and the magistrate could be seen by anyone passing in the street below. It occurred to him that the magistrate, Arnold Leach, wanted it that way.

Leach was regarded with resentment and suspicion by the planters. The slaves, whose welfare it was his job to safeguard, were, so far, unaware of his existence. They were likely to treat him with distrust as a lackey of the planters because he was white. Casey's presence on his balcony was a significant step forward in his campaign for acceptance by the villagers.

Casey was dressed in his most formal clothes. He wore a coat, a stock at his throat, and a freshly laundered cotton shirt. His boots were highly polished. He was proud to be seen on the magistrate's balcony. But while Mr Leach spoke, he wondered where his daughter was.

Mr Leach paused indulgently. "Is something troubling you, young man?"

Casey grasped the question he had ready. "Does it matter how they are classified? A slave's a slave."

"Ah, yes!" The magistrate steepled his hands and gazed at him over his finger tips. "You've heard about apprenticeship? The agricultural workers, the field slaves, will be apprenticed for six years. Domestics, the house slaves, will get their complete freedom after four years."

"I see." He thought of Carl's scheme. "If a planter changes his field slaves to house slaves after August last year, they'll still be classed as field slaves. They'd have to serve six years instead of four?"

The magistrate looked puzzled. "That's right, young man, but not likely."

"Why not?"

"Planters want their slaves in the fields, you see. That's where the work is to be done."

Casey nodded. "What about those under six years old?"

"Immediate freedom in their mother's care." The magistrate sat back with a satisfied expression.

"What happens if they don't have mothers?"

Mr Leach considered the question carefully. "The child would be indentured on the estate of his residence until he reaches the age of twenty-one."

"That's slavery for a lifetime!"

"Indenture, young man. He'll be paid, work limited hours, be given food, clothing, lodging and medical attention. Stipendary magistrates, gentlemen like myself, have been appointed to superintend the conduct of apprenticeship."

Casey sighed. It seemed Carl was legally right in what he intended to do to the Roxborough slaves.

"You look very thoughtful, young man." The magistrate

gave him an avuncular pat on his knee. He flinched.

"I intend to be scrupulous in my pursuit of justice for your unfortunate brethren, young man."

Casey swallowed his distaste for the white man's patronizing attitude and stood up.

"Is there a particular problem you have in mind, young man?"

Casey shook his head. He couldn't say the whole process was unfair and biased in favor of the slave holders. He moved toward the door. "There is just one question. Do you believe a negro slave is a human being?"

"My dear chap, of course I do." Mr Leach clapped him on his shoulder. "It's the cornerstone of the campaign for amelioration. When slaveholders realize that slaves are not chattels but human beings, albeit black ones, freedom is inevitable."

Casey moved out of the shadow so that the lantern shone fully on his face. His eyes challenged Mr Leach. "Do you side with the slaves or their owners?"

Mr Leach peered at him, then spluttered. "With . . . with neither, dear chap. I shall judge every case impartially. Any person, black or white, who has a complaint can appear before me. You . . . er . . . might let people know that."

"I might." Casey frowned, casting his eyes around the drawing room, wondering if he would see the girl.

"It's been stimulating talking to you." Mr Leach held out his hand to Casey who took it in surprise. "My daughter has a very high opinion of you."

Casey was taken aback by the remark and withdrew his hand quickly. The magistrate laughed.

"Lucy is an intelligent girl. I trust her judgement. Perhaps it runs in the blood!" He chuckled again and Casey waited, not seeing the joke.

"Yes . . . er . . . well," said Mr Leach. "I believe you'll find Lucy downstairs. She'll want to say goodnight."

Casey bounded down the stairs with the magistrate's words ringing in his ears. Perhaps the man wasn't a prejudiced and pompous fool after all. Lucy! Her name was Lucy!

"You're in a hurry." The girl's bright laughter halted him.
"I was --"
"In a hurry to leave us?" Lucy's blue eyes widened to indicate caution as her mother stood at the door to the street.
"I'm sure Casey has lots of things to do," Mrs Leach said, holding open the door.
Casey found himself being bundled out of the house without a chance to speak to the girl. Lucy! He stood under the balcony and gazed up at the sky. There was no moon and the night was clear but it seemed that the stars were mocking him. He walked home sadly.

15

Casey had been raised by women. Whites, browns, blacks; his entire life was spent in the company of females who, by nature of their profession, were hard. He never lacked affection and the whores doted on him. As a child, he slept clasped to their naked breasts for comfort. He was accustomed to female flesh and, until this moment, it never occurred to him how potent and desirable it was.
When his body stirred and his prick was stiffer than a green plantain, the whores gave him solace, shrieking with laughter at his youth. They treated him like a pet, and he was content to lie back while their hands and lips drained him.
He stared out at the sea from where he sat with his back resting against the trunk of a seagrape tree. In the darkness behind, he sensed someone watching him, waiting for him to call. He raised his eyes at the stars and sighed.
"Yo' does be sad tonight, Cas?"
Uraline eased herself down beside him. He was pleased to have her company and put his arm around her, resting his

head on her shoulder. She patted his hair gently, her fingers tingling the sensitive area at the back of his neck. He squeezed her, sighed again, and removed his arm, leaning back against the tree trunk. His legs dangled over the wall. Uraline snuggled against him.

He valued her friendship. She ran the kitchen with discipline and even though he was her favorite, she boxed his ears when he tried to steal some tidbit from her. She was a hearty soul, brash and vulgar, but she knew how to be quiet too. She listened to the sea with him, her hand idly running down his chest to unfasten the button of his coat.

"No!" He caught her wrist.

She chuckled and entwined her long fingers into his hand.

"I've met a girl, Uraline," he said.

She stroked his palm tenderly.

"She's English. She's sixteen years old, the daughter of the stipendary magistrate and she thinks I'm interesting."

Uraline's fingers crept up his arm, across his chest and to his throat. She pulled out his stock. He tried to keep calm.

"I met her today. She's wonderful! She has hair the color of . . ." He thought, unconsciously pushing away Uraline's fingers. ". . . Evening sunset! She's so modest, she blushes when I mention mam's whores. Her eyes, Uraline, her eyes!" He twisted restlessly against the tree trunk.

"You know how the sea is when it's a bright day and it's a deep blue. That's the color of her eyes."

Uraline moved closer and he smelled the odor of her warm flesh and the scent of a peppery stew on her breath. He lay back and concentrated his mind on the stars.

"She's seeing those stars too," he said. "Perhaps she's thinking of me."

"Perhaps." Uraline's voice surprised him.

"You don't believe me?"

"I believe you, Cas. Why not?" She opened his shirt and slipped her hand inside, under his trousers.

He squirmed. He was stiffening as Uraline's fingers edged lower. He wanted to turn away from her but it was too late.

"Uraline, what can I do? She's a respectable English girl. She'll never want me, I'm nothing."

"You are, Cas!" Uraline's fingers stopped probing and she pushed her head close to Casey. He saw her dark eyes were blazing with anger.

"You're the grandson of the Bondmaster. This white girl is nothing beside you!" Her hand cupped his crotch and squeezed him gently.

He chuckled. "Leave me be, Uraline."

"Oh law!" She fingered him and he stiffened in her hand.

He pulled away and leaped to his feet. "I love you, Uraline, " he said, panting. "But I can't do that. It's her. She wouldn't like it."

"Oh law," said Uraline again, shaking her head wisely. "You've got it bad, Casey. Be careful! That white man will cut off your balls if you touch his daughter."

It was his intention, Arnold Leach told Lucy, to visit every plantation in his parish. Lucy wondered how he would manage without a guide. Her father said he hoped to find one.

"Which is why you're being considered for the job," said Lucy, laughing delightedly. "I hope you'll agree."

Casey was sitting opposite her in the drawing room of the magistrate's house. Her mother was elsewhere while her father sat shuffling papers at his desk. He had been summoned for the interview a week after his first encounter with Lucy. He had thought of her every hour since then, mooning about the bordello in a dream, deaf to the teasing of the whores. Only Uraline didn't mock him, and she seemed preoccupied with thoughts of her own.

"Well, what do you say?"

He blinked. He had been watching Lucy's lips which were the delicate pink of anthuriums. He yearned to kiss them. "I don't know . . ." he stammered.

"Come on, young feller! Be an education for us both."

"He will, he will, daddy." Lucy fluttered her eyelashes. Casey lowered his head, not hearing what Mr Leach said. Lucy took his hand!

"Daddy wants to know if you'll go to Roxborough with him now."

"Roxborough?" He paled. Lucy's eyes pleaded with him to agree. "Yes," he said as though speaking from afar. He rose to his feet in a trance.

"I must help mother," Lucy said. "I'll see you when you come back."

"Yes." He gazed after her longingly as she swept out through the door.

"Come along, young feller." Mr Leach clapped him on his back. "Like to get there before dark."

They were received like visiting Royalty when they arrived at Roxborough Hall. Slaves in their liveries fussed around them, supervised by Dale and Sabina. Mr Leach was nonplussed by the reception. He gaped at Sabina who greeted him as if she was mistress of the house.

"I must send for Master Carl," Sabina said after Mr Leach was seated and had taken a glass of sangaree from Dale.

"In a while." Mr Leach moved his chair closer to Sabina's side. "I never expected to meet such a charming and beautiful hostess on a slave plantation."

Casey stood behind his chair, uncertain what to do.

"Forgive me asking," said Mr Leach, edging his knee closer to Sabina's so it brushed against her. "Are these dusky courtiers all slaves?"

"Oh yes." Sabina smiled politely and patted her bosom. She was dressed with the elegance of a lady hosting a salon. Her hair was drawn back accentuating the dark rose complexion of her flawless skin and the depth of her somber eyes. "I'm a slave, too," she said.

Mr Leach shifted his knee away. He coughed and glanced around for Casey.

"I'll look for Mr Carl, sir," Casey said, pretending he hadn't noticed. "Sabina can tell you a lot about slavery." He was glad to leave the magistrate and ran down the steps. Dale was waiting for him.

"Boy, you're the smartest slave in Dominica!" Casey punched Dale playfully and admired the scarlet broadcloth of his full-skirted coat.

"Maybe." Dale sounded gloomy.

"What's wrong?" Casey had known Dale since the slave

was a boy and they played together by the Layou River. Dale was four years older than he but he was too young to be burdened with problems. Casey linked his arm in his and accompanied him around the back of the house. "Don't see much of you now, Dale," he said.

Dale shook his head. "Things goin' bad, Casey. When Mas Carl done come, I was pleased. I got myself made the butler without any problem. Then I fix for Sabina drain him good so we does have him under our control."

"Sabina!" Casey rolled his eyes. "She's surely got Mas Carl in her clutches."

"Too much, Casey. That bitch got a spell on him now."

"Obeah?"

"She's a priestess, Casey. She encouraging him in his wickedness. She even does eat at his table!"

Casey frowned. By the unwritten code of slaves, a wench could share her master's bed, but to eat with him was blurring the dividing line between slave and master. It boded disruption in the traditional scheme of things.

"Sabina does be telling Mas Carl all about slaves and plantation life. Secrets. He wants to make us all into fancies, and sell us! Her idea. She wants the money, trinkets, everything she can get from him. She has him bewitched."

"He does seem to have changed since he arrived in Roseau. He was a nervous little man then."

"Something happens to white men in Dominica, Cas." Dale nodded his head sadly. "They starts good but then they gets wild." He shrugged. "De heat, de rum, de wenching? I don't know what it is but dey does come like animals."

"Carl doesn't live like an animal." Casey gestured at the slaves in their uniforms waiting by the kitchen. "He lives better than an English milord."

Dale sniffed. "You'll see." He left Casey and walked up the back steps leading a procession of servants bearing tea things for Mr Leach.

Casey was thoughtful as he strolled through a grove of coconut trees to the paddock, or Pen, where the children lived. He was listening for their shouts but reached the fence before he realized that the only sound was that of blackbirds quarrelling in the lamboyant trees.

He stared across the paddock and saw the children huddled together in the center. They were all stark naked. Carl and Laidlaw sat on chairs in front of them. Casey hesitated but Laidlaw saw him before he could dodge behind a bush.

"Get away from here, boy!" the overseer shouted. "You're trespassing."

"Casey!" said Carl in surprise when he looked to see what Laidlaw was shouting about.

Laidlaw spat. "Idle bugger! Pesters his mother's whores at night and sleeps on the river bank all day. Looking for some of your fillies to mount, I shouldn't wonder."

"Wrong again, Laidlaw. Casey ain't like that. Come, boy, you can learn how I examine my stock."

"Don't let him in here. He's a yeller snake. Watch his eyes. Shifty as a squit."

Carl beckoned Casey and he was obliged to open the gate to join him. "Mr Leach is here," he said.

Carl reddened. He glanced at Casey in despair. "That's obviously what Laidlaw intends to do," he said.

"Mr Carl? What is the purpose of this?" Casey asked softly.

"Breeding, of course."

"Those whelps are too young for that!"

"Laidlaw, I know what I'm doing. Of course, they're too young now, but in a couple of years time --"

"They'll be free then!" Casey gripped the back of Carl's chair as he interrupted him. "It's the law! The magistrate --"

"Shut up, Casey! Let's see the girls."

Laidlaw hawked and a glob of phlegm splattered close to Carl's feet. "No girls here, only a couple of fillies close to being on heat." He raised his short-handled whip and flicked the tongue in the direction of two young female slaves cowering at the edge of the semi-circle of naked children. The thong caught one of the girls on her breast. She flinched.

"Tsch!" said Carl. "Don't mark them."

Laidlaw shrugged and lashed out again. "You two!" The girls hurried forward, shoulders hunched to dodge the whip. They approached Carl, clutching themselves nervously. Carl slapped his knee.

"Come here, girls. Stand here in front of me."

The girls were trembling. Casey's fury threatened to erupt. He knew these two like they were his sisters. Their tiny breasts were heaving with fright and they stood together with their hands touching each other for comfort.

"Come here!" Carl shouted to one of them. She stepped forward and Carl clapped his hand around her thigh. "See," he said to Casey. "Isn't she beautifully proportioned?"

"It's the hips you want to check. See if they're broad enough to bear a whelp."

"Your advice isn't needed, Laidlaw." Carl scowled, and rubbed his hand roughly up the girl's thigh. Her eyes watered.

"Finger the conny!" said Laidlaw. "You ain't making love!"

Casey glared in disgust at the overseer but his attention was distracted by Carl who, with a gurgle of delight, thrust his hand between the girl's legs. To his shame, he felt a familiar stiffening in his own loins. He sheltered his crotch with his hand.

The girl's lips sprang open with a dry soundless scream as Carl poked his fingers into her. Tears streamed down her face and she bucked her body violently against the fist lodged between her thighs. Carl looked at Laidlaw with a self-satisfied smirk.

The girl fell in a faint. Casey leaped forward and caught her. He cradled her in his arms while Carl shrugged and sniffed his fingers. Laidlaw reached out suddenly and grabbed Casey's crotch.

"What did I tell you! A prick as hard as a branding iron."

Casey was supporting the girl and she hung limply in his arms. Laidlaw twisted his penis viciously and thrust his face close to his and leered.

"A filly ain't safe with this snake around!" He pulled the girl out of Casey's grasp. "I should geld you!"

The hiss of a whip slicing through the air made Casey duck. The lash passed over his head and caught Laidlaw across his cheek, raising a bright red whelk on his sallow skin. His hat flew off revealing his sparse hair stuck in ugly strands across his scalp. He swung the girl around as a shield.

Casey remained crouched on the ground. Carl was holding the whip and raised his arm for another blow. The tongue sailed toward Laidlaw but landed on the girl, slicing deeply into her breast. She was stung into consciousness and shrieked. Carl drew back his hand to strike again.

"Let the girl go, Laidlaw," he shouted.

"Not while you're bloody lashing me. Have you gone mad?"

"I think you have." Carl aimed again and scored another stripe across Laidlaw's cheek.

Laidlaw threw the girl to the ground and pulled out his pistol. Casey leaped at him. The two crashed to the ground and Carl's whip lashed out again. It caught Casey on his backside. He reared off angrily and jumped away from Laidlaw. The whip sliced across Laidlaw's fist and the overseer dropped his pistol. He rubbed his hand.

"I'm quite enjoying this," said Carl gleefully. "Get the pistol, Casey!"

"Do it yourself!" Casey ran off quickly toward the paddock gate. "I'm going for the magistrate."

"Yeller bastard!" Laidlaw rolled across the ground and recovered his pistol. He pointed it at Carl. "It's time I took what you owe me and got on my way." The girl was sitting up and weeping into her hands. Laidlaw walked over to her, keeping his pistol pointed at Carl. He kicked the child in her crotch. "Get up, wench," he said. Casey stopped at the fence and watched.

"I'll take this nigger with me." He gripped the girl's shoulder and hauled her to her feet. "You," he said to the other girl. "Pick up my hat and come here."

"Those slaves are worth a hundred sterling each," Carl said, flapping the whip but keeping a wary eye on Laidlaw's pistol.

"Aye, but you owe me a bonus." Laidlaw took his hat, shook the dust off it, and put it on his head. It seemed to restore his authority. The two girls stood nervously by his side.

"Walk," he said, slapping them across their buttocks. They shuffled in front of him toward the gate.

Carl ran across the paddock banging the stock of the whip against his thigh in frustration. "You're fired, you're fired," he said, almost screaming. "I don't need you! I don't need you or any one! I'm the Bondmaster!"

16

Carl was trembling when he reached the courtyard of the house. He had never been so angry. He slashed at the air in front of him with his whip, replaying in his mind his encounter with Laidlaw.

"What are you doing with that whip?"

He stopped in mid–stroke and looked up in astonishment. A white man stood at the top of his steps. Casey was behind him, whispering in his ear.

"Who the devil are you?"

"I'm the stipendary magistrate. I'm responsible for the welfare of all the slaves in this district."

Carl cracked his whip in the air so that the tongue snapped against the step below the magistrate's feet. Mr Leach stepped back on the balcony. The color drained from his face. Carl chuckled.

"Did any of my slaves complain to you, Mr Magistrate?" He ran up the steps two at a time and took in the scene on the balcony. Casey was at the magistrate's side. Two chairs were positioned close together with tea things for two on a table between them. Sabina was sitting in one of the chairs but she rose as soon as he glanced at her. Dale hovered in the doorway.

"You!" He pointed the whip at Sabina. "Did you complain to the magistrate?"

Sabina shook her head without speaking.

"You?" He dug Dale in his ribs with the stock of the whip.

Dale looked grave. "Ah done serve de massa correck, Mas Carl."

He spun around and sneered at the magistrate. "I see you've been enjoying my hospitality. Tea for two with this wench. What about her welfare, Mr Magistrate? Perhaps you want to probe into slave welfare under her skirts?"

"Really! This is preposterous." Mr Leach looked in alarm at Casey, seeking an ally.

"Don't believe anything that yellow bastard tells you. He and his mother want my plantation for themselves. He'll tell you any lies he can to discredit me. Now get off my premises or I'll have to report you for molesting this wench here."

"I never...!" Mr Leach gaped at Carl, and clung to the balcony rail for support.

"Come, sir." Casey drew him away gently and led him down the steps.

"You haven't heard the last of this!" Mr Leach shouted when he was safely on his horse.

"Then neither have you!" Carl threw himself into a chair as Leach and Casey rode off. He began to tremble again but he gripped the whip handle to steady his nerves. He hadn't defied anyone in his life before, not even Cook. It was an exhilarating experience. Now people would learn that he really was the Master of Roxborough.

"Carl . . .?"

He looked up. Sabina was standing beside his chair. She held a glass which she pressed into his hand. He took it and drank greedily. The strength of the sangaree calmed him. He smiled.

"Carl?" She seemed gently amused.

He insisted that Sabina call him Carl. He was infatuated with her. She was his mistress, not a slave bed wench for a white visitor to fool around with.

"Dammit, Sabina!" He pulled her roughly to sit on his lap. "Did you show the magistrate favor?" He knew what she was like.

She kissed him and stroked his cheek. "I was friendly, *oui?* Like you told me to be with guests."

He frowned, feeling the effects of the sangaree on his nerves and the mellowing of his anger under her caress. "I don't know why it is." He shook his head, quite baffled. "I've never used a whip in my life. Now this afternoon, I've seen off the overseer, the magistrate and young Casey."

Sabina's smile was enigmatic. "You're a man, Carl, the master. That's your right." Her voice was soft and sensuous.

"It was so easy."

She said nothing. Her hand toyed with his hair.

"I only have to raise my voice, snap the whip, and people do what I tell them." He laughed. "You should have seen Laidlaw scuttle out of the paddock when I fired him." A thought struck him. "Oh dear! I'll have to get a new overseer now."

"Why, Carl?" Sabina slid off his lap into the chair beside him. She began to stroke his thigh. "You don't need one."

"Don't I?"

"You are so strong and powerful. The slaves respect you. You can do it yourself."

"I suppose they do." He liked the idea. "I'll lash them a little. That's all Laidlaw ever did."

"You have changed," she murmured, her eyes glinting. "I like you better this way."

"You do?" He was throbbing uncontrollably as her hand brushed against his crotch.

"You're much more of a man." She leaned over him and lowered her lips on his mouth. Before he closed his eyes, he caught a glimpse of the dour face of Dale as the slave turned away from the doorway in disgust.

Carl was gratified to discover that Sabina was right. He could handle the running of the plantation without an overseer. He wasn't so gullible he believed her flattery that his success was due to his new sense of mastery. There were other factors at work.

He realized that the slaves respected Sabina. He assumed that it was simply because of her relationship with him but whatever the reason, the negroes were in awe of her. Every day she visited the slave quarters, wearing the gown he bought for her on credit, and looking every inch a dusky lady. The slaves were more malleable after her visits and she became the liaison between him and the negroes. He did what she suggested and the slaves remained tractable.

He was helped too, by the tradition and routine of plantation life passed from one slave generation to another. The day began an hour before dawn with the blowing of a conch shell to summon the slaves to work. They toiled from dawn till dark with two short meal breaks. Each slave belonged to a gang led by a driver who was provided with a whip to use on the lazy. Usually, a crack in the air above a slave's head was enough to get him working faster.

Carl enjoyed the countryside because of its contrast to London, but the idea of closer involvement with it was anathema, especially in the fierce sun. Fortunately, the pattern of plantation life begun by Carlton Todd was not disrupted by the lack of constant supervision from an overseer.

The field gang knew what attention the sugar cane needed,

and the garden gang tended the provision grounds efficiently. The roads were maintained by a gang under a female driver called Tency. The paddock was run by an old wet nurse whose tasks were defined by the antics of her charges.

Carl decided that an occasional stroll around the plantation was sufficient to maintain order. He took Dale with him on his tours of inspection. He sensed that there was some animosity between Dale and Sabina and he attributed it to jealousy. He saw no harm in it and discussed plantation affairs with them both.

"Such docile beasts, these Bondmaster slaves," he told Dale one day when the two of them were walking through the cane pieces after visiting the field gang.

"Docile," said Dale glumly.

Carl turned on the huge negro sweating in his heavy servant's livery. "For God's sake, boy, can't you say something yourself? Haven't you got thoughts of your own?"

"Thoughts?" Dale's expression was inscrutable.

Carl sneered with exasperation and pushed his way through the cane. He hated this part of it: the flies, the heat, the mentality of the slaves. They could only blame themselves for their fate.

The path led to the main avenue. An oddly familiar sound made Carl halt with surprise. He stepped behind a bouganvillea bush and held up his finger to Dale to be quiet. He listened. The noise was like Cook snoring in the kitchen of the Stephens' home.

"Do you hear anything?"

"Nossa!" Dale answered boldly.

"Shut up, you fool!" He waved his fist in the slave's face. "Where is the road gang working?"

Dale pursed his lips nervously. "Working?" he muttered.

Carl grabbed his shoulder and pushed him out on to the road in front of him. "Aha!" he said and pointed triumphantly with his whip. Across the road, seven slaves lay sleeping in the shade, their cutlasses on the ground beside them. Tency, the overseer, was leading them in sleep, her huge breasts heaving as the sound of her snores reverberated along the avenue to the river.

Tency was a formidable female with heavy thighs, fleshy arms and a tongue which lashed her gang with far more effect than a whip. In her youth she was a striking beauty but years of slave labor had given her features a hard, masculine quality.

She was regarded as a challenge to the plantation bucks. The boy who could boast of having bested Tency was treated with respect by the others. As Carl gazed on her with disgust, he saw a way to consolidate his own authority over the slaves.

Tency's gray osnaburg shift clung to her perspiring body. It was rucked up to her waist, exposing her massive thighs and a wad of hair. Her gang dreamed beside her.

Carl motioned Dale to keep quiet and sauntered across the avenue. He knelt beside Tency, his nose wrinkling at the goatish smell of her body, and picked her whip up from the ground beside her. He snarled and braced himself. With all the strength he could muster, he scythed the whip down onto her crotch.

Tency yelped.

He slashed again quickly and cut a stripe of blood into her thighs. Tency rolled on her side and struggled to stand. He flayed the whip at her enormous buttocks but he was no match for her now. She reached out and caught the tongue of the whip in her hand, snatching the handle from his grasp. He stepped back behind Dale.

"Why yo' lash yuh Tency?" she demanded, standing up. "Yo' done scratch me laps." She lifted her shift and stared at the blood oozing on her skin.

"You were sleeping!" Carl gripped Dale's arm and wondered what he'd done wrong.

"It does be mah mornin' break. I'se a right to sleep." Tency hitched up her bosom with a snort of outrage.

"Ten minutes break only, isn't it?" Carl turned to Dale.

"Ten minutes?" Dale looked perplexed.

"You had more than ten minutes!" Carl shook his fist at Tency.

"No, sah. Yo' done wake me wid de ticklin'." Two boys in the gang giggled.

Carl scowled. "How many in your road gang?" he asked, searching for a way to extricate himself without humiliation.

"How many?" Tency shook her head to show she regarded the question as ridiculous. "Sometimes six, sometimes eight, sometimes ten. It does depend."

His heart sank and he glanced longingly up the avenue to the house. Suddenly, he saw a boy bob his head down behind a bush. "Hey you," he called, stepping away from Dale. "Come here."

The boy stood up sheepishly and walked toward him. Tency wiped her thighs with her shift and started to grumble about how she was entitled to sleep. Carl sensed a weakness.

"Do you work in this gang?" he asked the boy.

"Yassa." The slave trembled with fright and a stream of urine trickled down his leg.

"Where have you been?" He knelt down so he could see into the boy's eyes. "Tell me the truth or I'll larrup you from here to Layou."

"Watchin' de cou, sah."

"What's the cou, Dale?"

"De cou? He does mean de house, sir."

"Why were you watching the house, boy?"

"For yo', sah."

Carl tapped the boy on his chest. "Why?"

"Tency done tell me to wake her when I see yo' come, sah. Yo' come de wrong way."

Carl frowned and stood up. "Tency, did you send the boy to watch for me?"

Tency scratched her cheek with her whip. The rest of the gang stopped giggling and watched with interest. Carl stepped forward.

"Take off your frock," he said.

"What?" Tency stared at him.

"Remove your frock and come here." He pointed to a spot in front of him.

"Yo' does be feelin' randy, sah?" She eased her shift over her huge bosom and let it fall to the ground. She put her hands on her hips and rolled her thighs mockingly.

Carl turned to one of the gang. "Give me your cutlass."

"What yo' gonna do, buckra?" Tency's brow oozed sweat and it mingled with the dirt and dust on her face. She took a step closer to Carl. He grimaced at the stench and the repulsive sight of her naked body. Her breasts were enormous, her nipples like crab apples.

"You must remember, Tency, that I am your Bondmaster." Carl plucked her right nipple with his left hand, tugging it and twisting. Tency grinned.

"You are to respect me at all times. You are not to sleep when you should be working. Do you understand?"

"Oh yas, sah!" Her bulbous face was bright and her eyes shone under the pressure of his fingers.

"Good!" He moved swiftly. Pulling her nipple out like it was rubber, he sliced the cutlass down into the stretched flesh. She fell back with a screech, blood spouting from her breast. He held her nipple in his hand.

"Here," he said, tossing the piece of flesh to Dale. "That tit says we'll have no more trouble from Tency."

Carl turned and strode rapidly up the avenue. Only when he reached the security of the balcony did he feel safe enough to look back. He was dismayed to see a carriage entering the avenue at the bottom of the hill. He shouted for Sabina. "Get me water, I want to wash."

"Yes, Carl." She hurried out, clapping her hands for a slave. "What is it?"

"If that's the magistrate again, I'll horsewhip him for trespassing. Go inside!"

"It's a grand coach, Carl."

The carriage pulled to a halt on its way up the hill. He guessed the occupants had discovered Tency. "Hell!" A boy brought him a basin of water and he dipped his hands in it, rubbing them furiously.

"You've cut yourself." Sabina's eyes sparkled when she saw the blood.

"Not me." He shuddered as the impact of what he'd done affected him. He held his hands out for a towel. The boy froze because he had forgotten to bring one.

"Damn nigger!" He wiped his hands on the boy's hair and cuffed him angrily.

The coach resumed its progress up the avenue. Carl was relieved to see that Tency was not on the coach box. "Who's visiting us now," he said. "Interfering busybodies!"

Dale came on to the balcony and whispered to Sabina. Carl swung around and glared at them both. "What the devil are you saying behind my back?"

Sabina smiled demurely and laid her hand on his arm. "Don't get vexed, Carl. Dale told me what you did to Tency. I think you're wonderful."

"What?"

"She's an evil bitch. She thinks she's the queen of the slave quarters. Such a bad influence. You were right to punish her."

"I was?"

"I'm proud of you, Carl." Sabina slipped her hands around him and stood on her toes to kiss him.

There was a rattle of wheels on the cobblestones as the coach drew up below the steps. Carl straightened his stock and Sabina released him. In the courtyard, Caliste and the footmen were helping the occupants alight from the coach.

A slave holding a baby emerged first, followed by a young lady of quality, if the elegance of her clothes and the charm of her manner were truthful indicators. Caliste and the footmen were in raptures, bowing and beaming with genuine solicitude.

"She's come back!" exclaimed Dale happily. He ignored Carl and cantered down the steps.

Carl gazed at the white lady and felt a strength pulsing through his loins. She was the most beautiful woman he had ever seen; exquisite, graceful, charming.

Sabina tried to slip her hand into his. He slapped her away viciously. "Get out of my sight, you black whore!" he said. "Don't show yourself while this lady is here."

17

"I'm Davril Gordon," said the lady, settling herself in the chair where only minutes before Sabina had been sitting. She smiled, not the cool smile of politeness but an expression of real pleasure. Carl gaped.

"I'm delighted to meet you," she said warmly and he knew it was true.

He was overwhelmed by her. Her eyes, the fine blue of a pure English maiden, intrigued him with their provocative allure. She exuded a sensuality more refined than that of Sabina, and more exciting.

He was unable to speak. Davril possessed an aura which smote him into inferiority. The stirring within him shrivelled and he knew that it would never be possible for him to screw such a lady. He blushed at his thoughts, dismayed that he was regarding a white woman in the manner he judged a slave wench.

"Ever since you arrived at Roxborough, I've longed to meet you, Mr Todd."

The emphasis Davril gave his name forced him to consider what she was saying, instead of wondering what delights were concealed by the generous folds of her traveling gown.

"Please call me Carl," he said, simpering.

"Carl! Such an evocative name." She appeared to be gazing right through him. He fidgetted.

"I see you inherited the Bondmaster's lust for punishment," she said. "Even if you don't look like Carlton."

"I take after my mother," he answered hastily. "What do you mean?"

"Tency. She's bleeding quite badly."

He swallowed anxiously. "Did you know my . . . er . . . father well?"

Davril arranged her dress. "I was to have married his grandson." The brightness in her eyes died and she bit her lip. "Mingoson killed them both here on this balcony."

"I'm sorry," he said, feeling the sadness of the tragedy for the first time.

Davril bowed her head as though to ward off a blow. "Brett left me a legacy, my baby son."

Carl became aware of the others on the balcony. Davril's maid was sitting in the shade by the door cradling a baby in her arms. Mercifully, it was quiet. Dale, the footmen and even some of the room maids were clustered at the end of the balcony eagerly listening to every word.

Carl snapped his fingers, glaring angrily at Dale and gesturing to him to get the slaves out of earshot.

Davril looked at her maid. "Take Tavron inside, dear. Put him to sleep somewhere cool." She glanced at Carl. "Oh do forgive me. I quite forgot my manners. I'm so used to coming here."

He waved his hand. "Yes, please, feel quite at home."

Davril smiled and he was momentarily struck by a feeling of uneasiness. "I wanted to visit you before," she said. "But I had to wait until the baby was old enough to leave home."

"Yes." He wondered how such a sensible young lady had got involved with a half breed.

Davril could have read his thoughts. She leaned forward. "My father wanted Brett as his son-in-law. He believed he was a future leader of his people. The Bondmaster was a difficult man but he loved Brett. We rather expected Roxborough to come to Brett's son, my baby."

Again the feeling of disquiet hit Carl. He gripped the arms of his chair and sat up. Davril's face was a vision of innocence. "I'm sorry," he said, wanting to explain, wanting to put her at ease. "I was in England, I didn't know . . ."

"I'm quite aware of the story, Carl."

The firmness of her interruption shook him. He was the one who was ill at ease. Davril's eyes had hardened. There was a clatter in the courtyard and Carl rose with relief from his chair and glanced down. The footmen were unloading boxes from Davril's carriage. They were carrying them around to the back of the house and up the stairs.

"Hey!" he shouted. "What are you doing?"

"Some things I've brought with me, Carl." Davril tilted her head to one side and flickered her eyelashes. "For the baby."

"Oh." He sat down and frowned. "Are you staying?" he asked after a pause.

"I rather thought I would."

"Without a chaperone?"

She tittered. "Oh, Carl! We're not in England. This is Dominica. We don't have silly ideas about propriety here."

He was out of his depth. The only thing that was reality to him was the erection straining against the broadcloth of his pants. He crossed his legs, praying she wouldn't see the effect her unspoken suggestion had on him.

"You're all alone in the house, Carl. There's lots of room for me and Tavron. I want Brett's baby to live at Roxborough."

"Live here?" His erection wavered.

"With us."

"With us?" He covered his crotch and moaned.

"Why not, Carl?" She looked hurt. "You're not married, are you?"

"No, but --"

"Then we shall be married."

He wondered if he was dreaming. From the house came sounds of Davril's boxes being deposited in one of the bedrooms and the excited chatter of the slaves. Dale's deep tones drifted through as he supervised them. There was the shushing of a woman's voice and the gurgling cry of the baby. Carl, soft again, uncrossed his legs and slumped back in the chair.

"I don't understand," he said weakly.

"I thought I'd made it perfectly clear." Davril's expression hardened. "We're going to be married."

He gulped. "Why?"

"To make sure my son inherits Roxborough, of course."

Now he saw it all! He jumped up. "Roxborough is mine, do you hear, and everything and everyone here is mine." He was frightened.

"Dale!" he shouted, dashing to the drawing room door. "Get those boxes out of the house!" He turned back to Davril, and was struck by how poised she looked. She hadn't moved.

"Kindly leave my house now, too. And take your black bastard with you!"

He stared unbelieving as she fanned herself and made no attempt to move.

"Daddy said you might be angry," she said, smiling coyly. "He didn't want me to come but it is the only way. Like this, Tavron can have a father. He can be brought up on the plantation and I can safeguard his inheritance." She paused. "He's not black at all. You only have to look at him to see that."

Carl thrashed the air with his hand. "You've got to go. Now!"

"Oh no, Carlington Brady, I'm not going anywhere."

"What?"

There was silence. The whole house stopped to listen. The birds seemed to be holding their breath. There were no cries from the children playing in the paddock. The only sign of movement was the sail of a schooner gliding noiselessly out of the river heading for the open sea. Carl wished he was on it.

Showing more presence of mind than he thought he had, he offered Davril his arm. "Shall we take a walk?" He nodded his head to indicate the slaves lurking inside the house. "Around the courtyard?"

"Is this a ploy?" Her eyes watched him mockingly but she rose to her feet and laid her hand on his own. He escorted her down the steps in silence as his mind raced with the implications of what she might know.

"Such a lovely afternoon," she said, as they walked to the edge of the cobblestones, out of earshot of the watching slaves. Carl sighed.

"Why did you call me Carlington Brady?"

"There's no need to be coy and think you can wriggle away." She fluttered her eyelashes. "Daddy happens to be very friendly with James Stephens, your former employer. He wrote to him and we've discovered the most extraordinary information about you."

He shook his head sadly. "I knew it wouldn't last."

"Mr Stephens was very puzzled that you claimed to be the Bondmaster's heir. He said it's impossible. Your father was Octavius Brady, his groom. He died insane. Your mother was a chambermaid. She never knew Carlton Todd. The letter you presented was a forgery."

"You know everything." Now he was discovered, he felt a sense of relief. He gestured helplessly. "What are you going to do?"

"Marry you, of course."

He accepted that according to the wheels of fate, it was his turn to be tricked and mocked. It was fitting that his retribution should be at the hands of the most desirable woman he had ever met.

"I'll go away. You can have Roxborough."

"Oh no!" Davril gripped his hand. "Where's the ruthless slave master who slices his niggers when they are lazy?" Her voice hardened. "Yes, I'll have Roxborough for my son. You'll be his father and the plantation overseer. It will be quite convenient."

He gazed at her and was dismayed to see she was serious. "You mean it?"

"Of course. Your secret will be safe with me. Daddy has agreed and so has James Stephens. He's quite pleased to be rid of you."

"I was a good butler."

"Always day dreaming, according to Mr Stephens. Lived in a world of your own, he says."

They completed one round of the courtyard and began another. The birds, Carl noticed, were singing again. "There's no money," he said. "Only the slaves."

"The Bondmaster left something for Brett, I know." Davril's lips which Carl thought were sensuous when he first saw her, hardened into a grim line of determination.

"You'll be marrying me for nothing." He squeezed her hand suggestively, feeling absolved.

"I'm marrying you for the Todd name!" She pulled her hand away angrily.

"We will have separate quarters!" Her eyes flashed. "You will never touch me, never!"

Casey said goodnight to Lucy and her mother. Mrs Leach held her sampler in her hand like a shield as she sat beside Lucy in the reception hall of her home. Lucy smiled fleetingly before he shut the door and stood, dejected, on the front porch. For eight weeks as Mr Leach's assistant, every time Casey made an attempt to be alone with Lucy, he was foiled by her mother.

He walked morosely down the street, grateful for the darkness which hid his misery from the prying of the village scandalmongers. Drunkards reeled in the road, staggering from one rum shop to another. Seamen bent on vengeance for the chastity they endured on board ship, lurched, arm in arm, to the casino and his mother's whores. He eyed them gloomily and slunk off the road to his lonely spot behind the kitchen.

He settled down on his haunches and gazed at the swelling sea where it rolled out of the starlit night and pounded the rocks. Spray spattered the black suit he wore daily in the humid heat while escorting Lucy's father around the parish. For all the opportunity his job gave him to be with Lucy, he would have been better off lounging naked on the banks of the Layou River where he first met her.

He groaned, gathered up some pebbles and flung them into the sea. The waves lapped up and drenched him. He didn't care. All he wanted to do was to hold Lucy, to lie with her and to share love.

"Yo' does be off yuh feed again, boy."

He wriggled his shoulders under his wet coat, and pretended not to hear. To his surprise, Uraline didn't pursue the point. She sensed his mood and hunkered down beside him.

"De sea does wash 'way many cares, Cas." Uraline tossed back her head and let the spray shower her cheeks.

"You're mad, Uraline." He gazed at her in surprise. "You're hot from the fire. You'll catch dengue."

"Won't," she said defiantly. "Fire burn out." Another wave crashed below them, the explosion of spray almost knocking them from their perch. "'Sides, don't matter 'bout Uraline."

"Say, girl!" Casey grinned and stood up, pulling Uraline up with him. "I'm the one who's pining, not you."

He put his arm around her stout frame and hugged her warmly.

"Drat yo', Cas! Yo' done wet me."

He was relieved to hear her scald him.

"I bake one nice piece of ham fuh yo', Cas, an' yo' done spurn it. Yo' got to mount dat beckey wench soon or yo' an' me gonna be real vex."

He shook his head and led her back to the kitchen. The fire was out, as she had said, and the only light was the glow of the lantern from the still room. He sat on a bench and Uraline settled beside him. Her fingers crept to his crotch.

"No, Uraline," he said kindly. "Not tonight."

"Yo' does need drainin', Cas."

"I know what I need."

"Den take it!"

"It's her parents."

Uraline's breasts shook with indignation. "Dey objects to yo'?"

"Not for the reasons you think. Lucy is precious to them. She's being saved so she can get a good husband. It's the English way."

"Ain't yo' a good husband?"

"Me!" He chuckled. "I couldn't hope to marry her. I'm poor. I've got no prospects."

"Dat's all yo' know." Uraline shut her mouth as though she had said too much. He was used to her ways and took no notice.

"I can't marry her, Uraline. I don't know if she'd want me."

"Why bother wid marriage, Cas. Jump her on de beach."

"We're not two breeding niggers rutting in the sand

because we're in heat. I have to be able to give Lucy something more than that. If I had a house, or a fortune --"

Uraline was tracing tiny patterns with her fingers on his thighs. He brushed her away. "I told you no."

"Would yo' do it fuh a fortune?"

"What do you mean?" He was tired, it was cozy in the kitchen and the proximity of Uraline's body was having an effect on him in spite of his determination. He crossed his legs. "No, gal!"

She moved away, her disappointment obvious from the slope of her shoulder. There was silence, then she spoke. "Years ago, when I was a chit with a conny so hot, only buck's water could out de fire, I saw de Bon'massa give Ma Gregg a letter."

"What are you talking about?" Casey uncrossed his legs and stretched lazily.

"He done tell Ma Gregg to give de letter to his heir."

Casey felt something being thrust into his hand. "I don't want any of your obeah charms, Uraline," he said, leaping to his feet, his tiredness vanishing. "Why can't you --"

"Don't worry 'bout me, Cas. My days fuh young bucks like yo' does be done. I got my man Tony and no obeah charm gonna make yo' do it to me 'less yo' want."

In the darkness of the kitchen, he couldn't see what Uraline was pressing into his hand. He stepped back uncertainly. "What is it?"

"De Bon'massa's letter, Cas. It's yours. Yo' does be his heir. Take it."

18

Casey opened the Bondmaster's letter that night. By the light of the flickering candle, he studied the shaky script scrawled across the old vellum. There were few words and when he deciphered them, he folded the letter thoughtfully and placed it under his mat. It was a long time before he fell asleep.

In his tours of the plantations with Lucy's father, he met many slaves. Their meek attitude dismayed him. The white man's control over them was fragile so, if they wanted, the slaves had the power to destroy the system that shackled them. At Roxborough, the deception was sustained by the conventional outlook of the slaves, who had been purpose-bred by the Bondmaster for docility. They hated change or an upset in their routine that would plunge them into the unknown.

Casey had discovered that they feared emancipation. How would they survive without their master? they asked whenever he explained the benefits of liberty to them. The Bondmaster's letter gave him the answer. He carried it with him, thinking about it, for days before he went to the slave quarters to meet them.

Dale was there, his countenance heavy with gloom. Tency, with her chest bound in a dirty cloth, squatted with her gang outside the huts. It was a clear night after a day of rain. The quarter moon caught in its shadowy light the rain drops rolling down the wide leaves of the banana trees. The pepper bushes, herbs and flowers which grew in profusion around the huts swayed in the night breeze.

First, Casey decided to test the slaves, to see if they had the spirit to defy Carl. He urged them to stop working. "There's nothing the white man can do," he said. "Freedom is coming by law."

"No, Casey." Dale was solemn. "Yo' ain' never been a slave. We know dat if we do what de beckey say, we have no trouble."

"It seems that you like being slaves!"

"It's our life." Tency shrugged. "Ain' no like about it."

"But look what he did to you! That's a crime."

Tency grinned ruefully. "Mah fault fuh gettin' caught."

Casey was exasperated by their refusal to help themselves. He scowled.

"Don' be vexed wid us, Cas," said Tency. "Roxbruh gonna be diff'rent nuh Miz Davril here." There was a stir of interest at her remark.

"How?" one of the slaves asked eagerly.

Tency cackled. "'Cause Miz Davril gonna drain de passion from Mas Carl," she said.

"Sabina did that."

"No, Cas. Sabina got Mas Carl's blood so hot he done things in a fury. To please her."

"De problem is," said Dale glumly, "dat Miz Davril won't allow Mas Carl to cover her. Her maid sleeps in her room and she makes me sleep outside her door to keep Mas Carl out."

"What about Sabina?"

Tency threw up her hands with a shriek of delight. "Dat bitch lost her pretty frocks, fuh sure!"

"Mas Carl tell her keep out of sight and Miz Davril tell her stay 'way too."

"So Davril does be de massa, nuh!" Tency scratched her crotch and chuckled. "Fancy shutting Mas Carl from her chamber . . ."

"Sabina de problem. She vexed like hells," Dale said. "She gonna use obeah!"

There was a hush among the slaves. The breeze rustled the leaves and shook rain on them. No one moved. Obeah was something they all feared. Even Casey shuddered in the sudden chill.

"What kind of obeah?" he asked.

There was silence. He watched the impassive faces of Dale and Tency. He was one of them, but he was not. They thought of him as being on the white side of the line that separated slaves from masters.

Perhaps he was foolish to think that he could help them with the Bondmaster's legacy. He knew where the gold was buried and it belonged to them, he believed. But they were an abject lot, spineless and superstitious. They deserved, and even craved, their miserable existence.

He got to his feet. "I don't believe in obeah," he said loudly. "You've got the power to do what you want yourselves. You don't need mumbo-jumbo for that."

"Hush, Casey!" said Tency. "De night spirits..."

"I'm not afraid of spirits!"

"Not spirits alone does be in de dark," said Dale, standing up beside him. "Sabina done send for Mingoson."

The slaves sighed and shifted closer together.

"Mingoson? I'd like to meet him," Casey said brashly. "At least he ain't soft and weak like --"

"Don't say dat, Cas!" Dale put his hand on his shoulder. "I know Mingoson. He's evil. He's eaten the liver of men. He has the strength and power of the devil."

"He's a man, isn't he? I'm not afraid of him."

"Oh, Casey!" Tency looked frightened as he moved away. "Take care!"

"Don't worry about me." He raised his eyes to the sliver of moon. "I'll walk home by the river. That's my protector."

"Safe walk!"

He left them hurriedly and the flowing of the river drowned their nervous voices. It was true that the river was his friend. After Uraline had given him Carlton's letter, he had spent hours walking along its banks or sitting in its glades considering the contents. He longed to discuss the letter with Lucy but when she joined him beside the rushing waters, he was tongue-tied.

Instead, impetuously, he kissed her, his lips brushing only lightly against hers for the first time. She jumped away and ran off leaving him watching the river alone and wondering why. When she came to the glade the next day, his nervousness kept him from sitting close, let alone touching her. She laughed and kissed him on the cheek before she left him again.

In spite of his experience with whores and negro wenches, he was totally confused by Lucy. She filled his thoughts as he walked toward Layou.

In the moonlight, the river sparkled like crystals over the rocks. He threaded his way slowly through the bamboo into the glade where he first met Lucy. He hunkered down at the river's edge and water lapped the dark sand, swirling around his feet. He wore old breeches and a cotton shirt. He removed them and flung them on the ground and stood, naked, at the water's edge.

"Lucy!" he called longingly. "Lucy!" He plunged into the river and propelled himself effortlessly under water.

He was at home in the shadows of the night, revelling in the river's flowing darkness. He swam with strong, steady strokes against the current until he was exhausted. Then he turned on his back and floated gently downstream to his hidden glade. He pulled himself out of the river and sank, his energy and anguish spent, face down on the sand.

"You're hung better than Brett, boy," a voice drawled.

He tensed as a foot pressed into the small of his back, pinioning him to the sand. He twisted and tried to peer into the darkness. A fist punched him between his shoulder blades and knocked the breath from his tired lungs.

"No tricks, now, pretty boy."

"Who are you?" he gasped.

A black shape loomed above him. A stench of decay drove out the scent of night. He gritted his teeth, reassured by the foul smell; it was unmistakeably negro.

"What do you want?" he said, feeling bolder.

"What do you have to give?"

The voice was laden with menace, drawn out and uttered with affected slowness. The ball of the man's foot ground into his back, sending spasms of pain shooting along his spine. He cried out.

"Did that hurt?" said the stranger. "Perhaps I should cool you down?"

A jet of hot water stung his neck and tore over his shoulders and down his back, trickling into the crevice of his buttocks. The odor made him retch. He gulped at the glimpse he had of the man in the moonlight urinating on him. The stream of foul water burned into him with the shocking pain of a slave brand. He felt sullied and wretched.

He squirmed to escape but the man fell on his back and pressed his knees into his shoulders.

"Such a little snake. Do you have poison in your fangs?"

"I'll kill you!" Casey trembled with rage at his impotence. The man's strength was twice his and he was unable to move under the weight of his body.

"Do you think you really will?"

The negro's mocking tone and educated accent puzzled Casey. He lay still, gathering his wits and wondering what he could do to escape.

The pressure on his shoulder eased and he felt his left arm being gripped and wrenched backward. He whimpered at the pain as the man rolled him over on to his side. The man swung himself over his body and lay on the sand beside him. He pushed his face close to Casey's.

"Do you see me now, pretty boy?"

"Yes," he said, relaxing as he realized that he could raise his knee and pound it into the negro's crotch and break loose. The knowledge gave him courage and he scrutinized the black face curiously.

The negro's hair was long and unkempt, the fine whorls extended into locks like rats tails, matted and caked with dried dung. His face was slender, his nose long and his eyes were sensitive, like a white man's. He was naked and Casey saw the outline of his broad shoulders and massive chest tapering to a narrow waist. He had the thick arms and thighs of a fighter and a grip like a manacle.

Casey shuddered and said in awe, "Mingoson?"

The negro nodded.

"Let me go!" He struggled more as a token than to be effective. Mingoson's arm was heavy and clamped him to the ground.

"You called me tonight." Mingoson's voice mocking.

"You were there?" He tried to hide his nervousness by questions. "What were you doing in the quarters, seeing Sabina?"

Mingoson twisted his arm and his eyes watered with the pain. "That hurts!"

"You sound like Carlton." Mingoson's voice was a whisper, his mouth only inches from Casey's ear. "Too many questions." Mingoson's chest brushed against his and the vibrations of his heart matched his own.

"I was curious," he said without thinking. "You killed my brother."

"I'm going to kill you, too."

A knot of fear tightened in his stomach as he knew it could happen very easily. Mingoson was in complete control but he was sniffing the air, and his heart beat faster. He seemed doubtful about something.

"Go on!" said Casey, calling his bluff. "Kill me if you want."

Mingoson lifted his head and listened suspiciously. The river swirled past their feet and high in the valley giant crapaud frogs croaked mournfully. "You're a smart buckra. Is this a trap!"

"No."

Mingoson sniffed again then nodded his head, apparently satisfied. "You've got Carlton's blood in you, Casey, so I don't trust you." Mingoson pulled him closer so that his nose was rammed under his armpit. He twisted away and Mingoson chopped him across his ear.

"Don't fidget, boy. You'll get me vexed."

"Since you're going to kill me, it doesn't matter what I do." He shrank from the fetid odor of Mingoson's body but with his nose and mouth forced against it, he couldn't avoid the stench.

"Hah!" Mingoson cuffed him on his chest. "I like you, boy!" He gripped his chin in his long fingers and peered at him closely. "You've got the Bondmaster fury in your eyes. That white bugger at the cou hasn't."

"Carl?"

"He's no more the Bondmaster's son than I am."

Mingoson's hand was creeping down his chest to his penis. Casey tried to back away but Mingoson's other hand locked him in his grasp. Mingoson gripped his penis viciously in his palm and began to rub it.

"See the prick dancing!" said Mingoson with a chuckle. "You have plenty of quem, boy!"

Casey twisted with shame as he felt himself stiffening in Mingoson's fingers. Suddenly he was flipped over so that he lay spread-eagled on his stomach with his head forced down into the sand. "What a sweet little rump," Mingoson said. A finger drove between his buttocks, piercing him with the agony of a knife thrust.

"Now I'm going to kill you!" Mingoson shouted and thrust himself down on to his helpless body.

"No!" Casey bucked backward quickly and bashed his buttocks into Mingoson's groin.

Mingoson laughed and clapped him roughly on his back, pounding him down into the sand again. He spread his legs apart with his knees and fell on him with a lazy sigh of triumph.

Casey twisted his mouth out of the sand in time to shout, "Gold!"

"What?" Mingoson thrust himself hungrily between his thighs.

"I know where Carlton's gold is hidden! I can help you."

"Huh?" Mingoson relaxed his grip and scratched in the matted locks of his hair. Casey scrambled out from under him but Mingoson held on to his leg.

"The two of us can get it," said Casey, sitting up.

Mingoson sniffed the air again. "Now?" he said suspiciously.

"Not now." Casey slammed his fist into Mingoson's jaw and yanked his leg out of his grasp. He rolled down the bank into the river.

He dove to the bed of the river without a sound. He emerged in the center with water churning around him and peered into the darkness trying to distinguish the outline of Mingoson under the mango trees.

"I'm behind you, Casey!"

A hand slipped around his waist and Mingoson's grim chuckle sounded in his ear. "Now what about that gold?" He ducked Casey's head under water and held it there until Casey thought his lungs would burst.

"Tomorrow night," spluttered Casey when Mingoson raised him up. He gasped for air. "Meet me by the mill at midnight."

"Ah yes." Mingoson held him firmly, water splashing around them. "I suppose you'll bring the militia too."

"No." Casey shook his head, feeling more confident. "I know you won't be there if I have anyone with me. I need you to help me. I want the gold too. We'll share it."

Mingoson's teeth glinted in the glare from the moon as the clouds cleared. He laughed evilly and Casey was flung backward into the depths of the river. When he surfaced, Mingoson had disappeared.

19

Casey lay on his mat on the floor of the darkened casino. He listened to the crashing of the waves and the cries of the morning street vendors. A mosquito droned around his ear.

He was naked and his body was drenched in sweat. He rolled lazily on his stomach, pressing himself into his mat. An image of Lucy flashed into his mind and he groaned. No!

He leaped up from the floor and flung open the shutters. The collision with the bright sunlight made him blink and he rubbed the tiredness from his eyes with the backs of his hands. He stretched, yawned, and focused on the sea below the window.

The fishermen in their canoes were rowing into shore with their catches; a small schooner darted from the river mouth and headed for the islands to the north. He watched it longingly, envying those aboard for their carefree life.

Lucy, he thought. She must never know what Mingoson did to him the night before. He imagined her safe in the haven of her parents' love, blessed with beauty and hope. He turned away from the window and rummaged in the corner for a piece of breeches. He pulled it on and slipped out of the casino.

Uraline beckoned him into the kitchen and handed him a dish. "Yo' still broody fuh dat white girl?"

He shook his head, then sipped the coffee. He grinned ruefully. "Something else on my mind now, Uraline. Trouble is, I don't know who can help me."

Uraline's eyes narrowed. "Yo' need special help?"

"How do you know?"

"It does be written all over yuh face!" She twitched her shoulders and her shift rippled over her body. She seemed piqued. "When yo' was a whelp, befuh yuh grain drop, yo' always tell me yuh troubles."

He sipped the scalding coffee and set the dish back on the table. "Who's the one for special help?"

Uraline drew herself up and her bosom shook. "Some of the slaves say I have special powers, *oui?*"

He put his arm around her and squeezed her waist affectionately. "You're too good for me. I need someone bad, really bad."

Uraline's black face grew somber. "Dere does be only one wench I know like dat."

"Tell me who!" He gestured with impatience.

"De one in de cou wid Mas Carl. Sabina."

"Sabina!" He was disgusted. "I can't go to her."

"Why not? She powerful wid obeah. De slaves say she curse better'n de devil."

He punched his fist into his palm. "Uraline, I can't. She's in league with Mingoson." He ignored her cold stare and began to edge out of the ajoupa. Perhaps he'd told her too much.

"Yo' ain't gonna work no good nor bad powers 'less yo' eat, Cas." She held out a plate of roast breadfruit and avocado mashed with farine. He took it reluctantly.

"I'm not hungry, Uraline."

"Sit down, Cas. Shut yuh mouth and eat!"

The remark made him laugh. It relaxed the tension in the ajoupa and he squatted in a corner with his plate and began to eat heartily. "I didn't know I was so hungry," he said.

"Prowlin' in de moonlight when yo' should be in some filly's arms gonna make yo' hungry, fuh sure."

He was curious. "Why did you say that?" He handed her the empty plate and rose to his feet. He filled a cup of water from a gourd and drank deeply. "Why?"

"Yo' was at Roxbruh last night?"

"Yes."

"An' yo' went for a river bath?"

He tensed. "How do you know?"

"I see yo' come back naked like a bozal from Afric' instead of a respec'able beckey."

"I'm not white; I'm not a beckey."

"Dat ain' give yo' no right to go ruttin' an' brawlin' like a plantation buck in heat."

"You saw, didn't you?"

"I don't know what I see, Cas. I regret I give yo' dat letter."

He put his arms around her shoulders. "You did what you had to do, Uraline. Now I must do my part too." He released her and flopped onto the bench. "God knows! I'd rather service my mam's whores and go fishing in the river all day. But it's what has to be done. Did you ever read the letter?"

"Law! Me read! Yo' does be crazy?"

"The Bondmaster's gold is in two wooden caskets buried in his father's grave."

Uraline sank to the bench beside him. Her face clouded with confusion. "Mas Carlton!" she whispered, letting the syllables slip from her lips like a prayer.

He slapped her on her thigh. "Do you want to come to the grave tonight and help me dig it up?"

Uraline seemed to shrink before his eyes. She drew away from him, the blood draining from her face. She gaped at him in terror.

"You can hold the lantern," he said, forcing himself to be jovial. The stark transformation in Uraline who was always so happy-go-lucky, unnerved him.

"Casey," she murmured. "Yo' ain't diggin' up no dead bones." Her voice quivered with fright.

"I've got to, Uraline." He stood up and paced the floor of the shack. "But I need someone to help me, someone evil."

"Why?"

"Because only an evil person is brave enough to molest the dead."

"Let de ol' man lie in peace."

"I need the gold. It's mine."

Uraline cradled her brow in her hand and rocked backward and forward in misery. "Don't be afraid," he told her. "I'll take someone wicked with me then no spirits will get me." He wished he was as confident as he sounded.

"Sabina?" She peered at him jealously.

"Mingoson."

"He'll kill yo'!" She yowled in the silence. "He'll take the gold."

"That's the risk. He's the only one who'll dig up the grave with me. The slaves haven't got the guts to help, and I need someone. It has to be him."

Uraline squared her shoulders and stood up. She straightened her shift, patted the braided whorls of her hair and glared around the kitchen. "I comin'!" she declared.

"No," he said laughing. "This is men's work."

"Den why a jackass like yo' doin' it!"

He glared at her. "I promised Mingoson, that's why."

To an observer hidden in the canefield, Roxborough Hall – with its shutters fastened back, lamps shining out into the night and people gliding about unhurriedly – was a picture of peace and domesticity.

Slaves moved graciously, performing their duties with the precision of a well-drilled team. A white man and a white woman, who an observer would assume to be master and mistress, sat correctly in chairs at either end of the balcony and allowed their servants to indulge them. Here was a picture of the confident authority of a planter and his wife enjoying a pampered life together.

The impression was a false one. Carl's rage had simmered for days. Tonight, he rose up from his chair and dismissed the servants angrily. He paced the gallery then advanced on Davril sitting demurely at the opposite corner. He was anxious that the slaves wouldn't hear so he leaned close to her ear and whispered crossly, "When will you come to your damn senses?"

"Get away!" Davril said, her eyes glinting, eager for argument. "You are my husband merely on sufferance, Brady!"

"Keep your voice down! I don't want the whole plantation to know what you've done to me."

"I'm sure my slaves are less interested in the affairs of their betters than are the servants of a certain house in a London crescent."

"They know I don't sleep with you!"

"Thank god!"

"But I'm your husband." He walked to the balcony edge and clenched the rail in his fists. "I've given your son a name!" he shouted as his fury made him forget his caution.

"It was yours to give by forgery alone," Davril said. Her eyes, which he once thought were blue with innocence, were deep with hatred.

"I've done everything you asked of me."

"Considering your only alternative was a prison cell had I exposed you to daddy's friend, the Governor, you had very little choice."

"But why, Davril? Can't you give me something? I'm a man, dammit." He hit his chest. "I have passions like other men."

"Then I suggest you act like other men and exercise some control over these so called passions."

"That's fine coming from you!" He spun around and glared at Davril. Her beauty made him weak. He dashed across the balcony and fell to the floor on his knees in front of her. "My God! I beg you. You are my wife! Let me come to your chamber tonight."

"I shall do no such thing!" She slapped his cheek and he reared up in anger.

"Why you little –"

"Dale!" she shrieked before he could get further. The slave must have been waiting in the drawing room for he was on the balcony instantly and advanced toward Carl.

"So you've bribed him too, have you?" He shook his head and retreated to his chair at the other end of the balcony. "I trained that nigger!" He turned on Dale who stared at him impassively.

"What did she give you, boy? A taste of white pussy?"

"Brady!" Davril shrieked in disgust. "How dare you!"

"Well it wouldn't be the first time. Your son's nearly black. Maybe you'll try for the whole thing next time."

"Tavron is not black. He's white!"

"As white as that nigger's arse."

"Control yourself, Brady. I thought you knew how to behave like a gentleman. I was mistaken."

"Oh, yes!" He grimaced evilly. "You'll find out your mistake. I'm your husband and I intend to have my rights."

"And I intend that you shall not."

"How will you stop me?"

Davril's smile was as warped as Carl's. She glanced at Dale before speaking. "That's so simple," she said. "A fall from the balcony, a heart attack. I could be a widow as soon as I want. Dr Farley is such a good friend. He'll issue the death certificate without question."

Carl went pale with panic. "You wouldn't . . ."

"To get what is rightfully mine? For Brett's son? Of course I would."

"But that's –"

"Justice!" Davril waved him into silence. "You claimed to be what you're not. The idea of being a widow is quite comforting. I hoped you'd be an amenable overseer. But if you plan to be a rapist, the sooner I'm a widow, the safer I'll be."

Carl glanced from Davril's genteel features to Dale's glowering black visage. He was aware of the slaves lurking in the drawing room, idling under the balcony and standing at the kitchen door. He had trained them all before Davril came. Were they all now allied against him and ready to obey her commands?

"It's preposterous," he said defiantly.

"Is it?" Davril gloated. "You'll find it no more outrageous than your assumption that you can batter your way into my boudoir."

He groaned. "Oh, very well!" He let his hand fall limply onto the arm of his chair. "You shall have your way."

"So I expect."

"But I shall have mine too."

"Indeed?" She watched him archly.

"If I can't have my wife, I'm not going to expire here like a eunoch in a brothel. I'll have my bed wench in my chamber."

"Spare me the details. Your morals are no concern of mine."

He leaned forward. "You're not serious, are you? About being a widow?"

She sniffed haughtily. "I'll consider it. Don't forget, Brady, you are expendable." She rose up and swept off the balcony, followed by Dale.

"By the devil!" Carl slumped in his seat and beat his brow.

A slave removed the lanterns from the balcony leaving him in shadow. No one took any notice of him now. The slaves knew he was an imposter, living in the house on sufferance, Davril had said.

He jumped up suddenly with a roar of anger and shouted across the canefields, "To hell with it!" He strode right around the balcony from one side of the house to the other, his spirits soaring. By the devil! He wasn't going to be murdered. He knew what to do – it was so simple.

It was Davril and her brat Tavron who would die.

20

Carl clattered down the back steps into the gang of slaves gathered outside the kitchen door. "Where's Sabina?" he demanded, fuming.

No one answered him.

He stood on the bottom rung so that he was head and shoulders above the slaves. "Sabina, where is she?"

He pulled a coin from his pocket. He knew how to make an awkward cuss cooperate. "A shilling for the one who takes me to her!"

The slaves whispered among themselves. All eyes turned to Dale. "Dat does be mah bitt, Mas Carl."

"When I see Sabina."

"Dis way."

"Where are we going?" He hesitated, his anger cooling.

Dale's teeth flashed in the light from the kitchen. "To de quarters. She does be visitin' she folks."

"Why are you speaking so niggery?"

"Dat de way ah does be, buckra. Niggery."

He was alarmed by the slave's animosity but he refused to be intimidated. "You certainly smell niggery," he said. The slaves tittered. "Get me a lantern if we are going to the quarters."

"Yo' scared de dark?" one of the kitchen women asked. The slaves laughed.

"Not of your dark conny," he said quickly. "Let's go."

A line of slaves followed him as he walked behind Dale along the path to the slave cabins. Too late, he realized the risk he was taking in not carrying a pistol or a whip.

"Walk faster, Dale," he ordered.

It was this boldness that gave him his authority. Slaves were trained to obey orders. Dale moved faster because Carl shouted at him. If he could keep his head and assert his superiority continuously, he would suffer no harm.

"What the devil is Sabina doing in the quarters?" Carl demanded of Dale. "I didn't give her permission. Neither did Mistress Davril."

As he expected, his reference to Davril confused the slaves. If they believed he was acting on Davril's authority, which they respected, then they would obey him faithfully.

The procession reached the quarters where the slaves lived in small, broken down, wooden cabins by the river. By the lantern's glow he saw about fifty of them squatting in the dark outside their cabins. The slaves seemed to be waiting for something.

"Raise the light, boy!" he shouted at Dale who held the lantern higher without a word. The expanding glow lit up haggard faces watching warily. He peered at them.

"Sabina's not here," he said.

Dale scratched his head. "She gone?"

"Call me master when you address me, boy!" The slaves shook their shoulders like vultures waiting to devour him. "Do you want to show these niggers that you don't know your job?"

There was a murmur of interest at his anger. "You will not have the shilling," he said, waving at the gathering of slaves. "It will go to them."

A torrent of patois greeted this suggestion. Carl understood only the words "beckey" meaning him, and "Sabina". The effect was disturbing. An old man spoke sharply to Dale and there was considerable head shaking before everyone lapsed into silence.

"Well," Carl demanded impatiently. "Doesn't anyone want the shilling? Where's Sabina?"

No one moved and he stared past them to a cabin at the end of the settlement. Spangles of dim light sparkled from cracks in its walls.

"Out of my way!" He thrust Dale aside and strode toward the cabin. No one followed. The cabin was old and dilapidated, surrounded by tall undergrowth. A smell encircled it like an invisible fence. Carl stopped and pinched his nose. It was the stench of rotting flesh, of decay.

"What the devil!" he muttered, but his curiosity about what was happening in the cabin overcame his growing apprehension. He crossed the unseen threshold into an atmosphere of foreboding. It chilled him and he halted nervously at the door instead of rushing in. He listened. There was a low murmur of voices chanting. Slowly, he lowered his eyes to a hole in the door.

There were two people in the cabin. Both were naked and had their backs to him. A flambeau flared on the floor of the cabin casting grotesque shadows on the walls and roof. Its bright flame illuminated the oiled skins of the two: a man he had never seen before, and Sabina.

Sabina's lissome body had haunted him since he banished her when Davril arrived. In vain, he had sent for her to return to him. He yearned to hold her close and to make love to her once more. The sight of her naked body only inches away from his eyes filled him with desire.

"Sabina!" he yelled, but his cry died on his lips. He was mute with a fearful lust. He shivered and he clung to the door jamb for support, watching in mounting horror the mysterious tableau enacted in the cabin.

Sabina and the man advanced to an altar at the rear of the hut. They raised their arms above their heads until their fingers touched the shingles of the roof. They lowered their heads in obeisance, dropped their arms to their sides and stepped back three paces.

They advanced again, and back, several times, accompanied by a high-pitched keening from Sabina. It was an ugly sound and Carl found it difficult to accept that it came from Sabina's dainty throat. Her whining was echoed by the roars of the man. With his sleek, muscular body and matted hair trailing down his shoulders, he was wild and lion-like to look at. Carl felt an evilness that made him nervous.

Sabina held a knife in her hand. It glittered in the bright flame and she advanced, alone this time, on the altar while the black giant waited. She raised her knife in the air and drove it down. There was a black shape on the altar which shrieked as the knife entered it.

Sabina stabbed and sliced until the shrieking died. She turned, her breast and loins smeared with blood. She beckoned and the naked man stepped to her.

"Aie bobo!" she cried, holding the knife at the giant's throat.

The man stood still, his legs apart and his massive thighs as immobile as a Greek statue in black marble. Carl gaped at the man's size.

Sabina slid the point of the knife down his chest, following the crucifix of matted hair to the center of his bulging muscles. She cut the knife across his skin in the shape of an arrow. The man neither flinched nor murmured. His face was a dark mask, gaunt in the fire and shadows from the flambeau.

Sabina stood on the tips of her toes and put her mouth to the incision. She sucked at it then moved back to the altar, her lips dripping with blood.

"Aie bobo!" she cried again and reached into the stomach of the corpse. She held up a bloody mass of entrails in her fingers and stuffed the liver between her teeth. She tilted back her head and the man leaned down and closed his lips over hers, sucking the liver into his mouth.

Carl fell back from the door and sank to his knees on the ground. The moon was dimmed by a cloud and his mind spun with confusion.

"Deliver us from evil," he muttered, and then stopped abruptly. His desire for Sabina was unabated, even heightened by what he had seen. She was the one for his purpose. A noise in the cabin alarmed him.

"Aie bobo!" Sabina shrieked and the growling of the man rose to a loud roar.

Carl dropped to his hands and crawled rapidly away from the cabin to hide in the long grass. The door of the cabin was opened and the glow from the flambeau spread out into the darkness. Carl crawled deeper into the bush.

The negro stepped out of the shack and stood upright. He was still naked and his shadow fell on the path in front of the hut. Sabina stood behind him, her hair flowing around her shoulders like a shimmering ebony mantle.

"Aie bobo!" the negro shouted, raising his arms into the air. A cloud drifted away from the moon and its light shrouded the glade. Sabina touched the negro on his chest.

"Mingoson," she shouted. "Kill!"

The negro brushed her hand away and loped like an animal down the path to the river bank.

Carl waited until Sabina had returned to the cabin, then he ran over and blocked the door with his foot as she tried to close it. "Sabina," he said softly. "Let me come in."

He saw the color drain from her face when he pushed his way into the shack. Her eyes widened and she staggered as though awakening from a trance. She fell back against the altar and the bloody corpse of the black pig tumbled to the floor. Carl kicked it away.

"What the hell are you doing, Sabina?"

She swallowed and perked up as she recovered her wits. "Ain't none of your business!"

"Yes, it is!" He shook her. "You're mine. What you do is my business."

"Hah!" Sabina sneered. "What does your wife say about that?"

He released her and stepped back. "She forced me into marriage because of something... She's not my wife. It's you I want!"

"Hah!" Sabina put her hands on her hips. The color returned to her cheeks and her lips were still bright with blood. "You told me to get out. What makes you think I want you? I don't!"

"You don't understand." Carl struck his brow with his hand. "Sabina, help me! I must get rid of Davril. She'll kill me if I don't." There was silence in the cabin as Sabina stared at him.

"I'll give you every thing. You can be my wife." He watched her face. "Please! You can do it. You're an obeah witch, aren't you? I've seen..." His voice died and he bowed his head under her gaze.

"Come," she said softly, her eyes sparkling in the reflection from the flames. She lay her hand, wet with blood, on his brow. He blinked, strangely calmed by her touch.

Her hands slipped under his shirt and ripped it off him. She rubbed her breasts, slippery with snake oil, against his chest.

Carl staggered and fell back against the altar. He gasped as Sabina's lips brushed the tautness of his throat. She clawed at his clothes until he was naked in the flame-light beside her. His heart soared with relief and he reached for her. She was gone.

He opened his eyes, suddenly fearful, and gazed around the cabin. The brightness of the flambeau showered stars in his eyes. Then he saw her. She was crouching in front of him with a knife in her hand pointed at his crotch. Her teeth were bared in an animalistic snarl.

He covered his penis and shouted. "Sabina!"

She swayed on her haunches and leaped at him. He flung himself to one side. He seized her wrist, twisting it until the knife fell from her grasp.

She slipped in the blood on the floor and he clamped his arms around her. She fought him with her body, each twist of resistance heightening his desire for her. He threw her to the floor and she lay spreadeagled beneath him. He fell on her and fastened his lips on her mouth, banging her head on the ground.

She gave in and her submission turned into a demand more furious than his own. She raised her thighs and wrapped her legs around his waist, squeezing him viciously. He drove into her, spiralling with each roll of her hams to an awesome climax. She sunk her teeth into his throat, drawing blood.

They relaxed, vanquished, in each other's arms.

Was it obeah or lust? Whatever it was, Carl's faith was restored. He tapped Sabina lightly on her cheek.

"You'll help me kill her?"

She nodded.

"How?"

"A potion. I'll gather herbs tonight. The moon is right."

"Poison?"

"It won't show."

Carl sighed with contentment and Sabina stroked him back to life.

21

Casey stood in a thicket of bamboo close to the mill wheel. His nostrils quivered at a goatish odor that wafted above the sticky stench of stale molasses. He tensed.

"Mingoson?" he said more bravely than he felt.

"Here."

Casey jumped. The tall maroon was standing beside him in the bamboo. "I didn't hear you come!"

"I'm a bush man. I know every path and trail here. The militia will never catch me." Mingoson spoke softly, his eyes and ears alert. "Did you come alone? I'll kill you now if this is a trap."

"No trap."

"You're smart." Mingoson cocked his head and listened. His body was smeared with snake grease and clotted blood speckled the bushy hair of his chest. Behind him, the water wheel creaked restlessly.

He seemed satisfied. "Why are you doing this, boy?"

Casey swallowed. He wondered himself. "Only you can help me. I want some of the gold, not all. We'll share it."

"Why do you want gold, boy?" Mingoson rubbed his hand over Casey's chest and arms, pinching his flesh in his fingers and thumb. He wriggled uncomfortably.

"That's my affair."

"You're a well built buck. Pity to kill you."

"There's enough gold for us both."

"Let's see it."

"Grave yard." It didn't matter what happened to him now, he thought. It was as though the Bondmaster himself was guiding him.

Mingoson laughed, a harsh, evil sound which was caught by the river and sucked into its roaring whirlpools. He embraced Casey, blood and grease smearing onto his shirt from his naked chest. He squeezed until Casey thought his ribs would break.

"Let me –"

"Only the Bondmaster would be smart enough to get the jumbies to guard his treasure." Mingoson laughed again and thrust him away. "No one would dig up dead men's bones."

"You would!" He held his breath.

"Which grave?" Mingoson's voice was sharp with a finality which caused Casey's hackles to tingle with fear.

"I'll show you when we get there." He waited for Mingoson's answer. There was no sound. The maroon had vanished, leaving the canes waving in the night breeze. It was eerie how Mingoson moved noiselessly, like a spirit. He shuddered.

After he had waited a few minutes and Mingoson didn't return, Casey walked toward the house. He wanted Mingoson with him when he entered the grave yard. If jumbies did exist, Mingoson would keep them off.

The brightness of the moon transformed the avenue with its overhanging boughs into a sepulcher. Casey cursed his fertile imagination and broke into a run. He was not worried about being seen as he crossed the courtyard in front of the house because slaves slept with their windows and doors tightly secured.

"Brett!"

The woman's cry startled him. He looked up at the gallery. Davril was staring down, her hands on her cheeks as though she had seen a ghost. He stepped into the shadows under the gallery.

"Brett?" Davril called plaintively.

Casey sighed and edged swiftly around the house. At the kitchen door, he stopped in dismay as another figure moved across the courtyard.

It was Carl, striding up to the grand steps with the authority of power. He seemed as unmoved by the mysteries of the night as Casey was disturbed by them. He climbed the steps two at a time and stomped into the house.

"Brady?" It was Davril's voice, shaky but assertive. Casey heard easily in the unnatural quietness of that late hour. He wondered why she called Carl by the name of Brady.

"Looking for a buck?" Carl jeered. "I saw Mingoson tonight. In the slave quarters. Are you waiting for him?"

Davril uttered a sharp cry of terror. "Then it's true!"

"What's true?"

"I thought I saw Brett. Out there in the courtyard."

"You were dreaming."

"But you saw Mingoson. They've returned to haunt us."

"Nonsense! You'll see Carlton Todd next." There was a bang as Carl kicked open the door to his bedroom.

"Brady, you don't understand. There is evil here tonight. I can feel it."

"Huh! It's too late to worry about that now." He slammed his door shut and Casey heard the muffled sobs of Davril weeping.

The noise in the house woke the baby and his cries were lustier than Davril's. Casey hurried away from his shelter under the gallery before the slaves were roused and came out of the kitchen to investigate. He scurried across the courtyard into the canepiece at the other side. The family burial ground was in a coppice of small trees on the mound of a hill.

It was dark at the edge of the wooded glade. No moonlight penetrated the trees to guide him through the shadows to the graves. He had heard the legend of a figure in a white cloak being seen floating through the trees years before. Fear chilled him and he glanced at the wood unhappily.

He found the spade he had hidden earlier that day beneath a tall saman tree. He glanced up at the branches of the tree and blinked as something moved. He fell to his knees, too scared to run. A solid shape jumped from the branches and landed on the ground beside him. His heart lurched.

"Get up, boy!" Mingoson seized him by the scruff of his neck and pulled him to his feet. "We haven't got all night. The cou's roused. That imposter's been prowling in the quarters.

"How –?"

"Come on!" Mingoson grabbed his arm and pulled him through the trees without any hesitation at the spirits they were disturbing.

"Which grave is it?"

He had to run to keep up with Mingoson. Low hanging branches clouted him and thorns snagged his breeches, tearing into his legs. "We're making too much noise," he called.

"Of course we are," said Mingoson. "It frightens the jumbies away."

"You mean . . ." Casey snapped his mouth shut in surprise. He hadn't expected that Mingoson was frightened as well. He pulled his arm loose from Mingoson's grasp and followed him at his own pace. The spade in his hand gave him more confidence than Mingoson's company now.

There was a clearing in the copse and Mingoson stood warily in the center. The moon was at its height, its full glow shining directly on him, highlighting his lean body. He was naked and the snake oil on his skin gleamed. He held a cutlass in his hand and pointed it at Casey.

"Which one?" He gestured with the blade at the piles of stones that marked each grave.

Casey hesitated, frowning. He had never been there before. "There's no knowing which is which," he said.

Mingoson laughed grimly. "I know."

"Why did you say Carl is an imposter?"

"Which grave, boy?"

"Answer my question first." He was delighted by Mingoson's nervousness. It showed he wasn't invincible after all. Casey stood a chance if he kept his wits about him. "We have plenty of time. No one will come here," he said.

Mingoson spun around, leaping anxiously from one grave to another. "It wasn't buried in Carlton's grave, that's for sure. Nor Brett's, nor Laura's." He stood in the middle of the piles of stones and scratched in his locks.

"You're a troublesome buck, like your dad," he said. "You can see Carl's an imposter. Look at his eyes. They're not the Bondmaster's eyes."

"Is that why Davril calls him Brady?"

"How should I know. Which grave, boy?" Mingoson advanced on him threateningly.

"Mas Carlton's father. Hayes Todd."

"Aie bobo!" Mingoson snatched the spade out of his hand and stuck the cutlass into the ground. He scraped the stones off one of the graves and started to dig.

"Aren't you afraid that something will happen to you?" Casey asked mischievously. "Disturbing the dead."

"Hold your tongue!" Mingoson's body shone with sweat and he dug with the energy of panic. Casey crouched down beside him.

"They say soucouyans come here. Witches floating in the trees."

Mingoson threw down the spade and glared at Casey, his eyes wide with fear. "Don't talk of such things! You dig!" He gazed up at the trees and gasped. A bat flew close to his head across the moon. "I'll keep guard," he said.

Casey smirked and took up the spade, digging slowly. He spoke while he threw up spadefuls of earth. "Spirits . . . dead men walking . . . we'll find out if they exist tonight."

Mingoson was growing anxious. "Shut up, boy!"

Casey grinned and pitched the spade into the hole. There was a clang as it struck metal. "I've found something. Maybe the old man's coffin."

"Come out." Mingoson pushed him aside and jumped into the grave. He dug feverishly with his cutlass and hands, scooping out the soil until a small casket was revealed.

"Aagh!" he said, nodding his head grimly. "You spoke the truth."

"Not me, Mas Carlton."

Mingoson broke into loud, evil laughter. His eyes danced wildly and he glared around the glade challenging the spirits to defy him. A bird, disturbed by the noise, cawed in anger and crashed through the branches in confusion.

"Perhaps that's a soucouyan," said Casey. Mingoson gulped into silence.

"I wonder if the Bondmaster put a curse on his gold?"

"What do you mean?" Mingoson let go of the casket and reared out of the grave.

"Oh, I'm sure it wouldn't worry you. Nothing will trouble you. Nothing living, anyway." He grinned.

Mingoson was feeling along the ground for his cutlass. It wasn't there. He glanced at Casey. "Boy, where –?"

A cackle of sinister laughter reverberated in the deathly stillness of the glade.

Mingoson flattened himself on the ground. Casey's spine tingled with fear. He'd tempted the devil too much by trying to frighten Mingoson. He began to pray.

"What's that?" Mingoson's teeth were chattering.

"I don't know." He clenched his fists.

"Did you take my cutlass, Casey?"

"No," he whispered nervously.

The laughter swelled around the grave yard again and Mingoson covered his ears with both hands. Casey listened carefully.

"Brett!" The laughter stopped abruptly as an anguished voice called again, "Brett."

"That's Davril," Casey said aloud, standing up. "She must have followed –"

Mingoson sprang off the ground at Casey's throat. His shoulder slammed into his chest and felled him to the ground. He rolled backward into the grave and Mingoson toppled on to him, his fingers clawing at his throat.

"You trapped me!"

Casey grunted for breath, pounding his knee into Mingoson's crotch. It was useless.

Mingoson's fingers tightened their hold on his throat and his thumbs crushed his larynx. Before he lost consciousness, he saw the soucouyan with flapping wings pounce into the grave onto Mingoson's back. He heard its insane shrieking and Mingoson's cry of terror.

He passed out briefly before the pressure on his windpipe was relaxed. Mingoson tossed the jumbie off his back and bolted out of the grave. The soucouyan gathered Casey in its arms and cradled him like a baby. He opened his eyes fearfully and found he was looking into the worried face of Uraline.

"How –?" he asked, choking with relief.

She laughed with the exaggerated cackle of the jumbie soucouyan.

"That was you?"

Uraline nodded.

"I heard Davril's voice," he said, then a shot stunned him into silence. Its report resounded over the hillside and a scream echoed it. There was the thud of a heavy body collapsing on the ground. Casey clutched Uraline and whispered into her ear.

"Who's that?"

A rim of light was glowing under the shadows of the overhanging branches. They heard the murmur of voices. Casey raised his head and peered out of the grave. Among the trees, flambeaux held aloft by solemn slaves flickered like fire flies. At the edge of the glade, Davril stood with eyes ablaze with hatred and a pistol in each hand. Dale was by her side.

On the ground by the grave, Mingoson lay wounded, blood spurting from a hole in his chest.

Casey scrambled out and rolled over to Mingoson's side. He crouched on his haunches and raised the maroon to rest against his thighs. Mingoson screamed, then choked on the blood which gurgled from his mouth.

"Never trust a white man . . ." he gasped, his eyes watering with pain. "Especially . . . a dead one."

Casey shook his head. "Don't blame me. I didn't know."

Mingoson made an effort to get to his feet. He clutched his chest with his hand and grimaced as the blood oozed over his fingers. Casey helped him to a sitting position. "Got to get –"

A shadow fell on them, blocking out the moon. They both looked up. Davril was standing over them, her cloak billowing in the wind. "Brett," she whispered huskily, gazing at Casey.

"I'm not Brett," he said, shaking his head.

Mingoson moved but he was weak and Casey's hands on his shoulders restrained him.

Davril raised her arm and pointed the pistol at Mingoson. She fired.

The flash blinded Casey and the shot deafened him. He

threw himself backward on the ground and waited for his head to clear. He opened his eyes to stars and blinked to clear his sight.

A hole was blown into Mingoson's crotch. His penis and scrotum were gone, his stomach was a stew of blood and his entrails bubbled to the ground. His hands clawed at his guts as his throat rattled with the gasp of death.

22

"You're not Brett!" Davril pummelled Casey's chest with her fists. She was moaning angrily with frustration.

"No," said Casey quietly, gripping her wrists and handing her to Dale. "He was my brother. I came for the gold." He gestured at the open grave where Uraline was scratching the soil away from the casket with Mingoson's cutlass.

Dale put his arm around Davril and called the slaves. "Come, boys," he said. "Dig that box out of the ground."

Davril eyed him suspiciously. "What gold?"

"The Bondmaster hid his fortune in his father's grave. He left a letter for his heir." He shrugged apologetically.

"His heir?" Davril's eyes took on a new gleam. "See the slaves dig up everything, Dale." She wriggled away from him and put her hand on Casey's arm, drawing him close.

"You have no right to this treasure, of course. My husband is Carlton's heir."

Casey grinned mischievously. "You know that's not true, Davril."

For a moment she appeared startled and seemed about to brazen out the lie, then she raised her hands to his chin and touched it lightly. "You're better looking than Brett." She ran her finger lightly over his lips down his throat and to his chest. "Better built."

"I'm not a slave, Davril. Nor a stud."

She removed her hand and smiled. "You don't talk like him. You're much more of . . . of a man!" She let her cloak fall loose, so that it brushed against his thigh. "It's a pity that you're not the Bondmaster," she said suggestively. "I suppose you should have been . . ."

There was a shout from the slaves at the graveside. He turned his back on her but she put her hand on his shoulder and whispered, "Roxborough could be yours, and the gold too."

He kept his eyes on the slaves as they pulled a second casket from the hole. Davril stroked the fine hairs at the back of his neck and stood on tiptoes beside him. Softly she said, "Carl has robbed you of your rightful inheritance. Why don't you kill him?"

The contents of the two caskets were tipped on to the floor of the drawing room. There were gold pieces of eight, reals, pistoles, crowns, dubloons, Spanish silver dollars, and joes from Barbados.

"It's a fortune!" said Uraline when the heap of gold glittered in the light from the flambeaux.

"Blood money," muttered Casey unhappily.

They stood by the gallery door as Davril ran the coins through her fingers. The nurse brought Tavron, and Davril jangled coins in his face.

"We're going, Davril," Casey said, turning away. He was ashamed.

"No!" Davril left the baby and ran to his side. "You can't leave me now, with this." She pointed at the gold but her eyes were on Dale and the slaves.

Casey understood her fear. He hesitated. Was this what Carlton Todd wanted?

He glanced around him. Night hung heavily over the hills. There were two hours to go before dawn. He saw movement in the canefields below the gallery. The field slaves, drawn like moths to the lights blazing in the house, were gathering in the courtyard.

"I can't stop them," he said. "Where's Carl?"

"Cowering behind his bedroom door, I shouldn't wonder."

"Cover the gold," he said. "It's liberty to them. They won't think."

Davril walked to the heap of coins and unfastened her cloak. She removed it and it fluttered to the floor and settled on the gold, hiding its glitter. The slaves in the room shuffled restlessly.

"Go to your quarters!" she said.

None of them moved. She turned to Casey, her eyes pleading.

He looked carefully from one slave to another. Dale was pursing his lips, his mind clearly obsessed with the pile of gold on the floor. The others were watching him too, waiting with an air of inevitability, just like the slaves in the courtyard. He felt that it didn't matter what he did now, everything was following a destiny planned by Carlton. He frowned and opened his hands helplessly.

"You found the gold," Davril shrieked at him. "You must do something!"

"Dale," he said softly. "All the slaves in Dominica are going to be freed next month. Only a few days to wait. The gold, properly used, can help make your future secure."

Dale grinned foolishly and rolled his eyes. He's playing his part, too, thought Casey.

"Plenty of gold there, Cas," he said, "for all of us."

"We gonna buy slaves of our own!" a kitchen boy said excitedly.

Dale rounded on him. "Hol' yuh tongue," he snapped. He turned back, his face serious. "Casey, you and Uraline take your share and go home to Layou. What happens here is nothing to do with you."

Casey bit his lip thoughtfully, watching Dale's eyes. There were only a few minutes before the slaves would get out of control and seize the gold. It was his own fault. Once, he had thought they were gutless. Now he knew they were right.

The bedroom door crashed open. Carl, naked to his waist, stood defiantly on the threshold, a bullwhip in his hand.

Before any of the slaves could run, he flicked his wrist and sent the rawhide lash sizzling across the room. It sliced into Dale's cheek and blood spurted out down his face. Carl gloated with triumph and turned on the slaves. They muttered among themselves and drew back.

Davril ran to Carl's side. "Dear," she said, "how clever! I knew you'd do the right thing."

"Get away!" He pointed the whip at her. "Over there with the slaves."

"Don't be silly, Carl."

He lashed out and the whip ripped the fabric from her bodice, exposing her breasts. She crumpled to the floor at his feet.

"Carl!" Casey stepped swiftly across the room and pulled the cloak off the heap of gold. The whip slashed across his hand, stinging his fingers. He gritted his teeth and tensed his body for another blow. It never came.

Carl seemed to know that the immediate threat came from the slaves. He struck out at three footmen huddling against the wall nearest to him. One tried to catch the thong as it cut through the air but it sliced a gash in his hand. He screamed and fell against the other slaves.

The bullwhip is the master of all whips. In the hands of a desperate man, like Carl, it is devastating. The iron bar in its short handle lent it weight and the tongue tore through the air into the flesh of every slave in the room. There was a scramble to escape and Carl chased them all from the room. They scurried across the courtyard and into the canefields.

When he returned to the drawing room, Davril was trying to staunch the blood oozing from her breast. The baby was crying.

"I hate that bastard," Carl said and snapped the whip. His face twisted into a warped smile when it sliced into the baby's tiny face. The baby fell to the floor and the nurse screamed and fled from the room.

Davril leaped for Carl, her hands outstretched to claw at his eyes. He flailed the whip in her face and the lash knocked her sideways. She crawled toward the child and stared in horror at the blood gushing from his cheek.

"Look, Carl!" Casey plunged his hands into the heap of gold and threw coins in the air. They glittered in the glow from the flaming torches, and the glimmer distracted Carl. He gazed at Casey suspiciously.

"What are you doing here?" he asked as though seeing him for the first time.

Casey grinned. "That's better," he said. He held out his hand. "Why don't you give me that whip, Carl?" He spoke quietly to calm him. "You've driven off the slaves. That's good. We can get this gold put away and everything will be all right. We'll send for the militia." He walked slowly across the room as he talked.

Carl backed toward his bedroom door. "Keep away!"

"All right." Casey stopped, lowered his head and bent down to pick up some coins. "Have you ever seen riches like this, Carl? These are dubs, Spanish gold worth over seven pounds in English currency. There must be hundreds of them!" He held out his hands.

Carl tucked the whip under his arm and reached out to touch Casey.

Davril lunged at them both with the flaming brand of a flambeau in her hand. Casey saw her coming and caught her wrist as Carl snatched up the whip. The flambeau fell on the floor, its sparks igniting the long curtain at the balcony window. Carl advanced on Davril, beating her with the iron handle of the whip, smashing it into her face and shrieking as the flames flared and fell on to a rattan chair. The curtain and chair blazed quickly.

Davril screamed and Casey flung her free. She ran back to her child and snatched him up from the floor.

"The house will burn down!" shouted Casey. "We must get water."

"Stay where you are." Carl's voice was icy.

Casey stared as the curtains became a blazing wall of flame. Davril was clutching the baby and shrieking hysterically. Uraline was crouched on the floor gathering coins into the pockets of her shift, and into a flour bag she had brought from the kitchen.

"Come on, Davril!" Casey defied Carl's flaying whip and

ran to Davril and led her out of the drawing room to the servants steps. The house was made of timber. It was old and dry and burned rapidly. When he turned back to the drawing room, it was already engulfed in flames. Uraline stumbled out into his arms.

"Where's Carl?" he demanded.

Uraline shook her head without speaking. He hurried them both down the steps. The slaves were forming a bucket chain. Tency dashed past him into the house.

"Look after Davril," he said to Uraline. "I'm going back for Carl. He's still in there somewhere."

"No, Cas! He deserves to burn in hell."

"He doesn't know what he's doing. I must try to help him."

The slaves were passing buckets up the back steps and throwing water on the flames through the door. Casey climbed the steps and tried to push through. Tency blocked the way with her huge body.

"Cas, yo' can't go in dere. De gold goin' stay 'til de fire done burn out."

"I don't care about the gold, Tency," he shouted. "I must get Carl."

Tency spat into the flames. Then she hoisted up a bucket of water and tipped it over his head. "Wake up, Casey!" she said.

He wiped the water from his eyes and dashed past her. There were gaps in the fire and he reached the drawing room safely. Carl was stretched out on the pile of gold.

"Carl!" he called. "This way!"

Carl didn't hear. His breeches were bunched around his ankles. He rose on his hands above the pile of gold and plunged himself down. His penis was hard and he stabbed it into the mass of coins, writhing in frenzy. The flames licked at his fingers.

Casey dived through the fire and landed beside him on the gold.

"Come with me!" he shouted. "You'll burn to death!" He pulled him up by his shoulder and helped him to his feet.

Carl grinned and steadied himself with one hand on

Casey's shoulder. Bending down, he picked up some coins and stuck them in his fist so they protruded between his fingers. He rose up and drove the fist into Casey's eyes.

The blow blinded Casey and he staggered back. Carl hit him again, the hard edge of the coins tearing into his flesh.

He slipped and toppled backward into the flames.

23

Casey's hair was singed and his eyes red. Blood was caked on the cuts on his face and legs. He stood with Tency, Dale and the slaves in the courtyard as the flames devoured Roxborough Hall. He had been lucky. Carl's blow had pitched him backward into the dining room where Tency was searching for him. She had dragged him out, leaving Carl behind.

Nothing could save the house. The flames burned through the floor to the slave quarters in the basement below. The four bedrooms were alight, flames leaping into the sky and curling around the shingles of the roof. The balcony girting the house was also ablaze.

"There!" Dale shouted. The slaves sighed as they saw what they had all been waiting for.

Carl had emerged from the flames and stood outlined starkly at the edge of the burning balcony. He was a darker part of the fire, his clothes and hair aflame. He thrust his hands into the air as though reaching out for the night, and a shower of sparks twinkled in the light from the fire and arced out from the house to fall with a clatter on the cobbles below.

"De gold!" Dale and the slaves dashed forward.

Under the flamboyant tree where she stood alone, Sabina smiled to herself with an air of grim satisfaction.

"Come," Uraline tugged Casey's arm. "Come with me."

"Where?" he asked dully.

"You'll see." She led him to the edge of the courtyard by the sugar cane. There were scores of people watching the fire; slaves, free blacks, even whites who had hurried up from Layou when the alarm was sounded.

"Casey!" said a familiar voice from the crowd. A girl ran to him and threw her arm around his neck. He blushed when she kissed him in front of everyone.

"Are you all right? You've been hurt! Your face, it's cut."

He grinned at her concern. "Lucy, what are you doing here?"

"Daddy brought me. Mummy's at home."

He seized her hand and squeezed it happily.

By Lucy's side, Davril was holding Tavron. The baby no longer cried. Mr Leach was talking to her. He turned to Casey and gripped his hand, shaking it warmly.

"You're a hero, I hear," the magistrate said. "Well done, young man, well done."

Casey smiled shyly.

"I'm taking Mrs Todd to my house. She's terribly distressed."

Casey looked at Davril and was dismayed when she held the baby out to him and mouthed so no one else could hear, the word "Ours." There was a chink of coins from under the baby's wrap. Mr Leach guided her away.

"May I walk back with Casey and Uraline," Lucy called after him. "I want to hear what happened."

Mr Leach, his mind on other things, nodded his consent.

Uraline spoke softly into Casey's ear. "Let we go now, Cas. Hell gonna break out when de fire done done an' de niggers search fuh de gold."

He let himself be led away by Uraline, with Lucy at his side. No one saw them go. The night was bright with the glow of the flames mingling with the moonlight. More white folk were scrambling up the hill from Layou, jostling with the slaves to get closer.

He followed Uraline obediently. Lucy held his hand close to her bosom. She was wrapped in a cloak, her head hooded against the night. Strands of blonde hair fell across her forehead and he could smell the lingering fragrance of verbena on her skin.

"Where are we going?" He was so engrossed with Lucy he had followed Uraline down a path that took them away from the village.

"Hush!" Uraline placed her fingers on her lips. She bade them wait for her by gestures and disappeared in the darkness ahead of them.

He turned to Lucy and put his arms around her. She held his waist. He kissed her gently on her mouth. She smiled.

"Casey," she said. "I thought you'd forgotten me."

"Never."

"Why? I haven't seen you for days."

He laughed. "Four days and eighteen hours to be precise. It was nine o'clock on Thursday morning when you waved at me from your balcony."

She kissed his cheek. "I love you, Casey."

"I love you, too," he said. The bushes parted noisily and Uraline coughed. He drew back.

"There ain't no one about," she said. "Yo' can go to de mill."

"Why?" Lucy frowned. "My father –"

"Mas Leach taking care Davril," Uraline said brusquely. "Come."

The mill was built of river stone; it loomed gray and mysterious out of the trees. The odor of molasses hung over it, adding to its forbidding atmosphere. Lucy clung to Casey.

"Don't worry," he said. "No jumbies can scare us with Uraline here."

"Dat foolish talk, Cas." Uraline grinned with delight.

The moon was nearly spent and they followed her with difficulty along the path around the mill. She stepped under an arch into the grinding hall where the massive wheels that squeezed the cane were housed. She pointed to a cask and Casey and Lucy sat down on it.

"What's this about?" he asked.

"Yo' make me vexed, Cas," Uraline said, putting down the flour bag. "How much gold yo' take?"

"Gold?" He gazed at Lucy and they both laughed. "By the devil!"

"Yo' ain't got none?" Uraline sighed with exasperation. "Lucy," she said wagging her finger, "dat boy Casey does be a lummox."

"I forgot." He gestured helplessly.

Uraline began to giggle. "Never mind, Cas. I have plenty fuh yo'." She tipped up the flour sack and hundreds of coins scattered to the floor. To these she added the coins she carried in her pockets and under her garments.

"Law, I think my waist gonna break," she said. She rubbed her hands over her breasts and thighs, wiping away loose coins that were stuck to her skin under the shift.

"That's stealing," said Lucy.

"It ain't. Dat gold does be Casey's. He the Bondmaster heir."

Casey gathered up handfuls of the coins and stuffed them in the pockets of his coat and breeches. "No sense in leaving them here." He smiled wryly at Lucy.

"I gonna keep five dubs, Cas. Yo' does owe me dat." She rolled her eyes. "No need to hurry, Cas. I wait fuh yo' by de trail." She hurried away into the darkness, sniffing loudly.

"Why is she crying?" he wondered aloud, taking Lucy by the hand. His pockets were weighed down with the gold.

"She's fond of you."

"She helped to raise me."

"Oh, Casey!" Lucy's sigh made him tremble.

He put his arm around her. "Why are you so sad?"

"I don't want to lose you."

He was silent. Her fingers touched his scorched hair and the puffiness around the bruises on his face.

"Davril wants you," she said.

Her remark forced him to face up to the source of the disquiet gnawing at him. "Not me," he said. "She wants my title. Without my cooperation, she has no claim to what's left of Roxborough."

"What will you do?"

He patted his bulging pockets. "I have some gold. We could go away."

She kissed him. "You're such a dreamer." She slid with him down the side of the cask and they lay together on the flagstones. He reached over and parted her cloak. Underneath, she wore only the cambric night dress which was what she was wearing when the fire was discovered.

He kissed her shoulder, and her body was alive in his hands, quivering like a butterfly under his fingers. He caressed her cheek and brushed gentle kisses on her eyes and nose. She sighed.

"Shall we go?" he asked.

"No, Casey, stay with me." She unfastened his coat and his shirt, touching his chest.

"Are you sure?"

"I love you!" she said, leaning back, using the side of the cask as a pillow. Her cloak was open and she shook off her hood so her blonde tresses spun around her bare shoulders like flames of gold.

His heart seemed to stop.

She slipped her arm around his waist and pulled him to her. She kissed him passionately. Her tongue slipped into his mouth and her fingers clawed at his back, sending shivers of excitement down his spine.

The gold in his pockets was like clenched fists between them. He opened his coat to lie more comfortably with her.

The scent of rum maturing in the casks laid down by the Bondmaster filled the air. Beyond the walls of the mill, the river gurgled beneath the water wheel. Above the mountain range in the east, the sky lightened and the gloom of night vanished.

"Wait," he whispered.

From the slave quarters, the lonely moan of a conch shell being blown by a Wagenie boatman announced the beginning of a new day. But this day, Casey knew, would be different.

He kissed her softly on her lips and rolled away from her. "Wait," he said again. He clutched the pockets of his coat close to him and in the dark of the mill house, slipped out through the door. He ran the few paces to the river bank. His face smarted from his cuts and his head was raw where his flesh and hair had been singed by the fire.

A canoe moved silently down the river. He hailed the two Wagenie blacks who were rowing and they pulled toward the shore. He waded into the water and climbed on board.

The Wagenies paddled the canoe out in to the center of the river and it scurried over the rapids and bore him away to the open sea.

Book Two

Bullers Fancy, 1834 – 1836

24

Gene W. Cable sketched rapidly. His hand flew over the pad and he was exhilarated by the drawing coming to life in front of him. Like Edison, he believed genius was nine-tenths hard work. This afternoon, with the boy leaning on the ship's taffrail watching the island recede into the distance, Gene Cable had the one-tenth touch of genius.

The boy's face, caught now in the sunlight, now in shadow as the ship breezed along, its sails full, was a study! Gene was thrilled. So often the negroes fidgeted too much for him to capture the essence of them. This mulatto remained motionless, his face reflecting some inner conflict and his eyes, with their pale luster against the tanned hue of his skin, bathed in melancholy.

"Farewell!" That would be the title of the sketch. "Farewell to the islands." A young man gazes forlornly at the home he will never see again.

"Yes," shouted Gene triumphantly, signing his sketch with a flourish. "I've got it!"

The youth nodded his head but said nothing.

"You can leave the rail now. I've finished." Gene held his pad in front of him and his nerves tingled. He'd got the boy's expression exactly right. Such a depth of experience in that young face. "Don't you want to see?"

A wan smile from the youth was the response before he turned back to gaze at the vessel's wake.

"Mon dieu!" said Gene, ripping the page from his sketch pad. "I'll have another shot since you're so pensive today." He began the outline of the youth's face, capturing his fine, straight nose, the lobeless ears like Pan's, and his dark, wavy hair.

"I've told you, Casey," he chattered, his eyes darting from the boy's face to the pad and back again. "New Orleans is the place for you! Once you've seen the girls in the Vieux Carré, you'll never think of the islands again."

The youth's muscles tightened as he gripped the taffrail more firmly. He was dressed like a seaman with his sleeves rolled up and his shirt hanging loose over his duck trousers. He was bare-footed having removed his boots when he came on board and stowed them in the cabin he shared with Gene.

The breeze played in his tousled hair and cuffed his chest, billowing his shirt like a sail. He didn't move.

Gene was ecstatic. His satisfaction came in nabbing a fleeting moment of naturalness and preserving it in his sketches. With Casey's features he believed he was portraying so much of the conflict of life in the Caribbean. 'Sketches in the West Indies' would be the title of his book. Casey's portrait would be its frontispiece.

Gene was on the last leg of his six month voyage around the islands. After Antigua which was already no more than imagination on the horizon, the ship was to call at Havana before sailing directly to New Orleans. He was glad Casey was accompanying him.

Gene had met Casey when his ship docked at St John's, in Antigua. He was perched on a bollard with the nonchalance of a seagull and Gene sketched him while the ship was tying up. This led to a conversation, with Casey responding cautiously at first to Gene's overture of friendship. They went on an excursion around Antigua together and Gene was intrigued by the sadness troubling Casey's spirit. But he was a good companion and when he accepted his invitation to join him for the voyage to New Orleans, Gene was delighted.

"I have money," Casey had said. "I can pay my way."

Even now, thought Gene as he added a few pencil strokes to indicate the ship's rail and deck, he knew nothing about Casey except his name. It wasn't surprising. The great wave of emancipation was surging through the British islands, and colored lads and blacks without ties were its flotsam and jetsam.

Gene had asked no questions, only enjoying Casey's company and willingness to be useful. He carried his easel and paints for him and discoursed with intelligence and curiosity. In New Orleans, Gene knew, Casey would be an irresistible success. His good looks and amiable personality were enchanting.

"Let's go below," said Gene, resting his pad on his knees. "I crave a glass of sherry."

"I'll stay awhile."

Casey's answer worried Gene. He wanted Casey to become his permanent attendant but there was such independence in the boy. He stood up and gathered his things himself.

"Very well," he said a little grumpily. "But, Casey, one day you could try sharing your problem. It would be a lighter load for two to bear it."

To Gene's surprise, Casey came toward him across the deck, smiling broadly. "Let me see," he said, taking the sketch book from his hand. "Hmm. Do I really look so sad?"

"Not sad. Wise."

"I'm not wise. If I were, it wouldn't have happened."

Gene longed to ask what. Perhaps Casey even wanted him to ask, but he didn't. There was time for that during the days ahead of them. "What about that sherry?"

Casey glanced at the horizon. The sun was setting and nightfall would soon be with them. "I wonder if I'll ever come back."

"Do you want to?"

"It's my home."

"New Orleans shall be your home. You'll live with me in my mother's house in the Vieux Carré. We shall have a perfect time."

"I'm grateful."

"For what?"

"For your friendship. And for helping me to escape."

"Escape?" Gene sighed. "*Mon dieu!* You sound like a runaway."

Casey shook his head glumly. "I am. Not from slavery. From myself, perhaps. Tell me, Gene . . ."

"Yes?" The use of his first name pleased Gene. It meant

Casey was to be his friend, but not his servant.

"Can a man do something to someone he loves, and he knows it will hurt that person, yet still he does it?"

"Man to man?" said Gene steadying himself by the rail.

"Yes," said Casey.

Gene sniffed. "I was in love once. Beautiful girl from a plantation. She loved me, so she said, but she jilted me. Her parents, you see. They didn't want her taking up with an artist. I was hurt for a while and then I understood. She was hurt too but she did it because she loved me."

Gene ran his hand through his long dark hair and his eyes flashed. "Do you see? Things happen, we don't know why, but it's for the best."

"For the best?" Casey smiled ruefully and punched Gene lightly on his chest. "I'd like that sherry now."

By the time the ship reached the Gulf of Mexico and entered the Mississipi River, Gene knew Casey's story. He drew it out of him while he sketched dozens of studies during the weeks of the voyage. He portrayed Casey in repose, helping the seamen on deck, laughing over a glass of wine, and in the nude.

Casey had a superb body and was so lacking in self-consciousness that he was an ideal model. Gene was ten years older than Casey and a famous artist, but he had never met anyone like him. He posed naturally, and while they worked, they talked. From the first, Gene had recognized the proud will lying beneath Casey's disarming smile. However, he had not foreseen that Casey would use that will to dominate their relationship.

As soon as Gene understood the reasons for Casey's despondency, he fussed over him hoping to get him to forget his confusion and sorrow.

"Thank your stars you left Lucy," Gene said one afternoon, chivvying Casey to laugh. "Can you imagine the heartbreak if you'd stayed. Disgrace for the family or, worse, marriage for you!"

"To Lucy or to Davril?"

"One as bad as the other," laughed Gene. "A young man

needs freedom, not matrimony. You'd know the Bondmaster's fury soon enough if you'd stayed. Now Lucy has a beautiful memory and Davril has the gold. You have your life ahead of you. Let's drink to that."

Gene pandered to Casey in an effort to restore the bright light of youth to his eyes. He grew fond of him even though Casey, instead of being the servant as he intended, was becoming the master.

"What would you like to do on your first day in New Orleans?" Gene asked when they stood on the deck watching the plains only six miles below the city. Luggers crowded the vessels surging upstream, and the cacophony of river traffic added zest to the sultry morning.

Casey shrugged. If he was excited, he didn't show it.

"I know!" Gene clapped him on his shoulder. "You're still dressed like a waterfront rat. We must find you a good tailor, new boots, a hair cut. You'll be the toast of the town." Gene slapped his back again at the thought of it.

"Tonight, I'll take you to a bordello. You've never seen such whores. They'll cure you of your melancholy."

"I don't want a whore. I was raised by them."

"Yes, and they looked on you as a child, didn't they? You were their pet prick to pull when they were bored. In New Orleans, the whores will love you as a man."

Gene paused as something occurred to him. "We won't worry," he said thoughtfully. "The whores are only concerned with the color of your money."

"Isn't it the same everywhere?"

"No." Gene frowned. "It isn't. White whores are usually reserved for, er, white clients. I –"

"Don't concern yourself, Gene. I know what you mean. I shall keep in my place."

"Casey!" Gene gripped his arm. "You must be alert here. In the Southern States if a man isn't all white, he's black. It's not the Caribbean, however charming and gay it seems. Beware of strangers, always."

"I can fend for myself."

"Don't be angry with me, Casey. The dangers are here. Negroes, even free men, have been captured on the streets and disappeared, sold as slaves in Georgia and Alabama. I know you don't believe me but take care!"

Gene's qualms about Casey's safety were forgotten in the excitement and bustle of their arrival. The river was full and their ship's masts towered above the houses beyond the levee. Gene was exhilarated to be home and hurried Casey along the wharf, through the streets, past the Cathedral of St Louis and the old Place d'Armes to Orleans Street.

"Rue D'Orleans," Gene explained. "So named when the city was founded." He waved his hand at the ground floor and garret houses of lime-stuccoed brick. Wooden doorsteps rose up from the worn flagstones.

"Down there is Rampart Street and can you see the oak and sycamore trees? That's Congo Square."

Casey took no notice but turned around to stare at the cathedral and its square where whites were promenading under the shade of its trees. He rubbed his eyes and Gene laughed loudly.

"I should draw you now! But come," he took him by his arm. "We don't want to gawp like strangers." He was aware of the attention that Casey was attracting. A white man and a quadroon were not an unusual sight in New Orleans streets but in their bedraggled traveling clothes, they looked a disreputable pair.

Gene hurried Casey along the Rue Royale and into the Rue Toulouse, keeping his eye open for awkward encounters. Casey, he realized now, would have to be protected, or he would soon be bailing him out of the calaboose.

"Don't talk to anyone," he pleaded to Casey. "Whites won't take kindly to it. To them you're a quadroon."

Casey looked down at his old canvas trousers and shirt open to his waist. "Should I buy a coat and fancy britches before I meet your mother?"

"Not for her. For dawdling, yes. Do come on!"

Gene stopped in front of a brick house with small balconies of wrought iron, like Spanish lace, at its upper windows. A recess above the heavy oak door resembled an arbor inundated with flowers and climbing plants. He took a deep breath and rapped loudly with the lion's paw doorknocker.

Suddenly Gene's misgivings at bringing Casey to New Orleans caught up with him. The boy was so ingenuous. How would he understand the codes that governed behavior in the city? He was a quadroon and as such wouldn't be accepted as an equal the way mulattoes were down islands.

The door swung open in the hands of his mother's negro butler, and he ushered Casey into the house. He only hoped his mother would understand.

Madame Eugenia Cable was half French with an influential position in New Orleans society, bolstered by an inheritance of several thousand dollars from her ship owner husband. She was an artist too and her convictions, although unconventional, were genuine and founded on a lust for life and beauty. She welcomed Casey as if he was a Prince.

Gene was astounded at the change in his protégé. Casey revealed such graceful manners and easy charm that he captivated his mother within minutes. Gone was the dourness he had shown on the voyage. Madame Cable was delighted. She took charge, declaring where Casey would sleep and what clothes, culled from Gene's own wardrobe, he should wear. She announced he must rest after the voyage and prepare to meet legions of her friends.

Casey's protests were to no avail and he submitted to Madame Cable's instructions with apparent good humor. When he had been led away to his chamber, his mother faced Gene in high spirits.

"Doudou!" she said. "Almost a year."

"The best year of my life, maman. So much to paint, and such color. I've got enough sketches for three books."

"I'm sure one will be sufficient." Madame Cable sat on the couch. "You must lend him to me!"

"Casey?" Gene was puzzled.

"But yes! He is divine. I will paint him in oil."

"We'll share him, maman. I was so worried about what you'd say. He looks a little unprepossessing at the moment."

"A nugget, darling. Out of nigrescence. A little polish, the right setting, he's a priceless gem!" She clapped her hands with pleasure. "How clever of you."

"I wonder how he'll fit in. You know . . ."

"We must launch him immediately! He must be recognized so people know who he is. At my next salon. When my circle have accepted him he will have no trouble anywhere in New Orleans. The city will be his! My dear," she giggled, "what the gossips will say!"

"That you have a quadroon paramour?"

"Yes, isn't it exciting. And who knows . . ."

"I don't want Casey hurt. He's not a street nigger who was selling himself. In a pouch under his shirt he has enough gold to buy a plantation. And he's sensitive and intelligent."

"So much the better. I adore him already." She frowned suddenly. "You must get the gold from him at once. For his own safety."

"Then you are worried?"

"We can't tell with a hot headed quadroon, can we? He must have girls! He's not an artist like you, Doudou. He's a gem but an animal too. A beautiful exotic animal but with passion, so much passion, in his blood. You can see it!" She sighed.

"His eyes are drunk with dreams. You must guard him jealously, Gene. If someone steals him from you, you'll never see him as he is again."

25

Place Congo, at the opposite end of Orleans Street to the Place D'Armes, was at the opposite end of everything. The square that formed Place Congo lay beyond Rampart Street where the palisade wall of the town used to run in Spanish days. Place D'Armes was the rendezvous of quality, wealth and authority while Congo Square was the haunt of the demi-monde, tradesmen and slaves.

"White at one end," Gene said with shame.

"And black at the other," Casey grunted, surveying the negroes and mulattoes parading around the square.

"But such blacks!" said Gene, his artist's eye following the people reverently. "You see the real African tribes here. Even though the shipping of slaves has been abolished for nearly thirty years, Africans are still landed in the bayous and lagoons."

Gene clapped his hands with excitement. "There's a troop of Sengalese," he exclaimed. "So black but such kind eyes. See those Foulahs! We call them 'poulards', fat chickens. They're like sable cherubs." He erupted with a childish giggle, but Casey scowled.

"What is the reason for all this?" he asked. "Are they on display?"

"You'll see."

Hundreds of blacks strolled around the square in the dying sunlight of the evening. There were slaves who wore ragged pantaloons and cotton shirts while their women were dressed in petticoats, some sporting a gaily-colored Madras handkerchief twisted into a turban. They mingled with free blacks and mulattoes and sauntered with an affected arrogance.

It struck Gene how similar some of them were to Casey, obviously dressed in cast-off clothing obtained from white patrons. He squirmed in embarrassment and hoped that Casey hadn't noticed.

"Do you know those people?" Casey's question alarmed Gene. He looked quickly over his shoulder at two white men who were standing under a balcony and watching them with obvious interest. One of the men spat eloquently onto the flagstones.

"They've been staring at us for several minutes," said Casey.

"Take no notice, Casey. I don't know them at all. Ugly customers, aren't they?" He tried to sound light-hearted. "Shall we move on?"

He led Casey around the square, glancing back to see if the men followed them. If they did, they were soon swallowed up by the crowds of blacks thronging the square. Gradually, everyone converged into the center, gathering around a crescent of musicians squatting cross-legged on the ground. A drummer, astride his instrument and riding it like a horse, slapped the end of it with a wild flamboyance. It was a signal.

A negro with a bare chest and rippling muscles, stepped into the circle formed by the crowd and raised his head. A song rolled out from the depths of his throat, its sounds steeped in the lore of the Congo. The shrill treble of a female responded, and the drumming rose to a frenzied beat.

A sinewy fellow with a belt of bells leaped into the air, followed by a sensuous Congo girl. They began to dance and were joined by another couple ecstatic in the fury of the music.

Gene tapped his foot to the music but Casey strode away angrily through the crowd. Gene ran after him.

"Don't you like it? I thought you'd like it!" He caught Casey's arm. "What's wrong?"

"Did you bring me to New Orleans to show me Africa?" Casey's face was twisted with disgust. "I want no more of slavery! Take me to a tavern!"

"We can drink absinthe at home. We don't need to go to a tavern."

Casey stopped so suddenly that Gene collided with him. He seized Gene by the lapels of his coat. "Why can't I go to a tavern?" he demanded.

"You can, you can. But let's not go tonight. Of course, there are places where quadroons go, but I can't actually take you there." Gene sighed. "I'm sorry, Casey. It's a bit difficult, isn't it. You must wait until you are introduced properly. Mother likes you. She'll present you to white people who can advance you in society. When you have their backing, you can go anywhere."

"So now I'm just a quadroon?"

"Yes."

"Then I might as well be a slave!"

"Now, Casey, don't sound so glum. Tomorrow, we'll start. You'll meet people. I'll paint you in oils. You'll pose in the courtyard with the sun dancing on your skin, and mother's friends will watch. You'll be a god in bronze and they'll worship at your feet!"

Gene was reassured by Casey's silence which he took for acquiescence. He chattered brightly to him and Casey seemed to be in better humor by the time they reached the Rue Toulouse.

Madame Cable had retired. Casey declined a drink of tafia saying he wanted to sleep. Gene saw him to his chamber and bid him good night. His luggage had arrived from the ship and he wanted to unpack it. There were so many paintings to look at but the best of them all were the ones he had done of Casey, his quadroon prince.

Gene's excitement at the quality of his own paintings was disturbed by the snap of a door shutting. He opened the French windows and stepped out on to the balcony in time to see Casey disappearing around the corner into the Rue Bourbon.

Two men emerged from the shadows opposite the house and hurried after him.

An instinct similar to that which leads a lost cat to its home guided Casey. He walked along the Rue Royale and turned right. He smelled the river and headed for it. He found the tavern in a narrow lane close to the levee. He knew it was the right one before he even pushed open the door. It smelled right.

The crush of people, the heat and the stench, the smoke hanging over the drinkers, the guffaws and curses of the men and the shrieks of the whores made him feel at home. He stepped inside with relief.

The bar was lit by a dim lantern throwing shadows over the tars sitting with their wenches. Casey sat on a bench to soak up the atmosphere. At last he was free of the cloying liberalism of Gene Cable and his mother. He felt at home in the midst of the drunken sailors and sweaty whores.

A girl's hand began to caress the back of his neck. She spoke to him in French. He crinkled his eyes in a smile of pleasure. The low neckline of her dress exposed the cleavage of a fine bosom and a sallow skin. Her hair was straight, black, and newly combed.

He didn't understand her question and replied in the patois

of Dominica. The girl shook her head so he said in English, "I don't want a whore, but if you want to talk, I'd enjoy your company."

The girl smiled. "I asked what are you doing in here?"

A negro set a bottle of whiskey on the table in front of him and moved away. The drinkers, Casey saw as his eyes became accustomed to the dark, were all white.

"To relax, what else?"

She was a mulatto, like him. He wondered if he was transgressing any law by being in the bar. He was dressed in Gene's clothes and the light was so dim, perhaps only the girl noticed him as an interloper. She poured a whiskey for him and took one herself.

"You take a risk."

"I'm a stranger. Arrived this morning." He accepted the glass but did not drink.

The girl nodded thoughtfully. "I'll say you are my brother. You have money?"

"Yes." He had some bitts but he had hidden his pouch of gold under the mattress in his room at Gene's house.

"Then there is no problem."

He sensed the tension that had been within him for weeks, beginning to leave as he spoke to the girl. He had missed the company of females, he realized. He was soon telling her about Lucy and his regret and confusion at having left her.

"It was for the best," the girl said, stroking his hand. "Better to leave her then than later, when her pain would be more."

He sipped at the whiskey slowly, warming to the girl's friendliness. "I'd like to go back for Lucy one day," he said. "When I've established myself here. A new life . . ."

"No," the girl shook her head sadly. "That will not be wise. Keep the memory. In a few years she will not be as you remember her now. You must live only for the present."

He put his arm around the girl's shoulders and she snuggled close to him. "If I don't plan to go back, what ambition will I have?"

"Ambition!" The girl mocked him with a kind of tenderness, even pity. "That's not for us. That's a white folk's dream. We're not white. We are playthings for the whites." She put her hand on his leg.

"We were born out of darkness and that is where we have to remain. In the dark."

"You're mistaken, I'm sure."

"No," she said with a sigh. "It is you who are mistaken with your talk of ambition. You must know your place in Nuorleans. I was mistress to a white gentleman. I lived in his house but I couldn't go anywhere with him. He kept me hidden away in the dark. I couldn't stand it, so I am here." She shrugged her shoulders and squeezed his thigh.

"I'm sorry."

"You will be if you have ambition. We are quadroons. The whites despise us, even when they seem to love us. We are a blot on their conscience." She looked at him sadly.

"You will become paramour to a white lady. She will give you money and her body, even somewhere to live and perhaps a carriage. But nothing else. You may not squire her in public. When you want to dance, you must go to the quadroon balls."

The girl smiled dreamily. "How I love our quadroon balls. They are so elegant and romantic! The most handsome men in the world! There is no finer combination in britches than a black man's physique topped with a white man's features. Like you."

He shifted uncomfortably. "I'll not be a paid paramour to anyone!" he said a little too loudly.

"Shh!" she said. "You are young, you'll learn. Whites have no respect for us. We are blacks to them, and blacks are slaves, animals. Not people."

The girl's bitterness shocked him. "Why don't you leave here. You're free. You shouldn't let your mind be poisoned this way."

The girl looked at him suspiciously. "Everywhere else is worse," she said.

The negro steward brought a glass on a silver tray and proffered it to Casey.

"What's this?" he asked.

"L'absint'." The negro's eyes darted sideways and Casey

glanced in the direction he indicated. In the gloom a man raised his glass, encouraging him to drink. Casey shook his head.

"No. Tell the gentleman I'm not drinking any more."

"You must take it!" the girl whispered anxiously. "He'll be insulted if you refuse. There could be trouble."

"I don't want it."

"Please," she said. "For me. I'll be in trouble too."

"All right." He took the glass. "Who is he?"

"I don't know him. He probably fancies you. We are only sex to them."

"I won't drink it!"

"You must; it's nothing. You'll please him."

He glanced at the man and raised the glass to his lips. "It's strong," he said in surprise. He placed the glass back on the table.

The man was talking to the steward. Casey saw some money slipped into the negro's hand.

"Don't look at him," the girl said. "He'll think you're interested."

"I'm not!"

The girl touched his hand. "Would you like me to show you the city? In the morning? I'll take you where the quadroons live. You will see plenty of beautiful girls there."

He chuckled. "The formidable Madame Cable wants to launch me on white society. I'd prefer to be with you."

"Good, we'll meet at –"

"Drink up, feller!"

Casey jerked forward as someone slapped him on his back. He withdrew his hand from the girl's and swung around. A white man with his feet planted firmly apart and his arms akimbo stared down at him. His jowls were dark with stubble and he wore a gold ring in the lobe of his left ear. His clothes were drab and his boots dusty.

Casey looked in vain for a sign of friendliness in his stern face.

"Don't yer like the drink I bought?"

"Yes, yes," said Casey. He picked up the glass and swallowed the contents with a grimace.

"That's right, feller. Have another."

Casey's head spun with the unusual taste, much stronger than Roxborough rum. He avoided the man's eyes. "No, thank you. I have to be going."

"Sure. When yer've had another drink." The man's voice hung over his head like a threat.

Casey glanced at the girl for help. She was inspecting the ruffles at her bosom. The steward loomed in front of him with a single glass on his tray.

"Take it," the man ordered.

He wondered what would be the consequences if he declined. The man was blocking a speedy escape for the door.

"Drink!" The man lowered his voice to a hiss that contained more menace than an angry shout. "Surely yer don't refuse a white man's hospitality."

"No, no," said Casey quickly. "I'll be happy to drink." He took the glass. "But not alone. Have one, too, sir. At my expense."

The man's eyes swelled and his chest puffed out like a bull frog's.

"Forgive him, sir," the girl said hastily. "My brother is new here. He doesn't know our customs."

"Drink!" The man's hand resembled a pistol as he pointed at the glass with his forefinger, his thumb upright.

Casey wanted to dash the absinthe in the man's eyes, kick his balls and run for the door. He didn't because of the girl.

"Your health, sir," he said, throwing back his head and pouring the contents of the glass down his throat. The raw liquor burnt his mouth and tore a course down his gullet. His eyes watered.

"That's a strong screw," he blurted out, feeling reckless.

"Aye!" The man's face assumed a grim smile of satisfaction. He seemed to be waiting for something.

"Won't you sit down?" It was foolish for him to be cowered by the man, Casey thought. Be hospitable. He's just a lonely white man who wants to talk.

The man scowled and passed his hand through his straggly locks.

"No offence!" Casey said, feeling his head loll forward unexpectedly. He straightened up and focused on the girl. She turned away in alarm, patting her bosom.

His head fell forward again. He felt whoozy. Can't take another, he thought, struggling to raise his head. His sight seemed to be going. Where was the girl? He lifted his head slowly, it took a lot of effort, and saw her rising to her feet.

"It's . . ." he said, trying to remember what he had in mind. The man's face loomed before his eyes. He remembered where he had seen him before. In Congo Square, watching him.

He swayed forward, checked himself, and swayed back.

"What's wrong, feller?" The man's voice echoed in his ears. A sudden thump on his shoulders sent him hurtling into space. He was falling a long way.

He put out his hands to save himself but they crumpled beneath him. His head struck the table with a thud.

"The buck's passed out," said the man. "Would yer believe it! So much lip but no head for liquor." The man put his hands under Casey's arms and pulled him backward off the bench.

"What are you doing?" asked the girl.

The man sneered. "Taking him where he belongs, of course."

He dragged Casey through the crowd of drinkers. Some of them turned and laughed. "Throw him in the gutter," said one.

"Yeller bellies pretending to be white," said another. "Hates them!"

At the entrance to the tavern, a second man held open the door. He chuckled.

"Never fails," he said. The two men lifted Casey into the carriage that was waiting for them, pushed him to the floor and jumped in.

The carriage moved off quickly toward the levee.

26

It was dark. His head ached and waves of nausea flooded through him. He was lying on his side on a wooden floor which rolled and swayed. It was stuffy, hot, and he seemed to be in a crowd; someone was pressing against his back and another body was in front of him.

Casey lay recovering his wits and trying to distinguish reality from the sickening pain in his head and guts. He farted and a mess of feces seeped between his buttocks, the stench adding to the foul odor surrounding him. He moved in shame and discovered that he was pinioned by his ankles to the floor.

He was appalled. He shifted slightly, twisting his moist body away from the person behind him. His hardness on awakening softened as the shock of his state swept through him. He was naked, his ankles were chaffed by the chains which bound them, and he didn't know where he was.

The constant motion of the floor suggested a ship. His condition implied a jail. He dredged his mind but could only recall the tavern, the drinks, and the stranger. He sighed with relief when he remembered that he had hidden his gold under the mattress at Gene's house. At least that was safe. He would get it as soon as he was released.

Naturally, he assumed his detention was temporary. Perhaps, he thought, when he'd drunk that absinthe, which must have been drugged, he'd caused a fracas and been arrested. Then why was he naked, in chains, with a man behind him and one in front and in a ship on a choppy sea? He decided to lie still and give his crapulence a chance to subside.

A hand wormed up to his crotch and stroked him. There were sighs and fidgeting around him. He flung the hand away and shouted, "Stop that!"

"Come, nigger," a gruff voice breathed in his ear. "I's hot." The man's hardness was thrust between his legs.

He bucked away in disgust but only succeeded in ramming himself into the willing flesh of the fellow in front of him.

"By the devil!" he shouted, twisting on to his back. The chains rattled and his unexpected movement caused a ripple of disturbance among the others in the hold.

"Yo's an uppity nigger, fuh sure."

"Who's a nigger?" Casey was dizzy with remorse.

"We's all nigger men!" A man's hand fell on his chest and massaged him roughly. "Yo' ain't a woman!" There was a guffaw in the darkness and a voice answered from his other side.

"His ass is tighter than a conny, too."

"Stay off!" Casey slapped away the man's hand and tried to sit up. His head cracked against a beam and he yelled in pain.

"Cudjo broke his maid!" a voice said with a grim chuckle.

He fell back and clutched his head, fighting the desire to cry out in protest. He was alone and confused. The hand slipped on to his chest again. He tensed.

"Take it easy, boy," the gruff voice said and the man patted him lightly.. "Yo's gwine get real blows soon enough."

"Where am I?" he demanded. "Why am I in chains?"

"Yo's 'quisitive. Buckree don't like that."

"Buckree?" Casey frowned. That was slave talk. Buckra they called the white master in Dominica. "I'm not a slave," he said, feeling uneasy.

The man patted him again. "No, nigger, none of we's slaves."

He sighed with relief.

"We's all free but buckree got we just the same."

"What the hell do you mean?"

The man sat up and Casey saw the outline of his woolly hair and pudgy face in the darkness. "Yo' speak like a buckree, nigger."

"That's right." Casey swallowed, remembering Lucy and Layou. "I'm from down islands. I'm really the Bondmaster of Roxborough."

"And ah am Cudjo de Prince of Bondage!" The negro roared with mocking laughter. Casey clenched his fists to keep back his frustration.

"It's true!" he shouted.

"We's all sumpin else," said another voice. "I's a carpenter. Born free an' workin' fuh hire in Saratoga."

"Then what are we doing here?" he asked. "I think I was drugged last night. I don't remember anything."

"I hear de buckree man say we's gwine Mobile."

"Mobile!" Casey stared wildly around him in the direction of the voices which came from the dark. "I don't want to go to Mobile. I'm staying in New Orleans."

"Not now buckree's got yo', yo' ain't." The mocking laughter was taken up by the other prisoners.

"Yo' shure was drunk when dey throw yo' in here last night. Yo' puts yo' arm 'round me and calls me Juicy."

"Yo' too bozal to be Juicy," another voice shouted amidst the laughter.

"I's no Afycan bozal. I's creole."

"Den why yo' only sell fuh nine hundred? I's a t'ousand dollar nigger."

Casey listened with dread to the banter. "I'm not a negro," he said. "I shouldn't be here."

There was a sudden hush.

"Yo's not a nigger?" Cudjo asked softly.

"No."

"Then yo's white?"

"Yes, I –" He felt Cudjo's hand on his hair, tugging at his locks. The hand rubbed down his face, pressed against his nose and fingers squeezed his lips. The hand fell to his chest, rubbed the hard muscles of his stomach then seized his penis.

Casey tried to move away but the hand continued down, feeling down his legs, squeezing his thighs and calf muscles. Then Cudjo's face loomed in the darkness and sniffed him.

"Yo's spunky and ranky like a nigger," Cudjo pronounced.

"My mother's white."

Another hush greeted Casey's statement. It gave way to muttering as the implications of that relationship struck the others.

"Yo' sire? Was he white too?"

"Half-white."

"Ah!" The men in the hold relaxed at Casey's reply. They seemed satisfied that he was, in fact, one of them.

"Makes no matter about yo' mam," Cudjo said. "If yo's black, yo's black."

"S'right," said another voice. "Black stronger'n white."

"Not when white have de bullwhip in his hand!" Cudjo laughed wryly.

Unexpectedly, a shaft of sunlight seared into the brightness of the hold, killing their mirth and making them blink.

Casey glanced around quickly. There were six of them squashed and bound together. Cudjo, on his left, was blue-black and stocky and the others ranged in shades from black to copper. There was no one as light as him.

A shape blocked the sun and filled the hatchway. "Shut up and get up here!" The man's voice was mean and cold. He thrust a key down.

They eased themselves carefully into sitting positions and the copper-colored negro took the key and unlocked the rod that held their chains to the floor. Casey wriggled his chain off the rod and followed the others up through the hatch to the deck.

He screwed up his eyes to accustom them to the sun. He saw the shore, a low green shadow, on his left. From the sun, he assumed it was early morning. They were sailing east on a brig, its deck cluttered with cargo; standing close to them were two men. They both had pistols stuck in their belts and whips in their hands.

Casey opened his mouth to speak but the man who had called them on deck handed the coppery negro a pail on a long rope. The negro dropped the bucket over the side, filled it with seawater, then, to Casey's shock, threw it over him. This process was repeated until the six captives were standing dripping wet on the deck.

Casey studied the two white men. One was thin with a face as lean and vicious as a cutlass. He was the one giving the orders in a high pitched, stern voice. His partner was taller and uglier, with a gormless expression that tagged him as a natural bully.

Casey spoke with deference. "Excuse me, sir. There seems to have been a mistake. I shouldn't be here." He waved his hand at the negroes shackled to him. "I'm a free man, a stranger to New Orleans. I arrived from the Caribbean yes–"

The slash of the whip applied with deadly accuracy struck his mouth and nose. His lips stung and his eyes began to water. He opened his mouth to protest and saw the bully raise the whip to strike him again.

"Stop!" The white man with the shrill voice squeaked and gestured to his companion to lower the whip. Casey licked his sore lip gratefully.

"We don't want to scar him."

The bully scowled. "Very well, Mr Steed," he said, eyeing Casey malevolently.

"I've told you before to place the blows so the skin isn't broken." Mr Steed turned back to Casey and said sternly, "You are my slave! I bought you in New Orleans."

"That cannot be, sir. I'm no man's slave. I'm a free mulatto from Dominica. Mr Gene Cable and his mother Madame Cable of Toulouse Street will vouch for me."

"You . . . are . . . my . . . slave!" Mr Steed said the words slowly, prodding Casey's chest with his fingers in time to each syllable.

He slapped the man's hand away. "Release me at once. This is an outrage!"

Mr Steed stepped back, his narrow face livid with rage.

"Yo's crazy, nigger," Cudjo hissed in Casey's ear. "He gwine lash yo' proper now."

Casey wasn't ready for the blow that crashed into the back of his head. He staggered forward and found himself being thrown over the hatch cover, face down. His companions in chains were forced to lie down on the deck beside him. His bare backside was pointing skyward. He twisted his head and saw the bully standing above him with an oar.

"I'm a free –" he shouted before a blow from the oar on his buttocks drove the air from his lungs. The man raised the oar and it smashed down on to him again. He winced.

"Do you still say you're a free man?" Steed pushed his nose against Casey's face and whined. "You made the mistake, not I."

"I'm free!" Casey said. The oar banged down again, beating him to the boards.

"Tell him yo's a slave," pleaded Cudjo.

He shook his head and the oar struck him a blow that almost drove him unconscious.

"Free," he gasped, his body shuddering with shock. The paddle hammered him until his buttocks were inflamed and burning.

"He be a slave, master," Cudjo cried out. "Same as we."

"Free . . ." whispered Casey.

Steed waved for the beating to stop. He inspected Casey's buttocks and clicked his tongue irritably. "He can't take no more, mustn't cut his skin," he said. He walked to the other side of the hatch and kneeled down to face Casey.

"Damn you, boy." He slapped him across his ear, giving way to his own anger. "You're a slave!"

"Free!" Casey glared defiance. Steed chopped him with his hand across his other cheek.

"Oh, we'll break you, boy. No mistake."

"Let me wallop him with the whip, Mr Steed. I can lash so it don't slice."

"Stay off him, Skerrit." Steed's lip curled cruelly. "He'll break some time," he said. "Sluice him down." He stood back while Skerrit thew a bucket of seawater over Casey. Its impact on his sore buttocks stung him as much as the paddle blows.

"You're damned lucky, boy. I can't beat sense into you the way I should because it will lower your price. Cost me two thousand, you did. Such a fancy! And a monster dangler on you, too." Steed shook his head.

"I aim to double my money on you, boy," he said. "You'll break, you'll break."

Skerrit was put to guard the six of them while Steed went

to his breakfast. The five negroes were each given a drink of water by one of the crew but none was passed to Casey. Cudjo squeezed his hand and tried to shield him from the sun.

Casey accepted his suffering, the pain and hunger and thirst, as his punishment for abandoning Lucy. As soon as he was free, he vowed, he would return to her. Somehow.

The negroes spoke softly amongst themselves during the long hours they were on deck. Cudjo and Loftus, the copper-skinned negro, tried to encourage him. They were all free, they told him, but they viewed their capture with fatalism.

"Ah never bin a slave," said Loftus, "but mah mammy was de slave 'cubine of she owner. Ma daddy was be white. He done free mah mammy when he die an' ah raise free."

"But now you've been kidnapped. You don't want to be a slave when you're free!"

Loftus stared at Casey and shrugged his shoulders.

"Yo's lucky," said Cudjo to calm him down. "De mastah say yo's fancy. Dat mean yo's gwine be house nigger."

"Or breedin' buck to mount de wenches!" said Loftus, rolling his eyes with excitement.

"But we're free!" Casey protested.

"We knows dat." Cudjo was losing his patience. "Yo's muh foolish dan buckree if yo' don' keep yuh mout' shut on dat."

"I can't keep quiet. I, all of us, we shouldn't be here at all."

"Sez yo'. I done see Mas Steed buy yo' on de wharf."

"I was drugged. In my drink."

"Ah tell yo'," said Loftus. "No one gwine believe yo' 'less yo' got white folks speak fuh yo'."

Casey bit his lip, thinking. "I'll never say I'm a slave," he said angrily.

"Yo' can say it," said Loftus grinning. "But yo' don' have to believe it."

The next two days were a blur of pain and sickness for Casey. His backside swelled and purpled with bruises. It was agony when he shuffled along the deck for exercise with the other captives or rolled on the hard boards of the hold at night. His bowels were sodden with diarrhea from the putrid water and foul food he was given to eat. Strangely, there was no new confrontation with Steed, and he regarded that as a victory. He resolved to swallow his pride and remain quiet and cooperative until the first opportunity came to escape.

During the long hours he was locked in the hold, while the others snored without the sensitivity to their cares such as troubled him, Casey realized escape would not be easy. He was now regarded as a slave even if he wasn't one. If he escaped, he became a runaway and because he was a stranger and easy to recognize, he'd be caught very quickly.

Slaves, he learned, were at a premium. Cotton, as the Southerners never ceased to tell themselves, was King. The more slaves a planter had, the more cotton he grew and the richer he became. And the more cotton he grew, the more slaves he needed. So great was the demand, and so lax the laws, that it was possible, and very profitable, for speculators such as Steed to acquire captured free blacks and, having made them tractable, to sell them to unquestioning planters.

On the third day, the ship docked and the six captives were brought on deck and told to put on breech cloths. Closely watched by Skerrit with his whip, they were trooped off the brig onto the wharf at Mobile. Casey shuffled in pain along the flagstones to a slave pen. The chain was removed from his ankles and he was locked in a cage with Cudjo and Loftus.

Steed came to gaze on them. He seemed to be in a quandry. "I shouldn't have bought you!" he muttered as he peered through the bars at Casey. "I knew you were too good to be true."

"Then let me buy myself," Casey said softly. "Send to Mr Cable in New Orleans and you'll get what you paid for me."

"Hah! I need double that," Steed whined. "Expenses!" His hands trembled. "I'll get it. Your ass is nearly healed. Damn Skerrit for causing this delay. Damn you!"

Casey stared at him coldly. "You know I'm not a slave. What kind of man are you to keep me here? Let me go!"

Steed flushed, spun on his heel, and hurried away.

That night, just as he had fallen asleep, Casey was woken

up by a blow on his head. Two men, whose faces he couldn't see in the darkness, seized him and hustled him out of the cage. Loftus and Cudjo murmured farewell. He was dragged, powerless to resist, across the sand of the auction ring to a building with bars on its windows like a calaboose.

The door was opened and he was thrust inside. A white man sat at a desk and a woman in a bonnet and cloak with her face hidden in shadow, sat opposite him.

"Good evening, ma'm," Casey said, struggling to stand up. He was cuffed across his ear by one of the men behind him. He turned but Steed emerged from the dark corner of the room.

"He's the finest colt you'll ever see," Steed said.

The woman glanced at him briefly and waved her hand in a gesture he didn't understand.

"Britches," said Steed impatiently. "Drop 'em!"

"Why? I'm not a sl –"

A blow to his face shut him up while one of the guards loosened his breech cloth. The garment dropped to the floor.

The woman raised a lorgnette and peered at him carefully. The guards turned him around at her instructions. She made no comment about his bruised buttocks. She lowered her glasses and frowned.

"He's not circumcized," she said.

"Er, no, Mrs Purdy." Steed stared accusingly at him. "That's his natural state," he said. "Untouched, unbroken. The finest buck . . ."

"Five thousand is too much," the woman said. "Three thousand."

"But Mrs Purdy . . ."

The woman rose from her chair without another glance at him.

"I'll take it," Steed shouted.

"Put him in the wagon with the others," she said. "I leave at dawn. I'll have to cut him when I get to Bullers Park." She swept out.

27

Casey was forced into a coffle with other newly-purchased slaves for the treck from Mobile, Alabama, to Bullers Park in Paxton County, Georgia. He planned to approach his new owner so he could explain his situation, gain her sympathy and win his release. However, it was three weeks before he reached Bullers Park and during that period he saw Mrs Purdy only when she rode by the coffle in her carriage. She never stopped so he had no chance to speak to her.

He found traveling with the slaves was loathsome and degrading but it fitted his mood. He had left Dominica and Lucy on a whim so he regarded the hardship and his bad luck as penance for his rashness. Having reconciled himself to his extraordinary circumstances, his good nature bubbled to the surface. It saved him.

His backside healed and toughened and he walked without pain. It was irksome to be chained by his ankles to the slaves but he rallied them and encouraged them to make light of their hardship. There were four of them, all strong, handsome youths, and they were soon a tolerably happy gang moving along at a fine pace.

The wagon, with a slave as wagoner and his wife as cook, led the way. The gang came next, followed by a dour white man, so taciturn that whole days passed without him uttering a word. He rode aloof on a roan horse, a shotgun at his side, pistols in his belt and a cowhide whip dangling from his waist. His very brooding added to his menace and the slaves, being intelligent and lively youths, chose not to rouse his wrath.

The coffle traveled about thirty miles each day. The

weather was good and Casey adapted to the routine. At night, the small party camped in the woods by the highway which was often little more than a trail through vast tracts of uncleared land. The wagoner and his wife slept in the cart while the white man, whose only name was Venables, slept on the ground wrapped in a blanket. Venables took turns with the driver and his wife to keep watch, although he never gave them a weapon. Mrs Purdy and her escorts put up at planters' houses in the neighborhood.

Casey began to organize the slaves on their halts. He made some collect dry sticks for a fire, others fetched water from the nearby creeks and in a short time Mimmey, the wagoner's wife, would be baking johnny cakes made from corn. Some evenings, boiled black-eyed peas were added to their diet.

The slaves were allowed to speak among themselves yet they were always conscious of Venables watching them and listening silently. When they had supped and cleaned up, Casey got the slaves to rake leaves into heaps under the trees for a mattress. They slept together, covered by gunny sacks and old clothes from the wagon.

At day break, if there was a creek nearby, Casey led his fettered companions to bathe. Venables, who never bathed nor removed his clothes during the entire three weeks march, kept guard. The journey continued until noon when they were allowed fifteen minutes to rest and eat the johnny cakes prepared the night before.

Casey tried to glean from Pompey, the wagoner, some information about Bullers Park and Mrs Purdy. Although he seemed prepared to speak, the presence of Venables inhibited him.

Casey did learn that Paxton County was north of Milledgeville, the capital of the State of Georgia. It was cotton country. To every question Casey asked about the plantation they were heading for, Pompey only replied, "You'll see." When the questioning went on too long, Venables cleared his throat with a growl and Pompey fell silent.

Casey wondered why Pompey and the slaves in the coffle were afraid of Venables. Apart from one, Tamba, who came from Africa as a child, they had all been born into slavery. So, by training, they were conditioned to fear whites. They were tractable slaves; conformist, docile and used to hard work. Only Tamba showed a spark of rebelliousness. He and Casey whispered together at night, a bond of friendship growing between them.

Casey's exuberance and leadership helped the journey pass quickly. Even Venables relaxed his grim watchfulness and showed trust in Casey by letting him take the slaves to the creek to bathe by themselves. After two weeks, he sensed from Venables' lighter attitude and Mimmey's whispered remarks, that they were getting close to their destination.

For days, the coffle plodded through land that was flat and dry. The climate became cooler and Casey shivered in his thin pantaloons and shirt. Tamba told him it was the season for seeding the cotton and Casey saw mules drawing plows along the ridges of the furrowed fields on either side of the trail. A boy or girl followed behind each plow with a bag of seed. The sower was followed by another plow which covered the seed.

The flat land, scarred for seeding, stretched for miles, broken only by pinetree windbreaks and, occasionally, a cluster of slave cabins and a plantation house. For Casey, used to the warmth and lushness of the Caribbean sugar plantation, it was depressing terrain.

"We on Bullers Park land!" announced Pompey late one afternoon, showing an enthusiasm that Venables didn't bother to check.

Casey gazed around. Something was wrong. He glanced behind at the manicured cotton land they had come through, and realized what. The fields that comprised Bullers Park were thick with grass and weeds, clumps of undergrowth surrounded lush woods and flowers were peeping through the unkempt hedgerows. Whatever it was, Bullers Park was not a cotton plantation.

Casey was driven with the slaves into a small cabin. It had an earth floor, the sides were of wattle and daub, and the roof was thatched. There was no window. For furniture, there were three planks suspended on a frame of sticks against the shingle that formed the wall. Loose straw was scattered on it for a mattress. This was where all five were expected to sleep.

They were released from their chains and locked in the cabin. They helped each other massage their chaffed ankles. A meal of black-eyed peas with bacon rind and johnny cakes, was served to them with some hard cider to wash it down. Casey's spirits rose after the meal and as he fell asleep that night, squeezed between Tamba and another slave, he resolved to demand an interview with Mrs Purdy the next day.

"Look lively now!" A white man threw open the door to the cabin, snapping his whip against the planks of the bed. It was day break, overcast and chilly. They hurried out. In the distance, behind a clump of oak trees and evergreen shrubs, was the house where Mrs Purdy lived. Casey craned his neck to watch it.

"Move!" The white man switched at Casey's thighs with the tongue of his whip. It took him by surprise and he broke into a run with Tamba by his side. They followed Venables who was riding ahead, leading them in the direction of the house. The overseer and another white man brought up the rear.

"Fine beauties!" Casey heard the overseer say to his companion. "Mrs Purdy can pick 'em."

"She can afford 'em, that's why. The yeller one cost . . ."

The man's words were lost as Casey and Tamba outran the others, chasing after Venables galloping ahead of them. It was good to run again, to feel almost free.

"Let's keep running, Tamba," he said. "Over the hills to freedom."

"I don't want a dog to bite ma balls off," the African said.

Casey grinned. "We could get away if we want to."

"An' go where? Back to Afyca?"

They followed Venables along a path with flowering shrubs to a flagstone courtyard beside the house. Casey was disappointed. He expected Mrs Purdy to live in a fine Southern mansion. The gardens surrounding it were prettily laid out but the building itself was a common boxed house painted white, with a long gallery across the front. It had a loft and four rooms.

"See dat place," said Tamba in awe. "De buckree lady is plenty rich."

"Maybe," said Casey with a sniff. "But my own house in Dominica is bigger than that."

"So's mine in 'Gola," said Tamba.

Venables reined in his horse and the five of them gathered around him. Casey was beginning to feel warm again. The overseer rode up and dismounted. He walked over and jabbed Casey in his stomach with his whip handle.

"Mrs Purdy gwine inspect you now," he said. "This whip tans clean but cleaves no mark. I gwine use it if I have to. You gwine do everything Mrs Purdy tells you, and don't speak to her 'less she asks you." He glared at Casey.

Tamba and the other slaves lowered their heads but he stared boldly back at the overseer. The man jabbed him in his waist again.

"Shuck off your pants now, all of you."

Casey hesitated, measuring the effectiveness of refusal. He decided to wait for Mrs Purdy. He stripped first and the overseer grunted his approval. When the five were standing naked in a line, the man signalled to Venables who rode up to the rear door of the house and knocked.

Mrs Purdy bustled out. She was a big woman in her late forties. Her dress was old fashioned, full across her broad hips with lace at her cuffs and high collar. Her hair was drawn up in a bun to which was pinned a cloth cap with a blue ribbon threaded through it. Her lorgnette hung on a silver chain across her wide bosom and she carried a cowhide whip dangling at her side where ladies usually wear their scissors.

She approached the five and stopped a few paces from them. With a speed surprising in a woman of her stature, she snatched up her whip and dashed it across Casey's ankles. "Dance!" she said, glaring at him.

The others jigged energetically but Casey stared at Mrs Purdy without moving. Behind him he heard Venables growl and the overseer cursing him. Mrs Purdy raised her lorgnette with her left hand and struck out with her right.

Casey was ready. He reached out and caught the lash of the cowhide in his fingers. It stung him but he closed his fist around the whip and pulled. It flew from Mrs Purdy's grasp and she dropped the lorgnette to her bosom in surprise.

He braced himself, anticipating the cut of the overseer's whip across his back. "Mrs Purdy," he shouted, quickly throwing her whip to the ground. "I'm not –."

His knees buckled under him and he crashed to the flagstones. A massive weight pressed on his buttocks and shoulders, pinioning him to the ground. He twisted his head and saw Venables sitting astride him. It was the first time he had seen Venables smile. His hand was raised to strike him.

"Let him speak," said Mrs Purdy, peering through her lorgnette again. Venables didn't move.

Casey took a deep breath. "Ma'am, I'm a free mulatto of substance. I was kidnapped in –"

"I know all that, boy!" Mrs Purdy smiled cruelly, showing the stumps of her decayed teeth. "Does that stop you dancing with the others?"

"I shouldn't be here. I'm not a slave!"

"Yes, you are. I've paid three thousand for your services." Her eyes glinted. "You won't find your life here unpleasant if you do as you're told. Now will you dance?" She accepted the whip handed back to her by the overseer and flicked it inches from his nose.

Venables climbed off his back and Casey got to his feet. He was bewildered. He glanced at the slaves but they turned away from him. Mrs Purdy's whip snapped at his ankles. He pranced.

Under Mrs Purdy's gaze, the five of them were directed to do various antics. They jumped, they ran around a great sycamore tree in the yard and they leaped over a broom stick held high by one of the white men.

Casey did as he was bid, too stunned to protest. He had been depending on Mrs Purdy to free him instantly he revealed who he was. She knew and yet she did nothing!

They came to rest, panting heavily after the exercise. Mrs Purdy passed along the line, followed closely by Venables.

She put her hand on the chest of each one of them, counting to herself. When she reached Casey, she lowered her left ear to his chest and listened carefully.

He took the scent of verbena and she reminded him of his mother. He wanted to speak but Venables' hand, vicelike, was gripping his shoulder in warning.

Mrs Purdy reached down and held his penis in her fist. He drew back sharply but Venables restrained him. She looked into his eyes and shook her head.

"I like my bucks clean," she said, fingering the rosette of skin at the end, "like the African." She indicated Tamba, "Done in the jungle, I suppose."

She toyed with his penis and inspite of himself, Casey was roused by her touch. Her eyes gleamed.

"I reckon I got a bargain," she said to Venables, withdrawing her hand and nodding at him.

Suddenly Casey was dragged backward. His legs were kicked from under him and he fell on his back on the flagstones.

"It's not my fault," he shouted, clutching his penis. "She shouldn't do that!"

"Sit on his chest," the overseer ordered Tamba.

The African hesitated then lowered himself on to Casey, straddling his chest so he couldn't move. Two slaves were put to hold his wrists to the ground, and the other two were positioned at his ankles.

Casey lay spreadeagled on the cold stones. He stared up at the gloomy sky and shivered in the sudden chill. Mrs Purdy moved into his line of sight. She dove into the pocket of her apron and withdrew a small box. She opened it and took a pinch of snuff which she stuffed in her nostrils with her finger and thumb.

Casey felt a rough hand grip his penis. He flinched but Tamba and the slaves held him firmly, according to their instructions. One of the white men passed a bunch of nettles to Venables. Mrs Purdy sneezed violently.

Venables squashed the nettles and rubbed them on to the tip of his penis, stinging him into numbness. All his feeling seemed to flow into his loins and he bucked at the mixture of pain and ecstasy. Venables sat on his thighs and another white man held his foot across his stomach. It was impossible to move. He whimpered with anger and frustration.

Mrs Purdy grasped her lorgnette and studied the operation with interest. Her mouth opened slightly and the end of her fat pink tongue protruded between her lips.

A knife snipped the numbness. Casey reared with pain. Venables cursed and Casey gritted his teeth and determined not to cry. Tamba's eyes held his own, trying to share his pain. The knife snicked again and the pressure was gone.

Venables got off his thighs, the two boys at his ankles released him and Tamba, at a curt command from the overseer, jumped off his chest.

Mrs Purdy took another sniff from her snuff box.

He raised his head slowly. Blood smothered his penis where he had been cut. The rosette and its sock of skin had been snipped back to reveal the bright pink head, glistening and bloody.

Venables dashed a pail of water over him and Mrs Purdy sneezed with satisfaction.

"Fine, Casey," she said, banging the whip against her thigh. "Rest now and in a couple of weeks you'll be fit to cover my daughter."

28

Jessica Purdy knew her own mind. She had buried two husbands and ran Bullers Park with more savvy than either of them had. People said she was mad but people always condemned someone with original ideas. She was not mad, the fortune she was making proved that.

"Hah!" Jessica turned her back on Venables whose mouth

was gaping open in astonishment. The bright-skinned buck with his cock bleeding didn't understand her either. He would!

She strolled to the house, leaving Marsden, the overseer, and the other white men to pen the bucks back in the barracoon. She was pleased with her purchases. It had been a long and expensive trip but good quality stock was getting hard to find. She needed the best to produce the prime slaves that fetched the top prices.

People had said she was mad twenty years before when she changed Bullers Park from growing cotton to raising slaves. Cotton was king, she reasoned, and a king needed slaves. So she decided to breed slaves and sell them to planters. She had made herself rich with her unique idea.

In the house, she settled herself at the bureau where she kept her stock books. She loved this part of the work, chosing which blood lines to cross to produce the perfect slave. With the importation of negroes from Africa frustrated by law, pure African bloodstock was a rarity. She was pleased she'd found one at last, as well as the quadroon fancy from the Caribbean.

She wrote their names and their prices in her book, ignoring the noise of a piano being pounded in the adjoining room. She had bartered two slaves for that piano, but it was worth it to keep Fleta amused. Her daughter had inherited a love of music, but not an ability to play, from her father, Thaddeus Purdy.

Jessica finished recording the purchases in her ledger and placed the quill pen in its holder. She smiled to herself. For all his obstinacies, Thaddeus would have approved of her new scheme.

Jessica had married Thaddeus when she was thirty-three and he was nineteen. She had Fleta by him before he fathered three mulattoes, a quadroon and a mustee in a year, and then expired of the venereal. This was a disappointment to her because she had married him to cover her female slaves and improve the stock.

Her husband's premature death had left her a widow again with a sickly and graceless child. She had done better by her first husband, Algernon Buller, who left her the Park and the few slaves that founded her fortune.

Fleta was now seventeen, a sighing virgin of no appeal to any eligible man. Jessica had a plan for her. It was not madness, whatever Venables might think. It was foresight.

Jessica Purdy rose with determination from her desk and strode through to her daughter's room.

Fleta was a rangy girl with a pallid complexion, a disconcerting squint and lack-luster hair flecked with dandruff. Her passion, when not murdering music, was for reading the romantic novelists of the period.

Jessica stood unnoticed by her daughter's piano. She reached for her snuff box, took a substantial pinch, and sneezed heartily. Fleta stopped thumping the piano keys and looked at her in surprise.

"Fleta, dear," said Jessica coldly. "You know I have only your interests at heart. Someday Bullers Park will be yours."

Fleta paled. "Mama!"

"Yes, it will." Jessica was comforted by her daughter's apparent concern that her life should be a long one.

"But I don't want Bullers Park!" Fleta's rogue eye flickered wildly and even after seventeen years of it, Jessica was tempted to turn her head to see what her daughter was watching.

"Of course you do! It's your sole asset," she said sternly.

"All those slaves! The park's full of them. I can't walk by the magnolias without tripping over naked niggerlings wriggling like worms in a nest. What would I do with them?" Fleta's face drained of what little color it possessed and she gasped for breath.

"For goodness sake, don't swoon, Fleta. You know what you'll do with them. You'll sell them for a profit."

"How will I care for them? All those wenches and . . ." The color returned to her cheeks. "Those rutting bucks!"

Jessica Purdy hitched up her bosom with satisfaction. She was right about her daughter and knew what she needed. "You will have a trusted slave to help you."

"A negro?" Fleta scratched her head in alarm and a shower of scurf landed on the lace of her high-corsaged dress.

Jessica picked up a copy of the Millidgeville newspaper from the table by the piano. "If you read what's here in the newspaper every week," she said, "you can see signs of what the future has in store for us."

Fleta's interest was aroused. "I didn't know you believed in the horoscopes, mama."

Jessica scowled and waved the newspaper. "Slavery abolished in the Caribbean! Isn't that shocking? How do you think our slaves will feel when they hear that?"

Fleta had the word on the tip of her tongue. "Jealous?" she said with a gasp.

"And damn restless. Someday, slaves will lose their respect for their owners and begin to make demands. You have to prepare for that."

"Me, mama?" Fleta's fingers toyed with the black notes on the keyboard.

"Yes, yes. You more than I. But your trusty negro will help you to protect your interests."

"But I don't have a trusty negro."

"Not yet." Jessica paused and gazed into Fleta's stationary eye, trying to ignore the antics of the other one. "Would you trust your own son?" she demanded.

Fleta fluttered. "Why, oh yes, well . . ."

"Exactly! What a perfect way of assuring the allegiance of our slaves if someone of our own flesh and blood, our own kin, is their leader. In other words, my grandson." Jessica gave up looking at Fleta and studied instead the boughs of the live oaks visible through the French windows.

Fleta glanced around the room anxiously. "Mama," she said in a soft voice. "You don't have a grandson."

"Your intelligence does you credit, Fleta. Imagine a grandson with your brains and the body of a black Hercules! A black who's one of us, whom we can trust."

Fleta giggled with embarrassment. "What if he has my body and slave brains?"

"Hah!" Jessica stood up, filling the room with her presence. "I've taken that into account. The buck I've selected for you has enough to compensate for your deficiencies in all departments."

There was silence, apart from the heavy tread of Jessica's feet as she strode around the room. "He's a fancy, a quadroon. That means your son will be a mustee. It's the perfect solution to preserve Bullers Park for the future."

"Mama!" Fleta's voice was small. "I'm not one of your breeding wenches. I don't want to lie with a fancy nigger."

Jessica stopped. "What nonsense, dear. It will do you good. Get me a grandson, Fleta, and I promise you . . ." She thought quickly. "A concert grand piano!"

"A new piano!" Fleta clapped her hands. "How lovely. I declare the one I have is quite out of tune. It makes my playing sound a trifle discordant at times."

"Yes, dear." Jessica sighed.

"Would you order it soon, mama. They take such a long time for delivery."

"So do babies. The buck's been circumcized. Give him a few days for the cut to heal."

"The cut?" Fleta seemed to have forgotten. "Oh!" Her hand clutched her throat. "Is he . . . is he very repulsive?"

"Nonsense, dear. He's quite attractive." Her eyes gleamed. "He's not only a handsome fancy, he's well hung too."

Bullers Park was run with the efficiency of a thriving cotton plantation inspite of its unconventional crop. Jessica Purdy believed in hiring the right man for a particular job and allowing him to do what he was paid to do without interference from her. She was astute in her choice of men and well served by them.

Marsden, a broad shouldered man in his fifties, was the overseer with responsibility for the general management of the plantation. The purpose of Bullers Park was to produce working animals and only a small part of the estate's four hundred acres was planted in cotton. This was to condition the slaves for field work and to occupy their time.

"An idle nigger," Marsden said, "is a wasted one." Like Jessica, he saw slaves as an investment of capital that must be exploited to get a good return. He was an educated man, not like the crackers and poor whites of the South who regarded slaves as inferior creatures to be abused.

Discipline was rigid at Bullers Park. Marsden understood that the key to a planter's control over his slaves was fear. "No amount of pistols and whips can keep a slave when he's lost respect for you," Marsden explained to his men.

"He must fear you. Be constant. Never utter a threat unless you can carry it out. Harry him. Intimidate him with your vigilance. And when you punish him, make sure that he and all the other slaves know why. Make him the example. But don't destroy him. The fields will do that."

Venables was Jessica Purdy's factotum. In the plantation hierarchy, he ranked under Marsden but the older man left him alone. Everyone did. There was in Venables a demon none of them understood.

The white men, isolated among hundreds of blacks, were a garrulous lot with a boisterous spirit of comraderie. Venables with his brusqueness and brooding silence unsettled them. Even Jessica was alarmed by the evil strength she sensed in him. It heightened his attraction for her.

For eight years, Venables had been her lover. He slept in an annex room attached to the house by a connecting door. When she summoned him, he came. His loving was hard and dispassionate and quite satisfactory. She asked no more and he gave no more.

It was into this well-knit organization that Jessica Purdy introduced Casey. She had sensed his uniqueness the moment she saw him in the auctioneer's office in Mobile. Venables' reports of Casey's behavior in the coffle during the long march from Mobile to Paxton County confirmed her intuition. He was ideal for her purpose, but she recognized the problems.

Southerners were traditionalists. Any violating of their conventions they took as a threat. There was only one race in the South: white. A man could be a red-necked, murderous cracker without a cent but, being white, he was tolerated. A negro was not, however, capable or intelligent. And a man with negro blood in him, even if only a slight proportion, was tainted for ever.

Putting Casey to cover her daughter, Jessica knew, would outrage people. It was worth the scandal. She believed a mustee with her own blood, raised in the mansion, was necessary for their survival. Jessica would train the boy. He could never own Bullers Park; it would be Fleta's. But the girl was weak and the mustee would be the strength she lacked.

Jessica, riding with Venables and Marsden to inspect the new purchases three weeks after Casey was circumcized, was aware of the fury she was about to unfetter.

"The bucks are ready," Marsden said when they approached the barracoon. He outlined the preparations to get them ready.

"Twenty days of hominy grits, hoe cake, hopping john with cowpeas and hog, now those bucks fitter'n a fiddle. I've exercised them, bathed them, oiled them. Bucks shootin' juice every night, they got so much." He chuckled happily.

"Real breeders, they are. Give you ten suckers apiece by Spring."

Jessica reined in her horse outside the barracoon. She had read that in Africa, the young males were separated from the females as part of their manhood training. They would understand.

"What about Casey?" she asked casually.

There was silence as Marsden dismounted and walked to the door. The old slave on guard shuffled and stopped nervously in his mistress' presence. "The yellow one?" Marsden hawked and spat grimly into the hard, red mud. "He's pining."

"You don't like him?" Jessica fumbled in her skirts for her snuff box.

"He doesn't belong here, Mrs Purdy."

"He seems like a breeder."

"Sure. But it's discontent he's breeding. Giving the niggers ideas. Working against me, Mrs Purdy. Working against you."

Jessica sneezed loudly. She looked from Marsden's sour face with its week-old stubble to Venables' impassive expression. "Very well. We must isolate him. He'll come up to the house."

Marsden shrugged. "You'll need to be careful. He'll skip

off if you bat an eyelid. He's slippery." He flung open the door.

"Out!" he shouted, holding his whip ready. Venables tensed and Jessica put her hand on the cowhide which dangled at her waist.

Three negroes trotted out, frisking like young colts, blinking in the sunlight and prancing restlessly. Tamba came out frowning. When he saw Jessica, he brightened and kicked up his heels the way Marsden had trained him. Casey slouched in the doorway.

Jessica blinked. In the three weeks since he arrived there was a change in him. She wondered what it was. He looked superbly fit; he bulged out of his pantaloons and shirt. Marsden's grooming had produced a sleek and formidable creature. But his eyes were dulled.

"Magnificent," she breathed, feeling a rush of interest stirring within her. Venables glowered.

"Dance, boy!" Marsden slashed irritably at Casey's ankles.

Casey shook his head. His sulky expression touched Jessica's heart. She edged her horse closer. Marsden's whip snicked the boy's ankles again.

"Is he sick, Marsden?" Jessica asked the question to divert the overseer's attention. He'd resent her interference if she told him not to lash Casey.

Marsden held the whip still and turned to Jessica. "Not that we know. He looks fit, as you can see."

"Why don't you ask me?"

Casey's voice, bold and arrogant, surprised Jessica. "Wait!" she said, raising her hand to halt Marsden's eagerness with his whip.

Marsden glanced at her with annoyance.

Jessica bit her lip at her impulsiveness. She could not afford to antagonize Marsden and Venables. She recovered herself and uncoiled the cowhide at her waist.

"You must learn, boy," she said, drawing back her arm and flexing her wrist so that the hide snaked around Casey's shoulders. "You must learn to speak only when you are spoken to." She lashed him again to mollify Marsden.

"Come with me, boy." She turned her horse hoping that

Casey would have the sense not to answer back in front of the overseer.

"Get the colts to their fillies, Marsden," she said. "Remember, ten apiece by Spring."

Marsden touched his forelock. Venables waited for Casey to trot along the trail after her then followed him closely.

Jessica smiled. Inspite of Casey's arrogance – or was it because of it? – she liked him. A grandson out of him would be a valuable asset indeed.

When they reached the house, she directed Venables to lock Casey in the privy. "Let him shake the shit out of himself," she said. It was important to have Venables on her side and she was pleased when he nodded in agreement.

Fleta was waiting for her when she entered the house. Her hair was dishevelled and she had been crying. "Mama! I've seen him," she said. "I can't practise."

"Why ever not?"

Jessica removed her bonnet and patted her bun. She stood before the hall mirror and wondered how she looked to Casey. She wore well. She was big-boned, not fat. Her skin lacked the sheen of youth but was not sagged and pitted like many women her age. Her nose was prominent and it was balanced by her chin. She was a woman who got what she wanted, and it showed.

"What?" She swung around to face Fleta.

"He makes me nervous, Mama. I don't know what to do."

"Nothing." Jessica glanced again in the mirror and sighed. She walked to the drawing room leaving Fleta open mouthed. "He'll do it all."

29

"What's that commotion?" Jessica roused herself. She had been dozing on the couch, dreams fooling her into feeling sentimental. The sense of pleasure was rudely shattered by the noise coming from the yard.

"Oh my lord!" she sighed. There was no one in the drawing room. She was at a loss for a moment wondering what it was. Ah, yes. The muffled voice she could hear from the privy reminded her. She pulled herself to a sitting position and shouted. A slave popped her head nervously around the door.

"Tell Venables to let the boy out and bring him to me."

"Yes, mistis." The slave bobbed hurriedly and disappeared.

Jessica snorted a heavy fingerful of snuff and braced herself. Her brain seemed to open wide and she felt mellow. She sputtered and wiped her nose just as the door burst open and a wild eyed Casey stood on the threshold. Venables was behind him.

"I will not be jailed like a criminal!" Casey said, gusting into the room with a force that caught Jessica off her guard. He seemed to sense that he had gained the advantage, for he changed his approach and bowed politely.

"You do yourself a disservice, Mrs Purdy," he said, "by treating me with a callousness surely quite alien to one so charming as yourself."

To Jessica, in her dreamy mood, the words were astounding. She sat back on the couch and stared. Venables coughed.

"Shut up!" she said, recovering her wits. She tried to

sound stern. "You do not seem to realize, boy, that you are a slave and must behave like one."

"Never!"

Venables stirred.

"It's no use beating him, Venables," Jessica said, thinking quickly. "The boy boasts he has a brain. I will convince him by logic." Venables' lips tightened in disapproval.

"Could you wait outside? He won't attack me, will you, Casey?"

"By the devil! I would if it would give me back my liberty."

"You see," she said to Venables. "He is quite sensible. Please go."

Venables scowled at Casey and walked out of the room without a word.

Jessica found that Casey standing in the center of her drawing room, tastefully furnished like a bedroom, was rather overwhelming. His overt masculinity dominated her.

"Sit down," she said, adding "please" involuntarily. It appeared to calm him.

"You may say your piece when you've listened to mine," she said, lowering her voice. "Mr Venables is in the corridor outside and he is a very violent man. He would snap off your neck at the slightest provocation."

"I'm not afraid to die."

"Oh, what a rash boy you are! If you're so stupid you might as well be thrashed."

He shrugged his shoulders and watched her warily.

"Your position, Casey, is that you are my slave."

"It's a lie."

"I have a bill of sale from Mr Steed."

"I was kidnapped and sold to him."

"Listen to me!" Jessica's eyes pleaded with him and she nodded at the door meaningfully. "I have a receipt for the three thousand you cost me."

"Let me reimburse you. Set me free and I'll find the varmits who tricked me. I'll have their hides."

"Casey!" She wagged her finger at him in exasperation. "Don't forget that you have no rights here. You are in the

South now, not the Caribbean. Your word is nothing against a white man's."

"What about Mr Cable's word. Let me write to him."

"Shhh!" She shook her head slowly, keeping her hand up in the air to quieten him. "Don't let Venables know you can write," she whispered. "He'll cut off your hand."

Her conspiratorial behavior at last communicated itself to Casey and he frowned instead of remonstrating. "Ah," said Jessica with a smile. "Now I see you understand that I'm not the one who'll stop you getting your liberty."

"Then why –?"

"Let me speak, Casey. I'm afraid your enforced stay with our Southern niggers has made you lose your good manners."

He pouted sulkily.

"That's better. I'm prepared to let you have your liberty in due course. I have a propostion."

"You must give me my freedom now."

"Impossible. Venables and Marsden wouldn't allow it. I could not allow it. I depend on their loyalty and earn it by my conduct. But here is a way . . ."

He was watching her but there was no expression in those eyes which had flashed so boldy when she first saw him.

"If you curb your insolence and behave yourself, and act intelligently, I shall keep you here in the house as my butler."

"If I am to be a slave, put me in the fields with the niggers!" He scowled.

"Hush, Casey. You want your liberty and I'm telling you how you shall have it. I bought you for a reason," she said. "I want my daughter Fleta to give me a mustee grandson. Cover her and get me a male sucker out of her, and I'll let you pay me four thousand, and freedom shall be yours." She paused and waited for his reaction. There was none.

"Of course, if you don't want to, then you can go to the fields with the niggers."

Casey was silent. She saw his chest muscles tensing and he clenched his fists. Behind his impassive eyes, a struggle was taking place in his mind. She wondered if beneath his hard exterior he was perhaps as young and naive as Fleta.

"You'd make me mount your daughter so she can have my child?" he asked, his voice flat.

Jessica laughed. "I'm a slave breeder."

"She's white."

"Oh dear, do you have our cracker morals? Does it make a difference?"

"I'll be lynched," he said, his face hardening.

"No, you won't. Fleta never goes anywhere and so no one will know. This is an investment, a business deal for me. When Fleta has the baby and you've paid me, you can have your liberty and leave."

Jessica drew eagerly on her snuff. Her own emotions were rioting against her commonsense. She was enchanted by Casey's ill-concealed, animal fury, his lean grace and passionate good looks. Fleta didn't deserve him.

"No!" He slapped his thigh. "I'll be damned first."

She sneezed in shock and her eyes watered. "Damn," she said amidst her spluttering. "See what you made me do."

The door clicked open and Venables glared at them both. Jessica waved him away. He withdrew, leaving the door ajar.

"It's your only chance," she murmured.

Casey was gazing behind her to the yard. He seemed not to have heard. His eyes lit up suddenly and he smiled.

"Your daughter," he said softly. "Is she pretty?"

Jessica hooted with laughter. "No, she's what nightmares are made of."

Casey stood up. "Very well, Mrs Purdy. I will serve you as you wish."

She was astonished. "Why have you changed your mind so quickly?"

"For my freedom."

"You accept?"

"Yessss!"

Jessica's flesh tingled. Casey's answer was as sibilant and menacing as a rattler's hiss before it strikes.

If Jessica had known why Casey changed his mind, she would have paid more attention to her misgivings.

It happened when Venables had entered the room. Casey

was ready to attack him, seize his gun and make a dash for it. He knew where the horses were stabled and reckoned he could ride away before Marsden and his men could catch him.

Instead, Casey's attention had been attracted by something happening at the window behind Mrs Purdy's back.

A girl stood there with her nose pressed to the glass, peering into the room. Casey saw her pale face with its squint and twisted mouth. He saw in her sad expression the loneliness and misery she suffered with her mother.

He smiled at her and she ran off.

If she was Mrs Purdy's daughter, he thought, he had found the ally he needed to help him escape. So he said, "Very well, I will serve you as you wish."

He slipped with ease into his duties as a butler. Mrs Purdy's household was one of women with the maids ruled by a diminutive black virago called Sack. Sack cooked, cleaned, polished and bullied the three girls who served under her. She adored Mrs Purdy, felt no sympathy for her daughter, distrusted Venables and resented Casey's intrusion.

"I bin serving Mistis Purdy since before de runt Fleta born," she told Casey. "We never had no butler before."

"I've never been a butler before." Casey beamed his most disarming smile and looked around the kitchen helplessly.

"Sack, you'll have to show me what to do. I don't want to upset Mrs Purdy."

His charm worked and when he made it clear to Sack that he regarded her as his better and had no plan to usurp her position, life in the kitchen became cheerful and pleasant. The new atmosphere spread throughout the house. He bowed to Mrs Purdy, flattered her outrageously and tended her with apparent devotion.

He suspected Mrs Purdy was too hard-bitten to be influenced by flagrant fawning but nevertheless he sensed a softening in her attitude toward him. He needed to create an atmosphere of trust in the house so he could move freely. He knew he was succeeding when Venables gradually relaxed his vigilance.

To Fleta, he adopted a pose of indifference. The girl trembled so much when he served her at table, he felt monstrous in her presence. He was sorry for her embarrassment.

The days passed rapidly. There were frequent visitors to Bullers Park in search of slaves to buy. With the weather getting warmer, Mrs Purdy entertained them on the piazza. Casey was kept busy bringing relays of whiskey or mint juleps to her customers.

Fleta remained in seclusion. Her music room adjoined her bed chamber at the back of the house and she kept the thick drapes drawn, shutting out the sun. Casey waited for Fleta to make the first move toward friendship but time was passing too quickly.

Eventually, in early summer, he was returning from serving guests on the piazza and stopped outside her door. The monotonous tones of a poorly played fugue were coming from the piano.

He knocked on the door and pushed it open. The playing stopped abruptly. Two candles burned in a candelabrum on the piano. Fleta's shocked face peered at him like she'd seen a jumbie. He ignored her squint and the eye which looked over her shoulder, and concentrated on her mouth.

"This," he said, placing a mint julep on top of the piano, "is for you."

Her hand grasped her throat. ". . ." The words stuck.

"If you don't drink, now is the time to start. Listen," he bent his head down, lowering his voice. "I need your help!"

Her wild eye swivelled in surprise and both of them lighted on him simultaneously for a fraction of a second. She began to tremble.

"I'm not going to touch you," he said. "Don't worry about that. Here, drink."

He proffered the glass and Fleta snatched it from him. She raised it to her mouth and gulped at it like it was medicine. She flushed.

"That wasn't bad, was it?" He grinned. "Fleta, I need a friend!" He glanced at the door which he had deliberately left wide open.

"I can't talk now. I'll come back when those foul-mouthed planters have gone."

He took the glass from her and noticed her hand had stopped shaking. He smiled again. "You will be my friend, won't you?" He kept his eyes on her and backed out of the room closing the door carefully.

When he passed the door a few minutes later on his way to the piazza, the notes of a minuet instead of the gloomy fugue tinkled cautiously from the piano.

It was afternoon when he visited her again. She sat by the French windows which were open onto the flower garden. The heavy curtains were drawn back and sunlight poured into the room. Two slaves were tending the flower beds and, in the magnolias, young birds twittered busily. She had a book open on her lap.

Seen in profile, Casey thought, she was almost lovely.

She continued to gaze at the garden while he stood beside her. "I want you to know," she said, her voice tremulous, "that I am my mother's daughter. I must do what she wishes."

"You can try," Casey threw himself into a tiny chair which skittered back on the polished floor under his weight. "One advantage of your mother's mad scheme is that she can't object to me talking to you."

"You don't approve of her . . . idea?" Fleta turned her face toward him. Casey wondered how much time each day she spent weeping.

"What your mother does is her affair. Just the same as what you do is your affair, or should be."

"You talk very boldly for a slave." Fleta's eyes were both watching him.

"Listen," he said, "I'm not a slave. I'm trapped, like you."

"Trapped?" She uttered the word as though its meaning was very familiar to her.

"Yes, and I'm going to escape."

"Oh!"

Her reaction of outrage showed Casey he had misjudged her. In his enthusiasm for winning her aid, he had over looked that she was a product of the South. To her, a slave speaking of escape was a personal threat.

Her pale face grew ashen and she gazed at the garden as though she longed to seek refuge in the magnolias.

He tried to calm her. "Look at me. Go on. Turn your head and look at me. Am I violent? Am I an animal? Look at my eyes, my face. Don't you see you can trust me?"

She didn't know what to make of him. Her eyes flickered over his face and her mouth fell open exposing her decaying teeth.

"See, I'm nothing to be scared of." He sighed. "Good lord! I feel so lonely here. No friends, only stupid slaves. If you would be my friend, we could talk to each other. You're so intelligent, you could help me improve myself."

"Oh!" She sounded alarmed.

"Yes. I like it here. You and your mother don't treat me like a slave. If your mother frees me, I think I'd stay."

"You said you want to escape."

"That's right. From the position she's put us both in."

"What . . ." Fleta hesitated. "What do you mean?"

"I don't want to be offensive, Miss Fleta," he said carefully. "Your mother is a great woman. Fine business, breeding slaves. Perhaps she's let her work cloud her judgement. Wanting us, you and I, to breed like niggers."

Fleta folded up like a discarded marionette. Her head dashed against her knees and sobs racked her frail body. A cloud drifted over the sun and the slaves in the flower beds continued scraping out the weeds. Casey touched her shoulder very gently.

"I'm your friend," he whispered. "We don't have to do what your mother wants. We'll pretend." His fingers crept under her hair and brushed against the nape of her neck. He tried to soothe her.

"It will be our secret."

Her shoulders stopped heaving. He withdrew his hand and crouched on his hams in front of her. "Cheer up," he said, taking her fingers away from her face and holding them tightly. "I often feel like crying too."

This startled her. She stopped sobbing and tried to look at him. "You do?"

"Sure. Why not?"

"You're a man."

"Is there any law says a man can't be frightened, or pleased?" He squeezed her fingers and stood up. "Let's be friends, Fleta?"

"Oh yes," she said, her voice mellowing with joy. "Yes, yes."

He smiled. "I'll wink at you when I'm serving dinner tonight. Don't laugh. Venables will have a fit."

She giggled.

"You're a wonderful girl, Fleta," he said. "You've made me happy."

She frowned and dabbed at the tears on her cheek. "That's what you've done for me."

"Good." He sauntered from the room, pleased that at last he was on the way to freedom.

"I said cover her, not love her!" Mrs Purdy stalked across the drawing room, twirling the cowhide in her hand. Casey watched blandly from his place by the empty fireplace. From Fleta's room, the melodious notes of a tune being played with a joyful flair, drifted to them.

In the weeks since Casey's approach to Fleta, a remarkable change had come over the girl. Her pious practising had become a pleasure to hear, her conversation brightened and her appearance, to which she previously paid no attention at all, had improved.

"Fleta is head over heels in love with you," Mrs Purdy said. "I thought it was rouge! When she sees you she blushes like she's got permanent hot flushes. Sack says she's eating twice as much, though in heavens name, I thought a girl went off her food when she's in love. And she's so happy!"

Mrs Purdy moved toward him waving the whip in exasperation. "Casey! Why aren't you mounting the girl?"

He spread his hands, palms upward, in a gesture of helplessness. "I wish I could, ma'am."

Jessica Purdy stopped in her tracks. "What? She's refusing you? I'll flay the girl alive."

"No, ma'am," he said with a grin, forcing his luck while

he had the chance. "It's Venables. He's always around."

Mrs Purdy heaved a sigh and retreated. "I see."

"He won't leave me alone with her, ma'am. The only chance we can be together is in the afternoon with the curtains wide open. He lurks in the garden with the diligence of a duenna."

Jessica inhaled her snuff and sneezed decisively. "There's an auction in Savanna next month. I've got a passel of strapping niggerlings ready for the hammer. Venables shall take them. He'll be gone at least three weeks. You'll have time to cover her then."

Her eyes glinted. "I shall be alone too."

30

Fleta walked to the door in response to his knock. She knew it was him; she had been waiting since dinner, incapable of practising or reading or doing anything. What preparations should she make? She had bathed three weeks before, at the beginning of October, so she was clean. She was wearing a dress which he must have noticed at dinner. It was white jaconet with lovely embroidery upon the skirt. The pink sash matched her hair ribbons.

"Casey!" she said, almost swooning with nervousness.

"Hello," he answered brightly, stepping past her into the room. She had lit all the candles in the candelabrum on the piano and the light seemed to sparkle at her from his eyes. He was wearing his butlers pantaloons of black, with a loose cotton shirt. He was bare-footed.

Without waiting for her to invite him in, he strode across to a chair and sat down. She settled herself on the couch and patted her newly-styled hair. It was drawn back with a center parting and tied with the ribbons. She hoped he noticed.

"Venables will be back in the middle of November," he said.

She remained silent, watching him demurely even though her heart was pattering at an alarming rate. Would he seize her and take her on the couch? Would he throw her on the floor. Would they do it on her bed?

"We haven't got much time."

She gasped and drew back from the candle glow so he wouldn't see her blushing. She had not anticipated that he would be so bold.

"Fleta," he said, lowering his voice in what sounded like passion to her. "I can't speak much. Your mother may be listening. Shall we write to each other?"

"Write?" It wasn't what she expected him to say.

"Yes. Can you get me some paper, ink and a pen?"

"Why?"

"I'll put notes for you where they'll surprise you. Little letters to say when I can come to see you."

"You can come any time."

"No, I can't. What shall we do when Venables returns? And there's Sack. If she knows I'm in your boudoir at night what will she say?"

It was beyond Fleta's comprehension. "It makes no matter what our slave cook says, does it?"

"Fleta," he grinned. "Perhaps you don't know how slaves love to gossip. Anything which happens at Bullers Park is known throughout Paxton County by dawn. We want our friendship to be a secret, don't we?"

"Yes." She was doubtful.

"Of course we do! You don't want me to be whipped to death by Marsden, do you?" He folded his arms. "That's what will happen if the whites hear of our friendship."

"Oh no!" She uttered a tiny shriek and gazed at him adoringly. He turned to see what had caught her attention behind his shoulder. She tried to focus both eyes on him but her squint betrayed her again.

"Then get me writing materials," he said.

How could she refuse that winsome smile? "It's all locked

in Mama's bureau. She'll ask why."

"Don't you write poetry?"

"Why no," she giggled. "I couldn't."

"You play so well, you read a lot. Surely your talents could run to a pretty poem. Write me one!"

She was astonished at the idea and clapped her hands with delight. "I'll try."

"Good. Just tell your mother you're going to write poetry. She'll be scornful, of course, but don't worry about that."

"You won't laugh at my efforts?"

"I'll treasure them. Get me some paper and I'll write poems too."

"Very well." She smiled. "You have such a lot of bright ideas. Everything was so dull here until you came."

"I know," he said, getting to his feet.

She was dismayed. "Are you going?"

"Yes." He raised his eyebrow in query.

"But you've just come . . . I mean . . . oh!" She blushed at how unladylike she was behaving. Her eye wandered hopelessly around the room.

"You're such a good friend, Fleta." He smiled and clasped her hands in his own.

He was so strong. She began to tremble with excitement. Was this the moment when he would sweep her into his arms and plunge his lips on her own?

"Don't forget a pen as well," he said. "Be careful, it's our secret." He let her hands go. She gazed up at him and her eyes moistened.

"I thought . . ."

He laughed and touched her playfully under her chin. It was a touch of fire; her body melted with heat. She didn't know where to look, what to say, what to do. "Casey . . ."

"I can't stay, Fleta. Tell your mama all is well when she asks. I'll say the same thing. We must make her believe that we are doing what she wants."

"Yes . . ." Fleta watched him stride toward the door. He turned, smiled and waved. She waved back uncertainly.

What had gone wrong, she wondered. Didn't he know that she wanted him?

Her yearning for Casey grew each day. She spied on him when he sauntered from room to room on his duties. She contrived to be wherever she knew he would be. She made a trip to Paxton, the county town, and ordered two dresses from a seamstress, Mistress Dundy. The woman was not much older than she was, and immediately understood Fleta's need.

"I'll make you something that will transform you," Mrs Dundy said, none too kindly. "A dress that will make your man your slave."

"Will it," Fleta wondered to herself, "make my slave my man?"

She was in despair. Every evening Casey came to her. He stayed half-an-hour talking, then left. At times she was so bewildered by her emotions, she was unable to understand all he said. She procured the writing materials for him, then waited for his poems. They didn't come. No time, he claimed.

The day came when her dresses were ready. She chose to wear that night the one in rose organdy, with a corsage skillfully tailored to enhance her miserable figure, and a voluminous skirt that emphasised the narrowness of her waist.

She felt very feminine and anxious and was unable to eat anything as Casey waited on her at dinner. She peaked at him when he was serving her mother, but he gave no sign of acknowledgement.

"Dammit, Fleta!" her mother exclaimed when Casey left the dining room for the kitchen. "You've more blood in you than a nigger sow on heat. Ain't you got enough of that buck's juice yet?"

"Mama!" Fleta stared at her plate, unable to say more.

"Why you bother painting yourself and putting on fancy silks, I don't know. You only have to lift your skirts and lie back. The buck don't want to look at you!"

Fleta wished she could sink through the floor.

"Tell me," her mother said, forking a lump of pork into her mouth and chewing it cautiously because of her decayed teeth. "What's he like? Can he use that pecker properly? I bet he . . . Why, in heaven's name, girl, what's the matter?"

Fleta broke into bitter sobs, tears streaming down her face and smearing her rouge. "Mama!" she said, choking back the tears. "Casey ain't a nigger. He's a gentleman. We don't do . . . we don't do that!"

"What!" Mrs Purdy peered at her shrewdly. "Dang me! he ain't burst your maidenhead yet? I might have known! You get him to get it up tonight, Fleta, girl, or I'm going to tan the backside off that fancy nigger. Venables due back this week . . ."

Fleta hid her face in her handkerchief and ran from the table to her room. She was still crying when she felt a hand on her shoulder. She jerked up her head in surprise, then hid herself in her handkerchief again in shame.

"I didn't knock," Casey said softly. "I saw you come in here. Try not to cry." His fingers were fondling her neck, shivering her spine. She choked, gasped for breath, and her heart lurched. She dabbed her eyes.

"My nose, my face," was all she could say.

He took a handkerchief from his own pocket and carefully wiped the tears from her cheeks. He steadied her face with his hand under her chin. His nose was so close, she felt his breath on her lips. She trembled.

"You look beautiful tonight," he said softly. His fingers stroked her face. "You have fine bones."

Her body tingled at the touch of his hand. His voice was the best music she ever heard, gentle and loving. She sensed his kindness, his affection, and his respect. She longed for him but she knew now her mother had murdered the love that could have existed between them.

"Casey," she said, pushing his hand away from her face. He sat on the couch beside her.

"Mama wants . . . I mean . . . she knows we're not doing what she wants. She's too shrewd to fool any longer."

"Don't worry, Fleta." Casey squeezed her arm. "I've made my plans. Some day I'll be gone."

"Gone?" She couldn't believe it.

"Yes. I've got to go to save you," he said. "You are a beautiful lady, Fleta. One day a handsome white man will come for you. He'll want a virgin, Fleta, not the mother of a nigger whelp."

She was bewildered.

"I'm going to write to my patron in New Orleans. When he gets my letter, he'll come here and you'll be rid of me."

She was close to swooning. "I don't want to be rid of you, Casey," she gasped. "I love you!"

"No, you don't," he said. "I'm the first person to treat you like a woman, that's all. Get out, go about some more. Hold your head up high. You're the heiress to Bullers Park, Fleta. You are somebody in this county."

"I love you!" There, she had said it again. Didn't he realize it was not easy for her to say? She clung to his arm.

"No, Fleta," he said gently, withdrawing his hand.

"Casey!" Jessica had been watching the door since he had gone to Fleta half an hour before. She emerged from the shadows in the hall and confronted him as he left her chamber. He looked startled.

"You didn't do it, did you?" she said.

"No, Mrs Purdy," he replied, quickly recovering his self-assurance. "Your daughter's distressed. She's delicate, Mrs Purdy. Not a nigger. A little time to get her accustomed . . ."

"What do you need to get you accustomed? A lick across your thighs?"

"Mrs Purdy!"

"Don't knit your brows at me like that, boy," she said, plucking at the cowhide. "I know bucks! Are you pulling your pudding?"

He looked baffled.

"You're built like a stud, bursting with sap. Ain't no reason why you haven't jumped that girl unless you're spilling your seed somewhere else. Sack swears you ain't pestering her or the kitchen girls."

"Mrs Purdy –"

"Don't try to charm me with your sweet talk, Casey. Get inside!" She held open the door of her chamber and beckoned him in with the handle of her whip. "I'm not slow to use this if I have to. Even on your gorgeous hide."

He walked past her and stood in the room by the door. Her bed, a huge four poster with the curtains tied by pink ribbons to the ornately carved posts, filled the room. She resisted the urge to rush at him and tumble him backward on it. She closed the door and fumbled for her snuff box instead.

He was a superb creature. Since coming to Bullers Park he had filled out. She knew what food to give her best bucks. His shoulders had broadened, his waist thickened and his thighs bulged under the thin cotton of his pantaloons. The pinched, angry look of his early days was gone.

Jessica was sure that, given encouragement, he was a wild and passionate animal under his formal manner. She supposed that Fleta's mooning was the wrong approach.

"Right," she said, sitting down on the bed and kicking off her shoes. She slapped the mattress with the cowhide to show she was serious. "Let down them britches."

Casey drew himself up like a cobra, his neck dilating. He said nothing.

"Casey." She kept her voice low and menacing. "Do you know how to satisfy a wench? Perhaps because you're a half-breed, you're a half-sex too? Should I put you in a shift instead of pants?" She was pleased to see his eyes flare with anger.

"Fleta's crying out for you in her sleep at night. I've sent away Venables. You can have Fleta whenever you want, but you do nothing. I thought you were a man!"

"I am, Mrs Purdy." His voice was strained. Jessica goaded him further.

"Not seen any sign of it yet. The Bondmaster's gets must be a line of cock suckers if you're a fair sample."

He took a step toward her. She raised the whip. "Britches," she said. "Let's see what you've got there."

He scowled, his eyes clouding with hatred. She knew he wasn't afraid of the whip. His pride had been hurt.

She sighed with excitement when he loosened his pantaloons and rolled them down his thighs to his knees. She had succeeded in rousing him but his penis, clean where Venables had circumsized him, was flaccid.

She beckoned him. His fists were clenched but he took a step toward her. She cupped his testicles in her left hand and held them securely so he couldn't spring back. With her right hand she began to massage his penis.

"Won't take five minutes," she said, "to see if you've got juice or not."

He was opening and clenching his fists with ill-concealed rage. Jessica knew that she was driving him to the edge of tolerance. Her fingers plied him expertly and she was rewarded by the hardening of the flesh in her hands. Casey groaned.

It was only seconds, she knew, before he would throw himself on her, lift up her skirts and drive himself into her with a fury she wouldn't be able to control. She rubbed faster, spreading her legs, crooning for the moment when he would lose all control and jump her.

She released him and raised her skirt. She fell back on the bed and closed her eyes. Her hands clawed the air and her thighs churned as she waited for him to rape her.

There was a stillness in the room. She strained her body to meet his. She waited . . .

She blinked open her eyes. At first she could see only mottles of light. She blinked again, watching the shadows of the room taking shape. She sat up and looked around. He had gone.

"I'm going to the quarters," Casey told Sack when the cook stared at him with surprise. She had been sleeping when he burst into the kitchen.

"What happen?" she demanded, wiping the sleep from her eyes.

"You've got a nose for trouble, Sack." He tried to laugh to soothe her. "I want fresh air, that's all. And I haven't seen Tamba for days."

Sack sniffed suspiciously. "Dat night air chill yo' to de bone."

"I'll be back before dawn."

"Mistis in bed?"

"I don't know!" he shouted angrily, slamming the kitchen

door behind him with such force that the house seemed to shake.

The night was dark and moonless and the cold air calmed him. He was grateful for it. He needed to clear his head, needed time to think. He strolled cautiously down the path in the direction of the slave cabins, skirting the wooden building where Marsden and the other whites lived.

It was a risk being out at night. Fear of slave uprisings kept whites alert. Even at Bullers Park where the slaves were considered docile, groups of armed whites, poor crackers hired for the job, patrolled the plantation every night. There had been several insurrections in the State, and Marsden was taking no chances.

Casey met no one. He threaded his way through the cabins to the one where Tamba was billeted with his current filly. The huts were in darkness. Casey scratched on the door. There was a sound of hasty movement inside then he felt the blade of a knife pressing into his back. A voice spoke close to his ear.

"Who are yo'?"

"I'm Casey. What's wrong?"

The knife was removed and the tall negro holding it tapped twice on the door. It opened about an inch. The negro bent forward.

"It Casey. Yo' want he?"

There was a whispered conversation inside the cabin before the door opened and Casey was pulled in. The negro with the knife stayed on guard.

"Tam –"

"Keep yo' voice down!"

"What's going on here, Tamba?" he said, speaking more softly although he was annoyed by the guard's suspicious attitude.

Someone held his hand and guided him to the side and, by pressing on his shoulders, indicated that he should sit. He squatted on his haunches and peered around the darkened cabin. Tamba spoke into his ear.

"We havin' a meetin', Cas. Are yo' joinin' us?"

"What kind of meeting?"

"We gwine escape."

"When?"

"Don' tell him no more," said another voice, harsher than the others. "He ain't swore."

"We can trust Casey."

"Hah! He half-buckree, ain't he?"

The slave's words brought back to Casey what Jessica Purdy had told him earlier that evening. He flinched. "Tamba," he said. "I came to tell you something. Can I talk to you? Alone."

"Yo' gwine tell buckree what we plannin'?"

"I don't know what you're planning, do I? I haven't seen or heard anything."

"Yo' won't join us, Cas?"

"Tamba, this isn't the way. Freedom will come some day for you all, by law. The crackers will kill you if you try to escape. They'll catch you even before you reach Maddocks across the creek."

"Dat don' sound like yo', Cas. Yo've changed since we met at Mobile."

"Maybe. I want to escape too, Tamba. Mrs Purdy can't risk an insurrection at Bullers Park. No one will buy her stock if planters know her slaves are troublesome."

"What that got to do with us?" The hard-voiced slave spoke again. "We want to be free!"

"Sure," he said, "but life here is better than bleeding out your guts in a ditch. Your way brings you freedom all right, freedom through death." Casey stared unseeing at the angry negroes who hissed back at him.

"You've got bargaining powers because Mrs Purdy can't take the risk of having discontented slaves. Use it. Tell her what you want. More food, better clothes, just ask for it!"

"Dat buckree talk!"

Tamba's hand touched his arm. "Let we go outside, Cas. Yo' can talk to me dere."

The two of them left the cabin while the slaves began to argue amongst themselves. They sat down in the darkness by the wall at the back of the hut.

"Are you really planning an uprising?" Casey asked.

Tamba shrugged his shoulders. "Lots of slaves in ferment," he said. "Lots ain't. If yo' join us, we could make it."

"I want to leave, Tamba, you know that. But I want to live too. I want to see Lucy again. There has to be a better way, one that is certain to succeed."

"Yo' still thinking of Lucy?" Tamba chuckled. "I don't know why Mrs Purdy doesn't give yo' a wench. That'll cure yo' lovesickness."

Casey gulped and gripped his friend's arm. "She wants me herself." Quickly he recounted what had happened with Jessica that night.

"Oh, boy!" said Tamba. "Yo' sure got to leave dis place now!"

"Whatever for?"

"Dat woman gwine hound yo'. Yo' shame her so she gwine lick yo'. She hot, Cas. Yo' gotta run before she nuts yo' or sucks yo' dry."

"I can't go."

"Yo' can. Join wid me. Yo's gwine be free when we rise up."

"I can't go," he repeated coldly.

"Why dat?"

"Fleta. She needs me."

Tamba stood up brusquely. "Cas, yo' more crazy dan a white toobub."

Casey cradled his head in his hands. "I ran out on a girl once, Tamba. I can't run out again."

"Den I's sorry for yo'." Tamba stomped off angrily, leaving Casey sitting on his haunches alone in the dark.

31

Why, Casey wondered as he chopped firewood outside the kitchen, did he remain at Bullers Park? Fleta had stolen paper and pen for him. It would take too long to send a letter to Gene in New Orleans and anyway, why should he pay for his freedom? Instead, if he wanted, he could write himself a travel pass to Millidgeville, forge Mrs Purdy's signature to dupe the patrollers, and be on his way.

He would have to borrow money from Fleta so when he reached the State capital, he could take a coach to Savanna. From there, he could get passage on a brig to New Orleans. It was simple… but could he really leave?

The plaintive notes of Fleta's piano playing swelled through the chill of the morning. He slammed his axe into the log with renewed energy, until the sweat was pouring off him and his shirt stuck to his back.

After the incident with Mrs Purdy, and because of Tamba's warning, he had expected some kind of repercussion. But Mrs Purdy had left him alone. Venables had arrived the night before, back from his slave-selling trip. He had spent the night with her.

He smashed the axe into the last log and chopped it vigorously. He stood up and wiped the sweat from his brow, comforted by the sounds of the piano trilling out over the garden. He bent down to collect up the firewood.

"Don't move!"

The voice shocked him as much as the blow from the whip which suddenly sliced into his shoulders. He dropped the chips and bunched his hands into fists, swinging around angrily to defend himself.

Venables was glaring at him. Jessica Purdy stood at his side, gloating.

The whip cracked again and landed on his chest with a force that made him stagger. Blood seeped out of the gash cut into his skin.

"Mrs Purdy . . ." he cried out, but Jessica ignored him. The sound of the piano died.

Casey turned away and saw Marsden and two of the white hands creeping out from behind the magnolias. One of the crackers carried a rope. He twisted around to plead with Mrs Purdy. Venables pushed her behind him and spun the tongue of the bullwhip in the air.

He dived for the axe.

The whip sliced into his waist.

"Leave it!" Venables ordered quietly.

Casey froze on the ground, his hand only inches from the axe. Jessica was shrieking.

"He'll kill me," she screamed. "The brute!"

Casey raised his head and stared at her in disbelief. "What have I done?"

A blow on the back of his head cut off the words. The two crackers jumped on him and his arms were wrenched behind his back and wrists tied together. Marsden spat at him.

"Got yer now, yer yeller snake."

Casey gritted his teeth to shut out the pain. Jessica sneered at him.

"Thank god you came, Ven!" she said. "I've been terrified out of my wits. Who knows what he would do. Ever since he . . ." She slipped her arm under Venables' elbow. "It's been a nightmare."

"Try to rape the mistress, eh?" Marsden glared at him. "We know what to do with snakes like you."

"I didn't!"

He was jerked to his feet and marched between the two crackers to the yard in front of the house. A wooden structure like a gallows had been erected under the oak trees. Casey looked at it in dismay.

Two upright posts, ten feet high, had a beam lashed across them at the top. A rope and pulley hung down from the center of the beam. A stake, about two feet high, its end sharpened to a fine point, had been driven into the ground underneath the pulley.

The slaves who had erected this curious machine were standing under it unhappily. They shuffled backward as Casey was led over to it.

"Dey gwine picket yo', Cas," said one.

"Yo' should've run," said another.

"Shut up!" Venables' whip snapped across their faces. His eyes gleamed.

"Now this bright-assed nigger will get what he deserves!" Marsden leered.

Casey was in a trance. He couldn't believe that this was happening to him. He glanced around for Jessica. She had taken a seat on the piazza and was watching the procedings with a warped smile of pleasure. He sighed. The crackers stripped his clothes from his body and his hands were jerked above his head and his wrists were fastened to a rope attached to the pulley.

Marsden instructed a boy to run around the plantation ringing the handbell to summon the slaves.

A gang of white men galloped up the driveway. They had ridden from Paxton. Casey recognized them with shock. They were the poor whites of the neighborhood, the crackers whose main occupation was hunting runaway slaves. They were ugly, mean and armed.

"Ain't he a beauty!" One of them whooped with delight when he saw Casey. He dismounted and strode over to him, drawing out his knife.

"Pestering Mrs Purdy, is he?" The white man laughed. "Let me cut his balls."

Marsden moved in front of Casey and glared at the cracker. "Your job is to watch the slaves," he shouted. "Line up there." He made them form a protective ring around Casey and the gallows. "If any of the niggers try to rescue him," he said, "you can shoot 'em."

"Whoopee!" A cracker discharged his pistol in the air.

Casey wondered how long it would take him to die. If he closed his eyes and thought of his mother, of Lucy, of

Uraline, of the broad course of the Layou River sweeping down to the sea, perhaps he would pass out quickly. He wouldn't shout or cry. He wouldn't let Fleta see him in pain.

He looked up at the house. Jessica Purdy was talking to Venables and smiling at him coyly. Casey knew he should have listened to Tamba. He was being punished because he had refused her. He scanned the windows of the house for a sight of Fleta. She was no where to be seen.

"Casey!"

He glanced behind him. The slaves were gathering. Tamba, hidden behind a row of worried women, raised his fist in greeting. "I's here, Cas," he said softly. "Yo' ain't alone."

Casey smiled ruefully. "Goodbye, Tamba," he said.

His arms were wrenched from their sockets. The pain stunned him. Two men were hauling at the rope on the pulley so that he was being raised by his arms into the air. Marsden steadied his feet.

"Higher!" he shouted.

Venables walked off the piazza and crossed the yard. He pushed through the circle of crackers and studied Casey. The rope had been tied to one of the uprights so that Casey was suspended above the sharpened point of the stake. Venables grabbed Casey's left foot, forced it up, and bound it with rope, toes downward, to his right leg.

His left knee now formed an angle that Venables gripped and used to turn Casey's body. He spun him around like a top.

Casey lowered his free right foot to stop the twisting. His toes contacted with the point of the stake and rested against it so that the skewer would not pierce his skin. Venables growled.

"You got the idea." He spun Casey again.

His weight dragged on his wrists, stretching the skin over his back. He closed his eyes to shut out the blur of faces. He wanted to vomit.

The first cut of the whip took him by surprise. He gasped. The second sliced through his skin and he spun wildly under its force. He struggled to steady himself on the stake but the point spiked his feet. The crackers laughed.

He bit his lower lip to stop shouting out at the pain. The third lash flayed him through his flesh to the bone. He twisted helplessly, his sudden scream warbling over the Park and chilling the slaves with its agony. The fourth cut across his chest, the fifth on his back, the sixth on top, the seventh . . .

He lost consciousness. His body was a bloody pulp, flecks of skin and flesh plopping to the ground. He dangled lifelessly.

Marsden shouted at Venables. "Give him time to catch his breath."

Casey stopped twisting and his foot rested on the top of the spike. Venables pushed at his knee and he spun again and the stake gored through the sole of his foot.

Venables chortled. His face and clothes were splattered with Casey's blood. He was panting.

"Let me lash him," one of the crackers begged Venables.

"My duty," he gasped. The crackers fell back knowingly.

"Watch the niggers," Marsden shouted at them with a roar.

The slaves made no move to protest. They watched stoically, singing to themselves. The low wailing of voices filled with the sadness of their African heritage swelled through the air. The whites glared and flicked their whips in the air but the negroes sang on.

Sack came out of the house with a bucket of water. She pushed her way to the picket and hurled the water in Casey's face. He struggled back to life.

Venables laughed and spun him again.

He puked, the vomit mingling with the blood spurting from the cuts on his chest.

Venables aimed another blow and it sliced into his buttocks, showering blood over the whites.

Venables still laughed and flailed the whip time after time into Casey's body.

He was no longer screaming. He was numbed by pain and nausea, twirling and spinning until his mind blacked out. His last glimpse was a blurred image of Fleta standing on the piazza behind Jessica Purdy.

She had a pistol in her hand.

"Make them stop it, mama!" Fleta said, holding the pistol steady in her mother's side. "I swear I will fire this if you don't."

"Ven!" Mrs Purdy shouted. "That's enough! Don't want to kill him. I need him alive to buy his freedom." She turned on Fleta.

"Give that to me, girl. What the devil do you think you're doing!"

Fleta burst into tears and let her mother take the gun. "You've stopped them!" she said. "Oh, mama!"

"I know." Mrs Purdy put her arm around Fleta and hugged her. "You don't understand, do you? It's for you, honey. He'll do anything we want now."

She gazed across the courtyard. A cracker unfastened the rope and let Casey's body drop with a squelch in the puddles of blood on the ground. The slaves stopped chanting and moved restlessly toward Casey. The circle of crackers tightened around his body.

"Sack!" Jessica beckoned the cook to her side, disentangling herself from Fleta and tucking the pistol into the waistband of her skirt. "Take Fleta to her room."

Tamba twisted past two of the whites and threw himself on the ground beside Casey. He held him firmly, defying Marsden and the crackers to stop him. Other slaves surged forward. The white men unleashed their whips and scythed into the slaves but they wouldn't stop. The crackers bunched into a group and backed up to the house. Some fired their pistols into the air.

"Let them have his carcass!" Marsden cried shrilly.

Tamba sensed the white man's fear and beckoned the slaves. They encircled Casey and Tamba and waited sullenly. The whips of Marsden, Venables and the crackers smashed into their shoulders.

"Back, back!" Marsden shouted. "Go to yer quarters."

The white men advanced in a pack and the slaves retreated, carrying Casey with them.

"We done scare dem! We rescue Casey!" Tamba yelled in triumph.

Casey was borne to Tamba's cabin and laid on his pallet. While the women keened softly to help him fight his pain, Tamba pondered what had happened. He was shaken by his discovery of a flaw in the mastery that the whites claimed to have over blacks. Whites were scared! Tamba saw his freedom lay in that knowledge.

"We gwine take revenge, Cas," Tamba said as soon as his friend was conscious. "Dey weak! Yo' wid us now?"

Casey's wounds were bound with poultices applied by the midwife. The slave women, their eyes dark with sorrow, hunkered down by his side to watch and comfort him through the long night of agony.

"It's not the way," Casey murmured.

"How can you say dat? Who know what happen next? We gwine rise up 'gainst de buckree before dey punish all of we."

"They won't punish you," Casey said, his eyes half-closed with pain and shock. "I shamed Mrs Purdy. You did nothing."

"Cas! Yo' have to join us!" Tamba gripped Casey's hand passionately. "We flee together, you and I."

Casey was silent. The cabin was in darkness and Tamba couldn't see his expression of forgiveness. "No," he said softly.

"Why not?" Tamba was puzzled.

"Because . . ." Casey's voice died as exhaustion and pain swept over him and he lapsed into troubled sleep.

Tamba shrugged his shoulders and watched him curiously. One of the women nudged him aside after a few minutes and he slipped quietly from the cabin. He joined a group of slaves squatting under the sycamore tree at the entrance to the quarters. They talked long and inconclusively among themselves until dawn rolled slowly over the plains.

32

Casey had been at Bullers Park for five hundred and twenty five days. He lay in the shade of the willow tree by the creek and counted again. It was hard to believe that so many months had passed since the day he arrived in New Orleans with Gene Cable. So long since he had left Lucy.

He rolled over on to his stomach and saw Tamba throwing stones one by one into the stream. "Isn't Marsden looking for you?" he asked.

Tamba shrugged his shoulders.

"Don't get lashed on account of me."

Tamba shot him a scornful glance.

"I'm grateful, Tamba, for what you've done." He put out his arm and touched the African. "I doubt if I'd have lived without your help."

Tamba sucked in air with a squawking sound of annoyance.

Casey dropped back on the grass and smiled. For months he had lain in a delirium on Tamba's bed while the African nursed him. It was Tamba who bound his wounds and forced him to eat when he wanted to die. Tamba made him walk and run when he thought he would never move again. It was Tamba who cajoled him back to life.

Now he was fit again; he could swim, run, climb and even laugh. But he would always limp where his foot had been pierced by the picket.

He chuckled softly. Tamba was a jealous guard, worse than Venables. He wouldn't let him be seen by the whites.

"If dey know yo's fit, dey picket yo' 'gain," Tamba said forcefully, throwing another stone into the creek.

"Mrs Purdy's forgotten about me," Casey said.

"She ain't gwine forget yo' 'til she dead."

He raised his eyebrows, surprised at the venom in Tamba's voice. Tamba stared back at him defiantly.

"Reckon yo's fit now," he said.

"Fit for what?"

"Yo's a buckree in truth!" Tamba threw the final stone and stood up. "Always axing questions. I gwine be late tonight. Yo' go back to de cabin 'fore sun down, yo' hear? Wait for me dere."

"Yas, marse!"

They both laughed and then Casey watched Tamba slip off through the trees. He wondered why he was moving so stealthily but he soon forgot about that and lay back on the bank, listening to the gentle murmuring of the stream.

Jessica was restless. Sack had served supper and Fleta had retired early to her chamber, as she always did. Venables was in Paxton. She opened the door on to the piazza and stepped out. The scent of the magnolias rushed to meet her and she breathed deeply. The moon was full, high over the live oaks, illuminating the long drive through the Park down to the road that led to Paxton.

She settled down on a rocking chair and swung herself backward and forward. Nights of the full moon disturbed her. She wished Venables would come early, she needed him tonight. She rose from the chair and walked to the edge of the piazza to see if she could see him on the driveway.

She listened carefully. There was a sound of something scuffling on the gravels of the path. She listened again. It was probably an animal foraging, she thought.

She strolled back into the house, banging the door behind her. It echoed eerily in the silence. Sack and the girls were already asleep. There was no light showing under the door of the kitchen. She lifted a lamp from its holder in the drawing room and walked with it to her chamber. She would lie down while she waited for Venables to return.

She gasped with surprise when she opened the door. Venables was in her bed, his head lolling on the pillows. The window was open and the curtains billowed into the room in the wind.

"I didn't hear you come in," she said, turning down the lamp and hanging it on a hook by the door. She rushed over to him.

"I was waiting on the piazza. Did you come 'round the back?"

He didn't reply. She threw herself on the bed and touched his face. "Oh Ven, don't sulk."

His hair was wet. She lowered her lips on his, pressing against his mouth, but it stayed closed. She ran her fingers down his cheeks and saw his eyes staring at her in a kind of terror.

"Ven?" she said uncertainly. "What's wrong?" She pulled back, suddenly afraid. She reached for his hand. There was nothing there.

She clambered off the bed and the abrupt movement dislodged his head from the pillow. It rolled to the edge of the bed and dropped to the floor by her feet.

The bed was empty.

Before Jessica could scream, a hand blocked her mouth and nose, choking her. An arm smashed into her stomach. She lashed out with her elbow but the solid flesh she contacted was unyielding. She was lifted off the floor and carried to the bed. Inspite of her weight, she was tossed on the bed as though she was a child. She glared angrily at her attacker.

Tamba leaned over her, grinning. His black face was dripping with sweat and drops of it showered on to her. His chest was bare and his hard muscles gleamed in the dim glow from the lamp.

Jessica slapped him across his cheek with all the strength she could muster. He didn't flinch. "What do you want? Who are you?" she asked.

Tamba crinkled his eyes, shaking his head from side to side with amusement. "Buckree always axing questions," he muttered. He placed his hands firmly on her breasts.

"Let go of me!" She glanced toward the open window.

Tamba laughed flatly. He pulled her skirt up to her waist.

"I know you," she said accusingly.

Tamba shrugged. "Dat good. I's yo' buck." His eyes wandered down to her thighs.

"Release me," she said. "I'll do what you want. I'll give you money so you can escape. I'll –"

He lifted his hand from her breasts and dropped it casually over her mouth, knocking her head backward to the pillow. He plunged his other hand between her legs.

"Shut up, woman," he said, beaming. He plucked at her with his long fingers. "My! That conny old and dry." He wrinkled his nose with mock disgust.

Raping Jessica was not part of the slave's plan. Since the day he watched helplessly while Casey was strung up on the whipping gallows, Tamba was determined to get revenge. The brutal punishment was the catalyst that finally enabled him to recruit other slaves to join the uprising. Casey hadn't been told of the scheme even though Tamba longed to ask his advice. Instead, he concentrated on building up Casey's strength for the long run to freedom.

The slaves waited patiently, bearing each new indignity in silence, until the day arrived when Casey was considered fit, and the moon was full.

The night of vengeance began with the murder of Marsden. He was overpowered and chopped to death while he sat on the veranda of his cabin smoking his pipe. Three other white men in the quarters were butchered with similar efficiency.

They ambushed Venables as he returned from Paxton by himself. He was stripped and his hands and feet were hacked off first. Then Tamba, who had planned this execution for weeks, plunged his knife into his crotch and cut up, slitting his belly in two. Venables didn't seem to stop screaming until they cut off his head. Now it was Jessica's turn.

"What yo' thinkin', Tamba?" The negro standing at the foot of the bed with his eyes riveted on Tamba's hand between Mrs Purdy's thighs giggled wildly.

"Same as yo', Dukey." Tamba swung himself up on the bed beside Jessica.

"Casey say yo's partial to prick," he told her. "I's never eat white meat."

"It sweet." Dukey's giggles became a deep-throated gurgle. "See de hair on it. It big an' pink."

Tamba fumbled with his pantaloons and pulled himself out. As soon as he took his hand from her mouth, Jessica struggled to sit up.

"Spare me," she said. "Do what you want, but spare my life." Her eyes widened when she saw Tamba kneel over her.

"Hold her face," Tamba told Dukey. The slave released Jessica's ankles and Tamba spread her thighs. She offered no resistance.

He slammed into her with the fury of hatred. There was no love, no lust, only the desperate need to defy, as though by shooting his seed inside this white woman he was somehow destroying her.

She cried, she moaned, she thrashed, and then she screamed. Dukey stuffed his fist in her mouth, as Tamba thundered to his climax.

"Me nex'," Dukey said, pushing at Tamba's shoulder. "Ou' de way, quick."

Tamba pulled out and rolled off. Dukey wriggled his hips between Jessica's thighs. He thrust into her and she moaned, tossing her head from side to side on the pillow. Her hands were free, clawing at Dukey's buttocks.

"De bitch like dat," chuckled Tamba. He reached down to the floor for his knife, honed lovingly to a cutting edge sharp enough to shave with.

"Now! Now!" shouted Dukey.

Tamba held Jessica's nose between the finger and thumb of his left hand and sliced the knife sharply across her throat with his right. Blood spurted over Dukey's shoulders and Jessica's body twitched with spasms.

"Aye!" Dukey was astounded, still buried within her. "Dat sweet! Dat sweet!" he gasped.

Casey limped through the Park. He was panting and stumbled often in the darkness under the trees. The moonlight dappled the boughs of the live oaks waving in the night breeze and the house looked serene. Lights shone dimly from Mrs Purdy's bedroom, and from Fleta's. He prayed he was in time.

Only a few minutes before, he had been on his plank asleep. Sack had woken him, shrieking hysterically with the news that Tamba was at the house.

He crouched under the magnolias and listened. There was a scream. He wasted no time to think. He hobbled to the back of the house, pushed open the door and hurried down the corridor into Fleta's room.

She was lying in bed, staring in terror at two negroes sitting on either side of her. One had his hand over her mouth and the other was pulling off the covers.

"Get away from her!" Casey's chest heaved as he caught his breath. The two slaves eyed him jealously.

He looked at them, trying to gauge their strength. "Primus!" he shouted. "You and Dandy, let her go. What's happening here?"

"You want her, Cas?" Primus drawled. "Tamba say to keep her 'til he come."

"Tamba gwine burst she!" Dandy said, spittle drooling down his chin.

Casey walked over and smashed his fist into his jaw. The slave released Fleta and put up his hands to defend himself. Fleta jumped out of the bed and flung herself at Casey. She clung to his chest. She was weeping and unable to speak.

He held her tightly, patting her shoulders to calm her and drawing her away from the two slaves.

"Casey!"

He turned toward the door. Tamba stood there, his pantaloons in one hand and a knife, smeared with blood, in the other.

"Why ain't yo' in de cabin? Yo' don' belong here."

"Why, Tamba, why?" Casey cried.

"For yo', Cas! We all gwine get we freedom now. We's gwine burn dis house den I's gwine take yo' to Nuorleans."

Casey shook his head, still clutching Fleta to him. "This isn't the way!" he shouted.

"It de slave way, buckree!"

Casey glared. "Why are you so damn stupid, Tamba. You won't get beyond Singer's plantation over the creek. The patrollers will hold you before you pass Maddocks' gates."

"Dey ain't gwine know. We kill all de whites an' no nigger gwine tell dem."

"You're the nigger who'll tell them!" Casey patted Fleta's shoulder as she wrapped her arms around his waist.

Tamba gaped. "Me?"

"Listen!" said Casey, "If you set fire to this house, the whole of Paxton County will be here in minutes. What chance will you have then?"

Tamba stuck the knife between his teeth and pulled on his pantaloons. He said nothing.

"I'm not going with you, Tamba. I'm staying here with Fleta."

"No!" Fleta pulled away from him. "You must go, Casey," she said between her sobs. "I'll come with you."

Tamba removed the knife from his mouth and grunted. He scratched his head and turned to Dukey. "What do you think?"

Dukey scratched his head and gazed at Primus and Randy.

"Makes no sense burning de house?" Tamba asked doubtfully.

Casey was emphatic. "No, not if you want to run."

"Got to run now, Casey." Tamba shrugged his shoulders. "We kill Marsden and Venables an' de mistis."

Fleta shrank away from him and Casey held her tightly.

"Seem like yo' gotta come wid us, Cas. Dey lynch yo' if yo' don't."

Casey's brain raced. "I've got an idea. If Fleta pretends she's our owner, I could be the driver and you and the niggers could be the coffle. We'll have a few hours start. We could be clear of the county by morning."

"No!" Tamba shook his head and advanced toward him. "Give me the wench, Cas."

"Why?" Casey backed against the bed. The slaves closed in.

"We swore to kill all de whites, Cas."

"That's madness. Fleta's done nothing. I'll look after her." He pulled Fleta behind him.

"We want she, Cas." Tamba put his hand on Fleta's elbow. She twisted out of Casey's protective grasp and leaped for

Tamba, clawing her fingernails into his eyes. He was taken by surprise and fell backward on to her bed. She jumped on him, banging her knee into his crotch and beating her fists on his chest.

"Come away, Fleta. You'll get hurt." Casey brushed her aside and fell on to Tamba himself. His hands locked on to his friend's neck and he pressed his thumb into his larynx.

"Give your word that she can go free," Casey demanded, squeezing. "Then I'll let you go."

Behind him, Primus and Randy grappled with Fleta.

"Casey!" she screamed. "Cas –!"

Dukey plugged a bedsheet in her mouth as a gag.

Casey glanced behind him to see what had happened to her. Tamba raised his knee and slammed it into Casey's crotch, pitching him across the room. He fell clumsily crashing his head on the brass fender of the fireplace.

Tamba leaped to his feet, picked up his knife and advanced on Fleta. She was twisting and bucking to break away from Primus and Randy.

"No!" Casey staggered up from the floor and threw himself at Tamba's shoulders.

Tamba raised the knife then fell forward under the weight of Casey on his back. Primus and Randy jumped aside. Tamba collapsed on to Fleta. The three of them fell against the wall.

Tamba tossed Casey off his back and crawled away. The knife was protruding from Fleta's bosom, blood seeping into the clean lawn of her corsage.

Casey seized her hands. "Fleta!" he cried, "Fleta!"

Her eyes wandered separately, then focused together and lingered lovingly on him. She smiled and tried to speak but a clot of blood bubbled between her lips and she gurgled to death.

"Tamba!" The shout of warning came from someone running along the corridor.

"In here." Dukey threw open the door. A negro stopped and stared at him in terror.

"Buckree!" he gasped.

"Where?" Tamba turned away from Casey.

"Two patrollers riding up the drive." The slave ran back down the corridor.

"Run!" said Tamba to Dukey. "Primus, Randy, get out."

"What 'bou' yo'?"

"I'll bring Casey."

"No, you won't." Casey knelt on the floor clinging to Fleta. "I'm not leaving her. I ran out once..."

"She dead, Cas."

"No, she's not!"

"Come on, Tamba," pleaded Dukey. "Leave him. De patterollers."

"They'll get you anyway," said Casey.

Tamba reached down suddenly and pulled the knife out of Fleta's breasts. He held it to Casey's neck. "Get up, Cas. We's runnin'."

"Cut me, Tamba. What have I got to live for now?"

"Come on!" Dukey shrieked in panic.

"I ain't saved yo' to lose yo', Cas." Tamba stuffed the knife in his waistband and punched Casey across his jaw. "Help me, Dukey."

"Why?" the slave shouted.

"Do it!" Tamba pulled Casey's limp body to his feet. Fleta slipped slowly from his grasp and fell to the floor.

With Tamba supporting him on one side and Dukey on the other, Casey shuffled down the corridor and out of the house, not caring if he lived or died.

Casey stumbled across the fields, urged to run faster by Tamba who gripped him under his arms. Dukey had disappeared into the darkness ahead.

"We got time," Tamba said, panting as he ran. "Dey ain' gwine search for we 'til dey got mo' patterollers."

"Leave me," said Casey, repeating the same words he had uttered since he left the house.

"No." Tamba yanked at his arms, forcing Casey to keep running. "We soon be off Bullers Park. We can cross to Maddocks by de creek."

"Leave me." Casey summoned his strength and pulled his arm free. He sank to the ground.

"Get up!" Tamba tugged at his shoulders, trying to raise him to his feet.

"Hear that?" The sound chilled Casey's blood. They were finished!

"Dogs!" Tamba jerked Casey up and they began to run again. "Where dey get dogs?"

"Sack," Casey panted. "She told me. She must have warned the patrollers too."

"De creek." Tamba pointed to the shadow of trees ahead of them. "We's gwine crawl 'long de water. Dogs gwine lose de smell."

A shot rang out, blasting near Casey's ears.

"Dat close!" Tamba's fear put strength into Casey. He ran faster.

"Leave me," he pleaded again, his voice stronger. "You can run faster without me."

Another shot sounded close to their heads. Casey stumbled and fell to his knees. The dogs barked louder. Tamba stood over him. "Come on, Cas. We's nearly to de trees."

A cloud that had dulled the brightness of the moon while they scrambled across the field, drifted away. Tamba's silhouette stood out starkly against the sky line.

"Get down!" Casey hissed.

An armory of guns fired in unison. Tamba dropped across Casey, a hole the size of a melon blasted in his chest. The dogs howled.

"Stupid nigger." Casey dragged himself out from under Tamba's body and ran, crouching low, into the coppice. Minutes later he heard the dogs yelping as they discovered Tamba's corpse.

He reached the creek and scrambled down the bank. Tamba's idea was a good one and he had about five minutes respite before the patrollers would look for him. Perhaps longer if they thought Tamba had been alone.

He tumbled into the stream and pushed himself out into the center. The water was cold and he felt cautiously for a firm foot hold. The overhanging branches of the trees gave him cover from the moonlight.

He thrashed his way along with the current, half-walking,

half-swimming. He remembered another time, almost another life, when he had fled by wading into a river. Perhaps it was that memory or simply the cold water soaking his body that revived him. At the point of capture and death, he wanted to live!

The left bank of the creek was Maddocks land, a cotton plantation run by Leo Singer. He had never seen the planter but knew from his slaves that he was a hard master who punished severely. He would find no sympathy there. In fact, he realized with despair, his chances of escaping were hopeless. Every Bullers Park slave would be hunted throughout the State.

He paused in the stream to listen above the rushing of the water. There was no sound. The dogs hadn't picked up his scent. If he continued down the stream he would emerge close to the quarters of the Maddocks slaves. Perhaps someone there would hide him until the furore died down. It seemed unlikely, but he had no alternative.

He was shivering. The water rushed over his shoulders. He was tired and lifted his feet from the bottom to let the current carry him. Exhaustion swamped him. He rolled over and lay on his back, floating wildly in the rushing water, bobbing and twisting in the eddies.

His mind drifted back to Layou and the afternoons he spent wallowing without a care in the river's vast waters. He linked his hands behind his head, as he did in those days in Layou, and relaxed. The stream bore him relentlessly.

Water splashed in his mouth. He gulped. When he breathed through his nose, water rushed in. He choked, and more water filled his mouth. His lungs seemed to be bursting. He wondered, drowsily, as he lapsed into unconsciousness, if he was drowning.

His hands slipped apart and his head lolled below the surface of the water. He twisted in the current, dropping slowly to the river's bottom.

Lucy stretched out her arms to welcome him.

33

Leo Singer lowered his tall frame into the chair, rested his elbows on its scrolled arms and steepled his fingers. He contemplated the long-limbed negress standing by the bed. She had been with him three years, since he first came to Paxton County to build Maddocks. A bright yellow turban hid her hair and she wore her long dress with an air of authority. She was straight backed and slender, her brown face creased with concern.

Leo Singer, who didn't like women, was a bit afraid of her. "Well?" he demanded sharply.

Mammy Mable shook her head with worry. "He wore out." She leaned over the bed and touched the cheek of the fair-skinned youth lying on it. He didn't move. "He need rest."

"Will he live?"

Mammy Mable drew herself up to her full height and fixed her eyes on his stern face. "Only yo' an' de Lord know dat, Marse Leo."

"Yes, yes, yes," he said, uncertain what to do. He had found the boy lying by the creek when he rode out before dawn six hours earlier. He put him across his horse and brought him back to the house. Mammy Mable had helped carry him to the guest room.

He folded his arms and regarded his housekeeper. "He's from Bullers Park, of course."

"Dat a terrible t'ing."

The news of the slaughter of the whites had spread quickly. Leo Singer was an aloof man. He kept out of his neighbors' affairs and hoped they would keep out of his. His only reaction to the uprising was to tell his own whites to be extra vigilant with his slaves in case they got restless.

"What yo' gwine do wid him?"

"Mammy, what would you do?" He sighed deeply. "He's a good looking youth..."

Mammy Mable nodded her head. She understood. She sucked her lower lip and seemed to be checking the doubts in her mind.

"He sure is a mighty pretty buck," she said slowly. "Guess dere ain't no one knows he's here 'cept yo' an' me."

"Right!" Leo slapped the arm of his chair. "Coffee, quick!"

"Yes, Marse Leo." Mable moved toward the door. "Why yo' bring de buck in de house, Marse Leo? In yo' nice guest room. Maybe he one of dem killers?"

"Maybe." Leo kept his face expressionless.

Mable glanced again at the youth lying on the bed. "God bless yo', Marse Leo," she said, closing the door swiftly.

Leo scowled. It was not to earn God's blessing that he had brought the youth into his home. He rose from the chair and walked over to the bed. The room was in darkness. He reached over to the window and pulled back the curtains.

It was day light. In the vast plantation, where the cotton bloomed like fields of gleaming white snow, as far as he could see, the slaves were hard at work. He had a good team of men and slaves; he treated them well. There would be no uprising at Maddocks.

He gazed down at the youth. In the light filling the room, he could see his face clearly. It was beautiful in repose. His hair was long and unkempt, his complexion translucent like precious porcelain. He reminded Leo of the urchins of the Mediterranean, wild, unbound boys with teasing eyes.

Leo pulled back the covers. The boy was naked, his wet clothes had been borne away by Mammy Mable.

Leo frowned in anger. The boy's chest, abdomen and thighs were scarred with the dark weals of the bullwhip. The stripes crossed his body like the mesh of a sieve. What a crime to mutilate such a fine creature, he thought.

He leaned closer, admiring the youth's physique. Slowly, he put out his hand and touched him on his thigh. The youth didn't move. Gently, Leo stroked him, amazed at the beauty rising in his hands. He stopped and withdrew his hand, thrilled at having the youth in his bed.

Leo had thought he was dead when he saw him by the creek. When he hauled him onto his horse, he was astounded by the amount of water that spilled out of his body. Perhaps the bouncing as he galloped to the house helped save him. He was close to death, even now. Leo prayed he would recover. He wanted him.

He put back the sheet and blanket to keep the youth warm. He studied his face again, wondering what he knew. His mixed blood gave him an exotic cast. He looked intelligent, resourceful and, from the scars on his body, obviously had a lively spirit that someone had tried to break. Had they succeeded?

Suddenly, Leo was puzzled. There was something familiar about the youth's face. If he could see the boy's eyes, it would give him a clue. He stroked his chin and paced the room thoughtfully. He felt that he knew the boy and yet he was certain he had not actually seen him before. If he had met him, Leo knew that with his tastes in young slaves, he would surely have bought him. Why didn't he?

"Ah..." He let his mind reason it out aloud. "I didn't buy him because I couldn't," he said. "I couldn't because he was a dream; he wasn't real. That's it!"

Leo stared incredulously at the youth. "No!" he shouted with excitement.

He raced out of the room, clattered down the stairs and hurried into the library. It was cool and dim. He opened the jalousies then stood in the center of the room and gazed at the shelves of books that lined the walls.

Leo was unusual for a planter. Some plantation owners could not read a slave bill but Leo had been educated in Europe. He was wealthy and cultured and collected books with the affection parents devoted to children. Somewhere, he knew, he had seen that boy's face... in a picture. He dived for the shelves of travel books and found the one he wanted. He opened it eagerly.

There, forming the frontispiece, was an engraving of a

youth, half naked with his hair blowing in the wind, and the rigging of a ship and the line of a mountainous shore behind him. The caption read, "Casey leaves the islands."

"Mammy Mable!" His shout disturbed the tranquility of the house.

Mable ran down the corridor and stood at the library door, her eyes wide with fright. "Marse Leo," she panted. "Yo' all right?"

"Look at this!" He thrust the book at the housekeeper. She backed away in alarm.

"No, Marse Leo. Yo' knows I can't read."

"Don't be silly, Mable. This picture. Look at it!"

He watched bewilderment steal over her face. Her eyes widened and she gaped at him. "Lor' hab mercy!" she said.

"Do you recognize him?"

"Yes, Marse Leo." She wetted her lips. "De boy in de bed...he does by Casey . . ."

Leo laughed and slapped her on her back. "I knew you could read, Mable!"

The negress darkened. "Only names, Marse Leo."

He ignored her, running his fingers through the pages of the book until he found the place he wanted. Mable tiptoed from the room. There were more pictures of the youth and he read quickly, nodding and muttering to himself.

"Yes, yes," he said with a sigh. "It's him."

There was something about Leo Singer which Casey couldn't understand. The man was in his thirties, lean and rugged with close cropped dark hair, a broad hinge of a nose and hooded gray eyes. His mouth was a hard, red slit, his manner curt and his voice stern. He appeared to be a typical hard-hearted slave-holder, yet he fussed over Casey like a woman.

Eight weeks had passed since the night of the slaughter at Bullers Park. For the first few days, Casey had lain meekly in the bed, marvelling at the luxury of its soft mattress, pillows and clean linen. He saw only the negress who tended him, her manner growing stiffer as he got better, and the white man, Leo Singer. No one else.

Mr Singer told him of the hue and cry to find him. He flapped his hands excitedly when he described the search of the Maddocks slave quarters by the patrollers.

"Why didn't you give me up?" Casey asked.

Mr Singer looked at him quizzically and patted his shoulder.

"I must leave here," Casey said. "I'm putting you at risk."

"Nonsense!" Singer threw up his hands in alarm. "You are perfectly safe here. For as long as you like."

The days stretched into weeks without Casey noticing the time passing. He wanted to leave but he liked the security of Maddocks. It was an odd sensation, not having to glance behind him all the time for the overseer with his whip. To be almost free.

Mammy Mable treated him firmly but with kindness. He spent his days reading in Singer's library or wandering through the house and gazing across at Bullers Park, now deserted, from the window.

He was troubled. Would he have to stay at Maddocks for the rest of his life? He was a wanted man. He could only leave Paxton County with Leo Singer's help. This knowledge forced him to tolerate Singer's behavior.

Mr Singer spent the mornings on the plantation and the afternoons and evenings in his library. Casey joined him there and learned to play chess with him. Singer was delighted with his company and Casey knew it was doing him good to be treated as an equal again.

He answered Singer's challenges to his intelligence slowly at first, but was soon discussing slavery, politics, and all kinds of issues with confidence.

"What about sex?" Singer said one night, leaning over to him and squeezing his knee. "At Bullers Park you must have been in great demand to service the wenches."

"No!" Casey replied quickly and wondered how he could change the subject.

"I don't believe you." Leo slapped his thigh. "You must be bursting for relief after so long without it."

"No." He shielded his crotch and moved out of Singer's reach.

"Oh?" Singer withdrew his hand and sat back on his chair as though disappointed. "You want to leave here sometime, don't you?"

"Yes!" The enthusiasm showed in his voice, but Singer merely simpered.

"You could stay here with me," Singer said. "I'd pay you a decent wage."

"What would I do?"

"Nothing. Just, well, you know . . . keep me company."

"I want to get to New Orleans, Mr Singer."

"Not yet, surely? You must wait until it's safe."

"Will you help me?"

"Hmm." Singer moved close again, his hand dropping on Casey's thigh and rubbing it with a slow circular motion. "That depends on whether you help me."

Casey shifted uncomfortably in his chair. "How?"

"You know . . ." Singer's fingers touched his crotch. Casey stood up.

"Will you help me?" he demanded, sickened by what he must do.

"Yes." Singer's face blushed with anticipation.

"When?"

"That's up to you. Tonight?"

"I mean, when will you help me to escape?"

"It will take time. Planning. It's up to you." Singer's gray eyes pleaded. "Tonight?" he whispered.

There was the rattle of wheels coming up the driveway to the house. Visitors were frequent at Maddocks since the slaughter. Neighbors called to bring news of the latest outrage in the county, and to check if all was well at Maddocks. Mr Singer discouraged them but he had to be careful not to arouse suspicion that he himself was harboring a runaway.

"Go on," he said, patting Casey's backside. "Upstairs to your room. I'll get rid of them quickly and come up."

"I'm grateful, Mr Singer," Casey said, shying at the wildness in the man's eyes. "Really I am."

"Show me later in bed. All right?"

"Yes," said Casey softly, resigned to doing whatever was

necessary to get free. He hung his head with shame and hurried out of the library to hide.

He lay naked in bed, the candle snuffed out and the door ajar. He dreaded hearing the heavy footfall on the stairs and feeling the clammy hand of Leo Singer pawing at his shoulder. But he was trapped.

He slipped into sleep. He didn't hear the door opening softly, nor see the trembling hand that held the candle and the eyes that peered at him.

"Casey."

The cry of joy roused him and he sat up in dismay. He stared at the face looming close to his, saw the tears, the hair, the lips and felt the arms that seized his body.

"No," he cried in disbelief.

"Casey!" The cheek, moist with tears, brushed against his, then a mouth pressed onto his lips.

It was real.

He tore himself away from the clinging embrace and blinked. "Lucy?" His voice was soft and small, doubting.

"Lucy?"

"Casey."

Lucy lowered herself on to the bed and wrapped her arms around him. "We've found you! At last!"

"What, I . . ."

"Don't speak, Casey. Thank God you're alive!" The sheet fell away from his shoulders as he pulled himself up from the bed.

"Your body!" Lucy touched a welt in horror. She began to cry.

"Don't," he said. "The time for tears has passed. Let me hold you."

"Yes," she said, "for ever." Her lips closed over his and he put his arms around her and pulled her close to him. She snuggled down on to the bed beside him.

He broke away and looked at her, passing his fingers over her face, touching her tiny nose and the curve of her lips. "You haven't changed," he said.

"Neither have you." They both laughed at the lie.

"It was Mr Cable's book," she said after a silence. "Daddy bought it. There were drawings of you in it. The book told how you'd disappeared. We came to New Orleans to see Gene Cable and then a letter arrived from Mr Singer saying he'd found you." She smiled.

"Gene and Daddy are downstairs."

Casey kissed Lucy hungrily and a new spirit swept into him, filling his brain with joy and swelling in his loins.

He laughed, and Lucy laughed with him. "My gold?" he asked suddenly.

"In the Louisiana Bank in New Orleans."

He giggled again.

"Come down and meet Daddy and Mr Cable," she said.

"Later," he said softly, drawing back the covers. Lucy blushed and turned her head away. He slid past her out of the bed, padded over to the door and closed it, twisting the key in the lock.

"Daddy –"

"There's only us," he said, taking her hands and lifting her to her feet. He loosened her bodice.

"Casey," she said when she stood naked before him, her hands on his shoulders, "I . . ."

"I know," he said, leading her to the bed. "I know."

A selection of bestsellers from SPHERE

FICTION

THE STONE FLOWER	Alan Scholefield	£1.95 ☐
TWIN CONNECTIONS	Justine Valenti	£1.75 ☐
YOUR LOVING MOTHER	Deanna Maclaren	£1.50 ☐
REMEMBRANCE	Danielle Steel	£1.95 ☐
BY THE GREEN OF THE SPRING	John Masters	£2.50 ☐

FILM & TV TIE-INS

THE PROFESSIONALS 14 & 15	Ken Blake	£1.25 ☐ each
E.T. THE EXTRA-TERRESTRIAL	William Kotzwinkle	£1.50 ☐
E.T. THE EXTRA-TERRESTRIAL STORYBOOK	William Kotzwinkle	£1.95 ☐
THE IRISH R.M.	E. E. Somerville & M. Ross	£1.95 ☐

NON-FICTION

THE HEALTH & FITNESS HANDBOOK	Ed. Miriam Polunin	£5.95 ☐
ONE CHILD	Torey L. Hayden	£1.75 ☐
GARBO	A. Walker	£5.95 ☐
BEFORE I FORGET	James Mason	£2.25 ☐

All Sphere books are available at your local bookshop or newsagent, or can be ordered direct from the publisher. Just tick the titles you want and fill in the form below.

Name ______________________________

Address ______________________________

____

Write to Sphere Books, Cash Sales Department, P.O. Box 11, Falmouth, Cornwall TR10 9EN

Please enclose a cheque or postal order to the value of the cover price plus:

UK: 45p for the first book, 20p for the second book and 14p for each additional book ordered to a maximum charge of £1.63.

OVERSEAS: 75p for the first book plus 21p per copy for each additional book.

BFPO & EIRE: 45p for the first book, 20p for the second book plus 14p per copy for the next 7 books, thereafter 8p per book.

Sphere Books reserve the right to show new retail prices on covers which may differ from those previously advertised in the text or elsewhere, and to increase postal rates in accordance with the PO.